Praise for the works of

D1525141

Being Emily

Winner – 2013 Moonbeam Children's Book Award in Young Adult Fiction – Mature Issues
Winner – 2013 Golden Crown Literary Award in Dramatic / General Fiction
Finalist – 2013 Lambda Literary Award in Young Adult

Engrossed... Enchanted... Rachel Gold has crafted an extraordinarily poignant novel in *Being Emily*... The unique mechanism of depicting Emily's speech as computer code is striking, defining the character distinctively. The careful and deliberate spacing of Claire's chapters are extraordinary; resulting is a pacing of action that is gripping. There is definitely gold to be found in this well-constructed novel.

-Lambda Literary Review

It's rare to read a novel that's involving, tender, thought-provoking and informative... What's impressive is Gold's delicacy in handling the physicality of Emily's story. She smoothly navigates the more intimate parts of Emily's transformation. And the author can bring you to tears as you read about Emily's struggle with gender identity.

-TwinCities.com

I couldn't put it down... It's not a sad or angst-ridden story at all. Instead it feels incredibly honest, and there are moments of joy, anger, and sorrow, laced together in a way that will make you cry and laugh along with the characters. It doesn't shy away from the hardship but it also doesn't make the claim that this hard stuff is all a trans person's life is ever... All in all, I think this is an excellent book that captures an honest, painful, but ultimately hopeful and joyful story of a young trans teen.

-YAPride.org

Just Girls

Winner – 2015 Golden Crown Literary Award in Young Adult

The novel covers all manner of sex, sexuality and gender identities and is an excellent educational tool, as well as a very good read... This book sits particularly well in the teen/young adult audience category, but can be enjoyed and appreciated by a much older audience as well, especially those who are keen to expand their knowledge and try to understand a little more about what it means to be trans*.

-Curve Magazine

Brilliant, brilliant, and all kinds of brilliant... Written with a sure-footed and almost magical lightness... Like a great wine: a beautiful blend of different emotions and different people told with depth, and complexity. It is a richly layered novel, which leaves the reader enthralled and wanting more of this exquisite concoction.

-Lambda Literary Review

As I said for *Being Emily*, this is an excellent book for any young person to read as it is a story about people like them and unlike them, which is always the basis for a good tale... What comes across strongly is that, to use my favourite quote from that great woman philosopher Marge Simpson, "our differences are only skin deep but our sames go down to the bone." This is also another fine read for any age – we were all young once and as I always maintain, still changing, still evolving.

-Glasgow Women's Library

My Year Zero

Winner – 2016 Golden Crown Literary Award in Young Adult

Gold has skillfully written a story with timely topics for navigating the slippery approach to adulthood, ranging from sex and sexuality, relationships, self-discovery, overcoming difficulties with authority figures, parental bullying and neglect, and bipolar disorder. *My Year Zero*...will appeal to both young and more experienced adults, meeting difficult topics head-on with a compelling story (and a masterful story-within-a-story) written to both inform and entertain.

-Lambda Literary Review

In the Silences

Winner– 2019 Moonbeam Children's Book Award silver medal in Pre-Teen Fiction – Mature Issues
Winner – 2020 Golden Crown Literary Award in Young Adult

Rachel Gold has crafted a story that is both a sweet coming of age romance, but is also a treatise on societal issues that impact everyone. ... *In the Silences* is something I think could be and should be required reading for a number of people and could be used in a classroom setting. I absolutely loved this book and found myself learning new things. This book will leave you thinking and that is something that only great books can do.

-*The Nerdy Girl Express*

As many white people are starting a long-overdue education in whiteness and anti-racism, *In the Silences* is a great book to turn to. This is a YA novel equally about Kaz's exploration of their nonbinary identity and their awakening to how racism affects their best friend (and love interest), Aisha, who is Black and bisexual. I loved how both Aisha and Kaz educate themselves to be better allies to each other—they support each other while recognizing that their struggles are different. ... For both the nonbinary rep and the exploration of whiteness, this is a perfect addition to any high school library or teen's bookshelf.

-*BookRiot*

Synclair

Rachel Gold creates a conversation when you read one of her books. *Synclair* is no different as it is an intriguing talk about religion. I love the different opinions and ideas that Gold's characters engage in and express. It is actually a process that I am going through right now and Gold's book comes right on time.

Synclair is about more than religious introspection as Gold adds romance to the mix. Now is this done in a typical way? Heck no! It is a Gold book. First we have Kinz, the girl Synclair currently secretly crushes on and who just happens to be her best friend. Then her best friend from the past comes back and she is hot. She is not only gorgeous, but likes girls.

Easy triangle right? (laugh) Then there is an accidental kiss with someone else and talk about complications! I loved it. Gold takes on some controversial topics and does it splendidly!

-Phoebe, *NetGalley*

curious minds

For Emma,
To the moon!
Stay curious :)

rachel gold

Other Bella Books by Rachel Gold

Being Emily
Just Girls
My Year Zero
Nico & Tucker
In the Silences
Synclair

About the Author

Raised on world mythology, fantasy novels, comic books, and magic, Rachel Gold (they/she) is the author of multiple award-winning queer & trans young adult novels. Rachel is a Visiting Assistant Professor of English at Macalester College, a nonbinary lesbian, all-around geek and avid gamer. Their diverse writing career includes seven years as a reporter for a regional LGBTQ newspaper and fifteen years in corporate marketing. For more information visit: www.rachelgold.com.

curious minds

rachel gold

BELLA
BOOKS
2023

Bella Books, Inc.
P.O. Box 10543
Tallahassee, FL 32302

Printed in the United States of America on acid-free paper.

First Edition - 2023

Editor: Katherine V. Forrest
Cover Designer: Kayla Mancuso

ISBN: 978-1-64247-449-7

PUBLISHER'S NOTE

Acknowledgments

This novel is very much the outcome of me teaching LGBTQ2S+ Literature at Macalester College, where I was also an undergraduate in the early nineties. Huge thanks to my favorite professors—Linnea Stenson, Diane Glancy and Susan Hill—and my friends during those undergrad years! Turi, Susie, Alicia, Corie, Jenna, Margaret, Leslie, Janis, Bonnie, Heather, Jessica—you all did a great job keeping me as sane as possible!

Much gratitude to my students in six sessions of my lit class over the last three years—you've been a delight to teach. Thank you to the Macalester English Department and my friends there.

As usual, I don't have strong enough words to thank the core of my writing/editing team: starting with everyone in my household, plus my extraordinary (sometimes uncanny) alpha reader Stephanie Burt and my editor, Katherine V. Forrest. For a novel that includes so much lesbian history, having Katherine's insight and suggestions were crucial.

Big thank yous also to:

- Patrice James for a lot of consulting and brainstorming.
- Ashton Rose for helping me understanding disability from a student perspective, and beta reading.
- Qamar Saadiq Saoud and therapist La Gr LPCC for consulting with me for the characters of Kai and Sophi. La created the concept of "sensory dumping" that you'll see in these pages.
- Rugby team captain Noah Velilck.
- Beta readers Lenny Prater and Raikha Patel.

And thank you, dear reader! Connecting with readers through books, events and online is part of what makes writing joyful for me. I hope that joy comes through in these pages.

For Macalester—thanks for bringing me back.
And especially for my students, who teach me so much!

CHAPTER ONE

Maze

I fell out of love with this party twenty minutes ago and can't tell if I'm more disappointed by the party or myself. College parties should be a pinnacle of excitement after an all-remote senior year of high school. Mixed reviews so far. I attended two last fall and only one was a disaster. I want this party to firmly swing the balance in favor of group social events with same-aged peers—but this is not happening. I'll give the party another hour to produce wonderment or fascinating disaster, then I'm leaving.

My room on campus is about a mile away from this house. I don't know who lives here, but from the cheap décor and psychedelic paint colors I'm guessing all students. I'm sitting on a couch that smells like wet cat and watery ketchup, but it's enthusiastically firm despite its age. The two couches in this bright, mustard-colored living room have been pushed against the walls to make room for dancing. I don't want to awkwardly watch the dancers that are crammed elbow-to-elbow through the middle of the room, but if I look down the length of the room, I end up staring at the couple making out on the far side of this couch.

It's hard not to stare. One is dressed all in green, four different shades: sweater, shirt, jeans, boots. The greens in her shirt and sweater bring out the golden hue in her olive complexion. Her dark hair is about an inch long, so short I almost mistook her for my friend Bas—who invited me.

"Just show up for a few," Bas had said. "Meet my girlfriend, eat free food, do whatever passes for dancing. Then you can go."

Bas disappeared an hour or two ago. I'm assuming with the new girlfriend.

Three of the greens in this outfit I'm observing—the shirt, sweater, and jeans—match the necktie of the person whose lap she's in. That person is in a brightly flowered button-down shirt with a green and gold paisley tie—and wearing a "he/him" pronoun button that I appreciate. He's big-bellied and flat chested and has deep red hair in a short shag cut over tan skin with sepia undertones.

I'm imagining the coordination these two went through on the outfits. Did the paisley tie come first or the four tones of green? Did they text photos or get dressed together?

I could walk back to my dorm in the cold, but my roommate has her boyfriend over this weekend because I'm supposed to spend it at home with my moms. Except they figured I'd come in late and planned date night. They offered to change it to family movie night, but that means they'd still be trying to cuddle on the couch when I wasn't looking and I'd rather give them the space.

Plus I really did want to come to this ultra queer party since I dodged most of the official meetings last semester. Trying to decide now if I want to go to meetings this spring. Our school's lesbian lit treasure hunt is about to begin, which means there'll be literary madness and, honestly, that sounds great.

"You're staring," Bas says from behind me, half-shouting over the music. As I jump-turn, she waves a hand in the direction of the oblivious couple. "Which I fully support, but when they notice, things could get awkward."

Bas is an average sized white human wearing a probably ironic pink frilled shirt and a dark-gray wool pirate coat over skinny jeans and ankle boots. She keeps her light-brown hair buzzed to a quarter inch, which emphasizes her cheekbones and eyes—big and greenish.

"I'm trying to figure out what they fight about," I tell her. "Personal space? Astrology? Matchy-matchy outfits? Is one of them secretly plotting to dump the other since we're in the armpit of winter and everyone wants an upgrade?"

"Those two," she says like she knows all about them. "Probably fight about moldy yogurts someone left in the fridge."

I snort and apply that idea. Doesn't fit, but I like it. I ask, "Where have you been? It's hours."

"Only if you round up," she says.

"New girlfriend?"

"No, the rugby team just got here. I was checking the décor of all the rooms we're not allowed in. But Kai's here now. Have you seen the whole team together? Hot. But she's hottest."

I stand up and she leads me through the kitchen into the dining room where there's food covering the long table. The room is packed with people because they get talking as they're filling plates and then don't move out of the room.

"How so?" I ask Bas as we weave between bodies wearing jeans and tees or sweatshirts. I've heard plenty about how Kai is hot, but not hott*est*.

She stops and faces me, making the human traffic jam so much worse. "She writes and it's good! Plus she looks adorably cute running down the field. And she listened to me explain all the design choices I made in French House this year. Nobody does that. Except you."

"Totally did," I grumble as we get moving again.

When I started at Mindeburgh College last fall, I thought it would be easy and familiar. I grew up here in the Twin Cities—or at least in a suburb. But even though I was super smart in my high school I might only be average smart for this school. And last year being on video for classes all the time was nuts.

Bas and I met at the first queer group meeting in September and she stuck by me those scary, lonely first three months. Maybe she was as scared as I was, but she didn't show it. I cried on her a lot. In the middle of last semester, I thought we were best friends maybe on the way to dating. Then came the Halloween Party debacle of 2021 and we haven't talked much since then. I think she feels guilty but won't admit it—and the invitation to this party is part of her trying to apologize. Or she's trying to show me that she's got someone now and she's not going to try to hone in on my people. She doesn't apologize with her words a lot, but she's been bringing me random baked goods and inviting me to stuff the last few weeks. I think she missed me.

Plus all my high school friends went back to their colleges in other states after winter break. I'm the only one in our friend group who stayed in Minnesota for college. So I guess I missed Bas too.

Both of my moms say I need more real-world friends. I don't disagree. I had a good friend group in high school but they mostly stayed with my sort-of ex when we split up over the summer. It's been great being in person for school this year and I talk to plenty of classmates, I just don't stay interested in that many. I can't tell if my social muscles are out of use or if I broke something internally or if they're actually boring. I can't ask that, so I keep muddling through and trying to figure it out.

At least Bas isn't boring and I have high hopes for Kai, the new girlfriend. Bas navigates us through the mass in the dining room to the far side of the table. Three people in rugby T-shirts are trying to talk and eat. Bas comes up behind the shortest of these three, a stocky Black girl with green braids. She's wearing a Mindeburgh Rugby sweatshirt—our college logo with the word "rugby" in turquoise on a gold background—over what might be black-and-white plaid fleece pajama bottoms. This is Bas's new girlfriend, Kai. I've seen photos on Bas's phone of her bright smile, looking friendly and fun. Bas slides an arm around her.

Kai shrugs off Bas's touch and spins to face her.

"Hey, it's me," Bas says.

"I know it's you," Kai says.

"Why are you mad at me?" Bas asks, taking a cue from her tone and the tense line of her lips.

Kai asks, "Are you working for Mads Leland?"

Bas rocks back a half step. "Yeah, he asked me to be one of his spring research assistants. How do you know that?"

"On what project?" Kai's eyes have narrowed, her lips pressed together, but still turning up, like she never completely stops smiling.

"Something about disability accommodations. Data stuff. Why?"

As they've been talking, one of the other rugby T-shirt folks, not much taller than Kai, purple hair shading to violet at the tips, has edged back to the table and turned her focus to the food. Now with a glance I see that the food was an excuse and she's actually heading out through the kitchen, making an escape.

The other rugby person is a few inches taller than me, blond hair in a ponytail, broad-cheeked face that I half recognize. I don't have a class with her, but I've been in rooms with her and I can almost remember her name. She's leaning into this Bas and Kai conversation, maybe more than I am.

Kai says, "You need to quit—request another job. Do you know him?"

"Had two classes with him. He knows his stuff." Bas is defensive, arms crossed, jaw tight.

"That research project is trying to prove that a lot of disability accommodations don't work," Kai says. "It's utter shit."

Bas shrugs. "That'll show up in the results. Don't you think there should be testing to figure out what does and doesn't work?"

Kai's eyes narrow further. "You sound like someone who knows more than a little about the project."

"I read the summary. It made sense."

"Are you *serious* right now?" Kai lifts her hands, palms up, like a shrug and then out, pushing away. "How much do you even know about accommodations and Mads Leland? Have you read his bullshit think pieces?"

"You have?" Bas asks.

"Too many of them," Kai tells her. "I was going to try to talk to you about this, but the way you're defending this project, I don't think we can date. It's so far from what my life's about."

"What?"

"I'm breaking up with you," Kai says, hands crossing and flicking outward, like a referee calling a foul.

I guess despite all those photos, her smile does go away. And her stare is pretty fierce. Bas glares back like they're having a telepathic duel. The tension makes my skin itch.

The times Bas has come through for me, if I'm being honest, are more in number than the times she's screwed stuff up—it only doesn't feel that way because the screwups were so much bigger. I should stand up for her, right? She texted me about getting picked as a first-year student for this research assistant position, super excited. It sounds like a huge deal.

I say, "Don't be too hard on Bas, that position's a big opportunity. I don't think she can get another one like it."

Kai's gaze flicks to me and whatever she reads in my posture or appearance gets a nod. She tells Bas, "You do what you have to do. But I'm not dating you. Can't."

"Can't or won't?" Bas asks.

"Both."

"Dick move," Bas says.

The blond rugby player leans in more, close enough that her arm is touching Kai's. She's facing me as much as facing Bas. "Would you date someone who goes against your beliefs? Anti-queer or Republican or balls out for crystal healing, whatever it is you can't do?"

"Bas is kind of a superlesbian like me," I say. "I don't think anti-queer folks are trying to date her."

"How are *you* on her side?" this girl asks, like we know each other. Like she knows a bunch about me that I don't. This is possible. I skip the meetings, but I post fairly often in the queer student online spaces.

Where do I know her from? Queer group meeting, probably, but I have a memory of facing her. Ah, orientation week. I snuck out of the tour and went to watch a panel that she was on.

"Felicity?" I ask and she winces.

"Lys, everyone calls me Lys. Please."

"I'm Maze."

"I know. Everyone knows who you are. I thought with all your queer theory, you'd be cooler about accommodations."

A familiar feeling of sick vertigo rises in my throat. Once again, I'm in the middle of a fight I don't understand.

"I am," I say, though I'm not sure this is true. I don't know enough about this. "But I'm also cool about people testing assumptions. If something can't be tested, isn't that just dogma?"

Lys blinks at me. "Are you assuming the testing is unbiased?"

"You're assuming it is biased."

"Given the state of the world, who do you think is more likely to be right?" she asks.

I turn to Bas, wanting to ask her what this professor is really like, but she's still in that telepathic duel with Kai.

She tells Kai, "You can't break up with me. We had, like, three, maybe four dates. We're not even officially anything yet. You can't break up a couple that isn't."

"Well then it doesn't matter, does it?" Kai says. "I am not dating you, whether we were dating or not, especially not when you're defending the most biased 'researcher' on this campus and I am using the term loosely because it is not research when you go to fill in your assumptions about how the world works."

"I'm not asking you to date him!" Bas says.

"But you were asking me to date you?"

To me that sounds like a real question, but the way Bas's jaw clenches, she heard it some other way.

"Oh fuck off," Bas spits. She turns in a swirl of pirate coat and stomps out of the room.

The front door of the house slams and I turn toward the sound. Bas is my ride back to campus—or was. It's so cold out and I didn't wear my snow boots. I guess I can take a Lyft from here to my moms' house. I've got my toothbrush in my bag anyway and there's spare clothes and Adderall at the house.

Behind me, Kai sighs heavily. I expected her to stay angry, but the sound is resigned.

"Food?" Lys asks her.

"Dance for a song or two, then food, then…"

"Cathartically break shit?" Lys asks.

"Absolutely."

I turn around to face them, wanting to know if they're serious and where they'd go to break things. If that's for real, can I join them? But they're already walking away through a gap at the end of the table where all the veggies sit still piled high.

I do not want to walk back to campus. Maybe I can find an empty corner and doze for a bit, get a ride home after date night is safely concluded.

CHAPTER TWO

Lys

How did I end up under a boy in a strange bedroom at a queer party? Boredom. No, that undersells it. I do think he's cute, but cute for someone else's body to appreciate. I implicate compulsory heterosexuality in the decision-making process and the fact that I'd only dated girls in high school. Also I thought he was gay, but midway into our making out, I realize he's bi and I am not.

"Linc, I'm not into this," I tell him.

He's half listening, so I put my palm on his chest and push. He sits back, hands on hips, looking every bit as gay as I thought he was. Linc is a white guy with bushy brown hair and a patchy but impeccably groomed short beard. I'd never made out with someone bearded before and figured I wasn't likely to again, so why not.

This is why not: he's got his hands on his hips, while straddling my legs, saying, "I could *so* be making out with someone else."

"That's the idea," I point out.

He pouts with his entire face and shoulders. I consider kissing him a little more, for science. It wasn't a bad experience, only it didn't feel at all like kissing girls. I'd only kissed two girls but both times I felt that I'd charge through a wall to get back to the experience. If Linc were on the other side of wall from me—totally fine. I'd probably sit with my back against it and play games on my phone. Plus, I don't want anything else to happen. There isn't a place to go to from this kissing, not for me; he clearly wants this to go somewhere and has mapped that path onto our bodies already.

The door opens because Linc had not locked it the way he said he had—and a body outlines itself in the light from the hall. Hard to tell from lying down how tall or who, until she says, "Oh sorry," and I recognize Maze's voice. We were in that Bas vs. Kai argument/breakup downstairs an hour ago.

Maze is another first-year college student, like me. She'd stopped going to the queer and trans events by the time I started in late September, but kept posting on the student forums. I'd read her epic posts with warm enthusiasm, now chilled from her defense of Bas. And I was all set to like Bas. Kai had been praising her for the last two weeks for being clever and thoughtful about design and international politics, plus a good kisser.

"Come on in," I tell Maze, holding my hand out and waving her in. Linc and I are done here, so if she needs the room, she should have it.

Maze steps up to the side of the bed. I figure maybe she wants a make-out room, but she's alone. She's a bit shorter than me but from this angle she looks mega tall and casually elegant with a baby-blue bandana tied around her head and long, straight dark hair falling to her shoulders. She's got serious dark brown eyebrows and serious dark pink lips—a combination that makes me feel I can tell her things.

"Threeway?" Linc asks, hopeful.

"No," Maze says and wraps her fingers around mine.

I jerk with surprise and grab her fingers so she doesn't think I'm jerking away from her. Except now I'm holding her hand.

Are we supposed to be holding hands?

I mean, I want to—or wanted to until that conversation with Bas.

"Well you're both awful," Linc declares and climbs off his perch on my thighs. "But if you change your mind, text me." He half-slams the door on the way out, like he meant to slam it but slowed it with his foot before it could.

Maze sits on the side of the bed, hand still on mine. "You okay?"

The casual bandana over her hair clashes with her dark-rimmed, oversized glasses, but is supported by the worn collar of her brown and tan flannel shirt. Under that is a Henley, most of its buttons open, showing a thin T-shirt. She's a series of gift boxes waiting to be unwrapped.

Her mouth is set hard, lips pressed in. With my free arm I push up, halfway to sitting. She must think I was in a dire situation. I guess I would too if I walked into a bedroom and saw a guy on top of an uninspired girl in the middle of the night.

I try to explain. "I hadn't kissed a boy and I wanted to try it. Not my thing, turns out. Thanks for the save, though, you're very noble."

She snorts. "Hardly."

"I got bored," I say, my chest burning with worries about what she thinks.

"Same," she says. "Not enough to kiss boys, though. But no judgment. I'm still riled about the whole thing downstairs. I feel like I should apologize for Bas."

"Cool. Thanks." I don't know what else to say or even which part I'm thanking her for because she's still holding my hand and that feels shockingly familiar, but also brilliant and new, so all my attention is in my hand.

Bass from the living room vibrates the floor and bed. And me.

I find my voice. "You're walking into bedrooms after midnight at a lackluster party and you were *surprised* to find people in the bed—what were you looking for?"

She says, "'When action grows unprofitable, gather information; when information grows unprofitable, sleep.'"

That sounds like a quote, so I ask, "What's that from?"

"Le Guin, *The Left Hand of Darkness*."

"Are you prepping for the literary treasure hunt?"

"Le Guin won't be in it," Maze says. "She doesn't count as lesbian literature despite the queer themes in some books. Because also: husband. The treasure hunt doesn't have enough science fiction, though."

"How do you know? Nobody has this year's books yet—not until we work through the clues."

For the past six years, our college queer/trans group has hosted the most iconic lesbian, bisexual, and queer women's literature treasure hunt. Only first-year students participate. At the start of spring semester, which is now, we sign up and pick teams. We'll get the first book and first clue next Thursday.

We have to read the book and use the clue to figure out a location on campus that would point us to the second book and its associated clue. The hunt proceeds through six classic works of sapphic, lesbian, bi, and queer women's lit—and if a team decodes the last work and its clue, they'll get the combination to a lockbox with some kind of valuable collection in it. My roommate thinks it's coins, maybe even gold coins.

The only catch—other than having to decipher six clues and six novels—is that the team also has to *find* the lockbox. Over the last six years, two teams have made it to the combination. No one's found the lockbox. I bet Bas in her pretentious-ass pirate coat already thinks this treasure is hers and that adds to the whole pile of reasons why I need to win this thing.

I ask, "Do you know who else signed up? Whose team are you hoping to be on?"

"If I had signed up, I'd want to be on yours," she says and my heart goes through two doomsdays and a cataclysm before being resurrected and ascending to the heights. I guess the dining room argument wasn't enough to put me off this crush. She was defending a friend. That's noble, right?

"Why?" I squeak.

I mean, does she even know me this well? We've only said hi in passing. The most interaction has been my rambling comments to her posts in the queer student forum.

Maze says, "I like how your brain works. Or were you asking why I didn't sign up? Nobody's going to win it. I don't know if it's winnable. Do you know two years ago they got all the clues and the combination, but they couldn't find the lockbox?"

"Please sign up. We could be a team. You'd be great at it. You're always putting smart quotes from books into your posts. You're like a Wikipedia of queer literature."

"I'm not sure I translate that well into the real world."

Her words come out so dubious and sad that I don't know what to say. Possible phrases flood my mind, but nothing fits, as if I'm the lockbox without the combination.

While I struggle with that, she answers the prior question. It takes me a moment to remember that I'd asked what she was searching for in her bedroom quest.

"I came in here hoping to find an empty bed," she says. "Maybe doze for a bit before I go home for the weekend. My moms live in a western 'burb, but it's date night and they're going to be watching some sappy lesbian period piece and draping over each other in a way that I do not want to have to sneak past, so I'm waiting for it to be late enough that they'll have gone to bed."

I know Maze has moms. It's the first fact I learned about her, the first fact anyone in Queer Club did. She's our legendary second-generation lesbian! Rumor was there'd been no sperm donor, that through the miracle of modern science they'd combined eggs from both moms and she was a superlesbian who would save humanity. Suspect, I know, but we wanted to believe. I did *not* know that her moms still did date nights and I could only imagine the awkward.

"I'm going to head back to the dorms," I tell her. "You can have my spot here."

Honestly, I want to stay and nap with her, but we haven't hung out before so that's too big an ask. She is number three on my current crush list. The top spot still belongs to Kai. We had a situation last September but then the semester got too heavy to keep dating. Maybe now that she and Bas aren't trying to date… But with Maze right here, I'm bumping down the hot young psych professor to move her up to number two.

Maze says, "Should I be helping you get home? Maybe access campus services? Talk to someone?"

"About what?"

"Linc?"

I raise both hands, warding and reassuring. "Oh, no. He didn't do anything I didn't invite. If I looked upset it's because I was bored, consented to kissing a boy and realized I was still bored. And it's late and my brain is laggy but wired so everything is too much and not enough."

"We could be talking on the way back. Do you want to share a Lyft?"

I don't have the money for even half a Lyft.

"I'm going to walk," I tell her. "I walk a lot and it's good for my knee right now. It's, like, the right level of reconditioning. I hurt it last fall. I mean, it was already hurt, but I made it worse. Long story."

To make the point that I'm good at walking, even with this knee, which is both aching and braced, I sit up and search over the side of the bed for my shoes. One has been kicked under and my sweater with it. Getting down to reach under the bed without bending my knee is intensely inelegant. I hope Maze isn't watching.

She is peering over the side, having scooted across the bed. She still has her shoes on—cute ankle boots.

She says, "I'll walk you. I can get a Lyft from there or sleep over in my room and face my moms in the morning."

"You sure? It's cold." I pull on my sweater and cram my feet into my big, unlaced boots.

"I grew up in Minnesota," she says. "And I'm not sure how safe it is to walk back alone at"—she glances at the bedside clock—"1:17 in the morning. Plus you can tell me about your plan for the treasure hunt."

I don't have a plan, but do not want to admit that to Maze. We walk downstairs together, to the den where everyone has tossed their heavy coats over all the furniture. Mine is an old Carhartt that my dad got used from one of his work buddies. It still has a big logo patch sewn on it for Can-Do-It Electrical in

Lansing, Michigan. The patch reminds me of Dad, so I put all my queer buttons around it rather than over it.

Maze's jacket is one of those modular three-in-one styles with a down layer for deep cold and a waterproof layer for less cold. It's blue and silver and looks like it came from the future. Her scarf is thin, probably a space-aged microfiber something, not the big knit I have from my great aunt.

I put on my big fuzzy hat and Maze pulls up the hood of her jacket. We step into the extremely crisp air and head for campus. The temp almost got above single digits today, but has to be hovering around zero now given the way my nostrils are freezing every time I inhale. The last snow was days ago, so the sidewalks are well-shoveled, a mix of ice and salt crunching underfoot. Now it's too cold to snow, so we'll have more days like this. The streetlights are small against the wide, dark sky.

"I don't have a plan," I blurt before we've gone ten steps.

"Cool," she says. "I'll make one for you if you want."

"You make plans?" I ask, because my brain tends not to. I always have tactics on the rugby field, or did before I twisted my knee during the fall season. I get ideas when watching rugby too. But having ideas and actions never turns into making whole plans that work.

"I make…" She trails off and sketches a shape in the air like tree branches. It feels so familiar that I grab her hand, my mitten around her glove, hanging together in front of us. She drops hers to her side, pulling mine with it, so we're walking, holding hands.

"Associative networks?" I ask. I heard this phrase in psych class and keep returning to it because it's so perfectly about the way every thought I have leads to other related thoughts, creating a network that I can get lost in.

She stops and the tug through our joined hands makes me stop. Tingles zip up my arm. A few buzz into my heart, but more wiggle down to my stomach and lower. The faint lights from the houses nearby highlight the darkness of her eyebrows and thick eyelashes. She stares at our boots or maybe the ground under them.

She asks, "Like trees linking roots underground?"

"They do that?"

"Whenever they can."

That also sounds like my brain, having big ideas and little ideas all connected together with roots. I might also need the trunks and branches and some squirrels to represent everything.

"My brain feels like a rugby team," I tell her. "I mean, that's my model for it. We have a small enough team that I play a bunch of forward positions, but I love being the open-side flanker. That's how my brain is all the time. All. The. Time. Always moving, looking at the field, whatever players are in front of me, and seeing possible tackles, opening, opportunities." Afraid I'm talking about myself too much, I ask, "Why don't you translate into the real world?"

We start walking again and pass silent houses.

She says, "The inside of my mind makes sense in a way that the outside does not. The inside space has my attention because it's more beautiful. The forest of thoughts, trees and their canopies and the roots and the mycelial network, all talking to each other, why *wouldn't* I pay attention to that?"

"Oh." My throat closes over the breath—an inverted sob I struggle to force back into my chest. That's too beautiful and I can feel how that is—understand why I've loved the big posts she's put in the queer online space, because they are rambling and branching, the way my thoughts are. "I wonder if trees are just rugby players moving in different ways."

"Sounds like," she says with a grin. The brown of her eyes turns infinitely deep in the low light.

She tugs my hand as we walk. With the glove and mitten between us, I only get the idea of her fingers, but they feel familiar. Maybe because of the way we're talking.

"If trees are rugby players," Maze says. "How long does a game take? Some might be hundreds of years long. But do they compete? Trees cooperate a lot." Her voice turns half teasing, half serious. "I'm not sure they do sports."

I have no idea how to answer that, but I love thinking about it.

"I'll teach you rugby and you can tell me," I suggest.

"Yeah, teach me."

"Have you ever watched a game?"

"Nope," she says. "I've walked by practice. Is it like football?"

I grin. "It *is* a full contact sport. The goal is to get the ball to the other side of the field to score, while other players use tackling to stop the ball. Unlike football, the ball can only be passed backward. Even if the ball hits your body and bounces forward, that's not allowed."

"Wow, harsh."

"No, it's fun," I tell her and then nerd out about the scrum and the ways it breaks and creates opportunities for tackles.

We arrive at the bright door of my dorm. I reach into my pocket for—nothing. Oh crap! I check my other pockets to find tissues and cough drops and a bunch of random non-wallet items.

Maze pulls out her keychain, student ID attached, and swipes it so the dorm door unlocks. She tugs me through into the warmth.

"My wallet's gone!" I tell her.

"Was it in your jacket?"

"Of course…no, wait, I had it in my sweater pocket and then in bed I took it out because it was bulky. That happened before I took off my sweater. I bet it's still on the bedside table at the house. I have to go back and get it."

"Okay," she says. "Let me get my toes warm."

"You don't have to come with me. You were going home. Your moms have to be in bed by now."

"Not leaving you to walk it alone. It's not even a mile. You sure I shouldn't get us a Lyft, though? They'd wait while you run in. Your knee?"

I've got it braced outside my jeans—a thick contraption of foam, metal and Velcro—so it's obvious there's something amiss. "I skipped PT this week and honestly walking a few miles is good for it. I really am okay walking alone. Not that I want to, I mean, I liked our walk here, but your boots are kind of skinny and maybe not the best in this cold."

"Wool socks at least," she says. "I'm warm enough if we keep moving. I'm a Minnesota native, honest. Plus we didn't plan our treasure hunt approach. I insist."

I set as fast a pace as I can manage safely on the patches of ice covering the sidewalk. The problem with my knee is probably early-onset arthritis—I'm waiting on the formal diagnosis—so I'm learning to keep it moving even when it hurts. Gentle movement like walking means less pain in the long run. Unless it turns out the surgery I got in high school messed up some nerves. Or it's a combination of all those factors and that's why I don't know when to move and when to rest.

By the time we've gone two blocks, I'm starting to worry that I'm pushing it too hard. I wish I could say yes to taking a Lyft back. It can't be more than a few bucks, but that means I won't have a cushion for emergencies next week and I'm not willing to give that up to get driven a mile.

"What's the starting book?" Maze asks as we walk quickly back the way we came. "They announced that last week, didn't they?"

"*Zami*, Audre Lorde. Do you know the first dozen times the group talked about it, I thought they were saying 'Zombie' and I was kind of disappointed."

"You haven't read it," she says. "You won't be disappointed."

"No zombies though."

"Are you that into zombies?"

"Not when you put it like that. What's *Zami* about?"

"Audre Lorde's life and her early erotic awakenings."

"How have I not already read this?"

"Straight parents?"

"Yeah. And they don't have a ton of time for reading, so it's mostly family TV when we can all manage it. Straight family TV, since I'm the only queer one as far as we know."

"Sucks," Maze says. "Though watching queer shows with sex scenes is deeply awkward with parents, just so you know."

"Oooh, hardships on both sides."

CHAPTER THREE

Maze

We're laughing as we reach the house again and I'm so glad I walked back with Lys. We still don't have a plan for the treasure hunt, but I know a bunch about where she grew up and the rugby team's recent adventures. Lys pushes through the front door, leading me into the blessed warmth. I could love this party again now that it's less crowded and Lys is with me, even if it does smell like someone burned a truckload of sage incense in a failed attempt to cover up the smell of weed.

"You can wait in the living room," Lys says. "It's warmer. Or in the dining room if you want food. I'll come find you."

I nod and she heads up the stairs. I don't feel like eating, so I wander into the living room. The couch where that couple was making out earlier tonight now holds three people who are laughing as they show each other videos on their phones. I turn toward the couch to my right, hoping for a place to sit.

Bas rises up from its worn brown cushions. Her coat is crumpled and her eyes bleary red. Her eyebrows are still perfect arches that echo the light brown bristle of her hair.

She asks, "Where've you been? You ready to go?"

The certainty in her voice pushes me to check my phone. It really has been three hours since she slammed out and I've received not one text from her in that time. I tell her, "You left hours ago."

"Correction: I slammed out dramatically and then came back. For you, of course."

"Why didn't you text me? I texted you." I find it profoundly doubtful that she came back for me.

"Did you?" She pulls her phone out of a deep jacket pocket and squints at it. "Huh. I was busy getting drunk to medicate my bruised ego."

"I don't think that's what you do for an ego."

Bas shrugs. "It's working, though."

"You can't drive," I tell her.

"Yeah, you're going to drive us back to campus. That's why I'm looking for you."

This is both a good and bad plan. Good because then Lys won't have to walk more, we won't freeze, and Bas will be safely back in her bed. Bad because I don't have a driver's license. My coordination sucks for maneuvering anything bigger than a pen.

Lys steps into the doorway of the room and jingles her keys. Her hair has been in a ponytail all night, but now she's twisted it up in a bun with wisps of honey brown poking out. My fingers tingle with curiosity about how her hair feels. I wave her over.

"Can we drive Bas back to campus?" I ask.

"Sure."

"I mean, can *you* drive? I don't have my license."

Bas shoves herself between us. She's a bit taller than me but I'm delighting in the way she's obviously shorter than Lys. She asks Lys, "Are you any good?"

"I'm shockingly good," Lys says and my heart does a thing.

I hope she's not only talking about driving. What I have in mind is more fine motor skills, but maybe she's good at both. This is ridiculous to consider since we haven't even kissed and I don't know if she's available. But I am getting that zing of energy between us and her body language is very open, lots of turning toward me, no closed postures.

We push into the cold again and Bas leads us down the street to where she's parked. She unlocks her aging Honda hybrid, gray and numerously dented on the outside but with sleek blue and teal seat covers inside. She separates her car key from her house keys, hands Lys the car key and crawls into the back seat. It's almost warm in the passenger seat, so Bas couldn't have been back at the party long. Did she go somewhere else to drink and then drive back to the party to find me to drive her back to her dorm? That doesn't make sense. Is she even drunk? Remembering to keep her house key is a level of precision I don't expect a drunk Bas to have.

"Bas, where'd you go?" I ask.

"Donut shop," she says.

I want to follow that up with a question about how she's drunk then, but maybe she hit the alcohol hard when she returned to the party, or she had some in the car. She likes to think of herself as a risk-taker, but last semester what I saw was a person getting all her assignments in on time and keeping her space neat. She's not even as chaotic as I am, but maybe that's why she acts out big sometimes.

"Which dorm?" Lys asks.

"French House."

"Where's that?"

"North side of campus," Bas says.

Lys's eyebrows are tight together, so I offer, "It's that right turn off the street that goes to the gym. Nobody ever uses it unless they're in one of the language houses. I'll tell you how to get there."

She pulls into the street and I give directions while Bas sprawls across the back seats, silently dramatic. Turning toward campus, the car slides on a patch of ice and Lys neatly turns into the skid, straightening out our path. I should ask her to teach me to drive.

After a few more turns, I point to the side street with the language houses and say, "French is the third one in. The blue one."

There's no room to pull up to the curb, so she stops in the street. "Can you get to your room okay?" she asks Bas. "And remember to hydrate?"

"Yes, boss." Bas rolls over, on all fours on the seat, and pushes the door open. "Text me what lot you park in. I'll get the keys from you tomorrow or you can drop them in my mailbox. The one at the student commons, not here."

She rights herself on the seat and swings her legs out the open door—then vanishes.

"Shit!" I shove my door open and look back.

Bas is lying faceup on the street, half under the car, one hand to her head, the other on her butt. "Fuckin' hurts," she grumbles.

A thick sheet of ice covers this side of the street. I step onto it carefully and shuffle to Bas. She must've slipped and the momentum of the fall carried her under the car.

"She's under the car," I warn Lys.

The car is in park, but now Lys turns the engine off. She comes around the far side of the car, one hand on the trunk for balance. Her big, square jacket exudes confidence, but her hat is askew, hair escaping one side, brushing her collar, more gold than brown under the streetlight.

"Did you hit your head?" she asks.

"Scraped," Bas says. "I hit my ass. Help me up."

There's no good place to stand on this ice for traction and my boots have slippery soles. If I reach out to her, I'm likely to end up under the car with her. Lys sees this problem too. She's bracing her legs, trying to find a spot beyond the ice, holding onto the car with one hand and reaching the other toward Bas. She's got bigger boots than mine and seems measurably stronger, even with the thick brace on her knee.

Bas grabs Lys's hand and tries to pull herself up, but doesn't move. I step toward the curb and crouch down.

"Your jacket is caught on something," I tell her.

Light sweeps over us as a car turns onto the street. It's narrow here and anything bigger than a compact car can't pass us.

They flash lights at us and Lys says, "I'll talk to them." She moves gingerly around the car toward the lights.

"Bas, can you see what caught your jacket?"

"Car stuff," she says.

"Try wiggling it loose."

"I can't see it. Might wiggle it worse. Get down here with your phone light."

"Can you get out of your jacket? Then we can pull it loose."

"Tried. I can hear it tearing. Stop screwing around and help me," she says, voice sharp, any edge of drunkenness—pretend or otherwise—long gone.

I thumb on my phone's flashlight. Bas and her obnoxious jackets. She has at least six of them. I don't know why she cares so much about tearing this one.

"Can't see," Bas says. "Shine it down here."

She's near the rear wheels, one side of her jacket up under the body of the car. My phone's light isn't reaching far enough to show what she's caught by.

"If you didn't have such an obsession with sweeping into and out of rooms with a flourish, you wouldn't have these problems," I snark at her.

"My obsessions are so much cooler than yours," she says.

"Hey, I'm trying to help you."

"You're eight feet away shining a light in my eyes, not helping," Bas snarls at me. "At least hand me your phone."

I crouch into a sit and then roll onto my belly. This puts my face about a foot from Bas's. She reaches for my phone but I don't let go of it, so she's turning the phone and my hand, searching the undercarriage.

"There," she says. "It's caught up by that rectangular metal thing. Can you reach it?"

"You want me reaching headfirst under a car on ice in the middle of the night for a fucking jacket?"

"Don't worry, if the car moves I'll stop it with my body," she says, the words hard-edged.

"I've got scissors in my bag."

"Don't you dare."

I squirm forward under the car, reaching for the area where the edge of her jacket disappears into sharp metal darkness. "Your knock-off pirate bullshit is not worth this," I grumble.

She's silent while I feel my way up the cloth to the place where the thickness of a button is wedged between metal and other metal. I start working it loose. Slow at first and then the button pops off and it comes free.

"There."

"Where's the button?"

"You can look for it in the morning," I snap at her. "It's not going anywhere it hasn't already gone."

I squirm backward, out from under the car, toward the curb. I grab her arm and tug for her to come with me. She does, pushing with her feet, but her other hand is slapping the ice, trying to find the button.

I say, "Starting to think you like that coat more than me, probably more than Kai, might want to look into that."

"You're the oblivious space case who blew me off over and over last fall," she flings back at me. "Don't pin this on me. You think you're less important than my favorite jacket? I was less important than finding the perfect fucking hand lotion and learning to cook green beans."

"I invited you—" I protest.

"To do all the weird shit you're interested in. And I got sick of it and kissed your ex and you can't grow up enough to put that behind us. Get over it."

"Get over your jacket," I retort.

"This jacket is more loyal than you are," she growls back at me.

We're free of the car now, so I scoot over the curb and sit in snowy grass. Bas pushes up and rests against the wheel of one of the parked cars.

Lys comes around the back of Bas's car and contemplates us. "You two okay? I'm going to move this so they can get through."

"We're alive," I say.

She waves and then the car crunches away on the ice, followed by the light-flashing folks.

"Your head," I say to Bas, peering at her in the dark street, trying to see if there's blood in the buzzed bristles of her hair.

"It's fine. Someone will be up. I'll have them check me out." She uses the parked car to pull herself to her feet and takes tiny steps until she's on the walk where salt has made the ice uneven and less slippery.

"I was having a good time with Lys," I tell her. "And doing you a favor. Why are you being this way?"

She turns, confronts me. "I got my ass dumped in front of the entire rugby team and as usual you're making it all about you."

I have to think about that. She did have a shitty night. But she's the one who left me at that party. Was I supposed to do something different? While I'm working that out, she turns and stalks up to the house.

Lys pulls up in Bas's car and leans over to open the passenger side door. I cross the ice carefully and settle into the seat.

"I'm parking this by my dorm," she says. "I think she owes us less walking. Are she and the jacket okay?"

"She got mad about the button," I tell Lys. "I don't understand."

"People are weird. Let's go get warm."

I could definitely get warm with Lys.

CHAPTER FOUR

Lys

We park Bas's car and trek the half block to my dorm. Our boots crunch and squeak in the snow. Maze has been quiet the whole way back. I heard her and Bas's voices under the car—sharp and then sharper—but I don't want to push to find out what was said.

This time, I unlock the door to my dorm building and usher us into the warmth of the lobby. Long tan couches sit empty. Maze pushes back the hood of her jacket and peers at her phone.

She says, "I scheduled a ride in the app while you were driving, to go home to my moms' house, but there's no car available for an hour. If I hang out in the common room, do you want to hang with me?"

Of course I do. I've already liked what I read from her online for the last five months and in person she's approachable, hot—long, dark hair falling to her shoulders, tied back with a careless bandana—but also awkward in her gestures. Plus I've seen her crawl on her belly on ice to help a friend. I want to stay close to her.

"Will your moms freak if you don't show up tonight?" I ask.

"Not if I text them. I'd hike across campus and stay in my dorm room, but I told my roommate she could have her boyfriend over all weekend because I'd be gone."

"So everyone around you is with someone, your moms, your roommate, and you've been trekking back and forth in the snow with me?" I feel fluttery and loose inside as I ask, "Do you want to stay in my room? It's so late. Just sleep and get your ride when it's light again?"

She peeks at her phone and asks, "Is it really okay to stay?"

I can't tell if her answer means that she's cold and tired and grateful for any nearby comfortable place to sleep or if, like me, she's leveraging the excuse of needing a place to sleep into something more. I hope it's the latter, but I brace myself to behave if it isn't.

"Of course. Be quiet, though. My roommate is a heavy sleeper but not that heavy."

"And she's cool with you having someone else stay over? I'll text my moms and let them know I'm staying on campus and cancel the ride."

I snort. "Last week she complained to me that I needed to get a girlfriend because she wasn't getting the real my-roommate's-a-lesbian experience."

"Good to know," Maze says with a grin.

She can't care that much about my roommate. She must mean that it's good to know I don't have a girlfriend. Warmth spreads from my shoulders down my back. Does she have one? I'm afraid of the answer.

We take the elevator up to my floor and walk the hall to my room in silence, like we're practicing for being inside the room. I turn the key slowly. Maze puts her fingers on the back of my hand before I can open the door.

"We're only sleeping, right?" she asks. "I'm not trying to turn this into…more than that. I mean not yet at least."

"Yeah." I breathe the word more than say it. "That's good."

I ease the door open. Maze follows me into the dimness of a room illuminated only by a shaft of light from where the window curtain doesn't completely block one of the all-night campus lights outside.

I strip off my jacket, hat, scarf, gloves and toss them into the beanbag chair in the corner. Then I sit on the bottom bunk, mine, and kick off my boots. Maze slides off her small backpack and mirrors my gestures.

It wouldn't be fair to change into pajamas when Maze couldn't, so I pull off my sweater, then reach back to unhook my bra and wriggle out of it without taking off my T-shirt.

Maze unbuttons her overshirt and shrugs out of it. She has a Henley on and another layer under that. She takes off her bandana and runs her fingers through her hair so it's an even, dark cascade. For a long minute, she gazes at me, then faces away, pulls off both shirts, takes off her bra, puts the shirts back on. My brain takes many photos of her slender, bare back and tucks them away for future contemplation. She undoes her loose cargo pants and steps out of them, revealing boxer briefs with thick horizontal stripes. I can't make out the colors, only that one is darker and one lighter.

I make myself stop staring, fumble at the clasps on the knee brace, slide it down my leg, then jeans off. I get under the blankets and arrange the pillows for two people, then hold the blankets open to her. She slips into the single bed on her back. This puts her elbow almost in my boobs; she rolls onto her side, one hand pressing against her mouth to constrain her laughter. If I keep looking at her, I'll want to kiss her so much I'll never get to sleep, so I roll onto my left side, facing away from her.

She shifts, settles on her pillow, the one I usually throw a knee over for comfort. Wow I hope it doesn't smell like the waist-to-knee region of my body. Too late now. I should've given her my head pillow.

Her hand rests on my hip. I reach for it and tug it an inch forward so she'll know I want her there. Better even than that light touch, she shifts her whole body forward, her chest against my back. I might never sleep now, but I'll suffer the insomnia joyfully.

How can she feel this familiar when we've only spent a few hours together? Is this one of those at-first-sight things that I don't believe in? But it's not only her body that feels familiar—that's actually the least familiar part of this. The whole time walking back and forth between the party and here, her voice and the words she used sounded like I'd been listening to her for months. Because I have! She speaks the way she writes and I've had her words in my brain since her first post last September. We have been talking for months, but not directly to each other like this. I sigh and press back into her.

Her hand moves forward again, to the lower curve of my belly. I hold my breath, afraid that she'll move it, but she relaxes—and minutes later her breath deepens with sleep. Listening to that soft rhythm, I follow her.

I sleep until my roommate, Char, creaks the bedframe repeatedly, waking up, rolling over like she'll go back to sleep. She doesn't manage to do that, because she keeps rolling side to side. Behind me, Maze jerks awake.

I turn over quickly. She's waking up in a strange place and might not remember to be quiet. I put a finger to my lips. Maze's sleepy brown eyes focus on my eyes, my whole face, my mouth and hand. She reaches between us and wraps her hand around mine so she can move my finger from my lips to hers. Very soft! Despite our walks in the cold last night. What was she using for lip balm? I trace her lips until they part under my touch and she kisses my finger. I'm grinning so hard my cheeks ache.

Char shakes the bed as she swings her legs over the side. I jerk the blankets up over our heads and listen. Plastic bottles clatter together as Char grabs her bathroom caddy and heads out into the hall.

"Do I need to grab my pants and run for it?" Maze asks as I lower the blanket.

The door clicks open again. Char forgot something. I'm about to explain Maze but Char sees us and shrieks, "Fucktrumpet!" Caddy and bottles clatter to the floor.

Maze sits up, hits her head on the top bunk, jerks back and slides out of the bed to the floor.

Char stares at this vision of a girl in boxer briefs with her nipples visible under her Henley and thin base layer. I stare too, of course, while scrambling to give her the top blanket from the bed, a threadbare Woolrich red plaid. She bunches it in her lap, like she doesn't know what to do with it. Her straight hair is frizzy at the back but not half as frizzy as my wavy hair gets overnight. Her calves jut from the bottom of the blanket, thin and pale, her shoulders broader than I'd have expected, like parts of her grew at different paces.

Maze turns bewildered eyes to both of us and asks, "What's a fucktrumpet and should I be worried?"

"This is my roommate, Char," I tell Maze. "She likes to add random words to swear words, especially when she's startled. Char, this is Maze."

"You have a girlfriend?" Char asks me. "When did you get a girlfriend? Yesterday you didn't have a girlfriend."

Char is cheerfully low femme in a way that blends the LL Bean and Victoria's Secret catalogues. She has shoulder-length hair that shades from dark to light purple and a face that's almost too long for her pert nose to make sense on it. Her morning wear is a flannel robe over a flowy sleep shirt and cute little shorts—plus giant slippers. She's the lightest player on the women's rugby team, but tackles like a pro because of her understanding of angles and momentum. Years of physics classes.

I don't know how to answer the girlfriend question. We haven't even kissed, but I want to—and I'd be her girlfriend for sure. Maze stares at her hands like the fingers are puzzle pieces.

Maze asks, "Would a fucktrumpet be a sacred trumpet that's blown to invite people to have sex? Or is it a riff on the fact that you *blow* a trumpet? But you're not blowing someone while you fuck them, assuming a narrow definition of that word, so then it's a threesome reference?"

Watching Maze's dark pink lips as she says sex things is profoundly distracting. I don't come back to reality until Char sputters, "It's *not* a threesome reference!"

"We're not inviting you," I tell her, and to Maze I say, "She's quite straight. Are we going to be girlfriends?" I regret asking as soon as I hear the question leave my lips and add, "Not that we should decide that now, we shouldn't!"

Maze's head tilts, sleepy eyes narrowing. "We probably will be, though," she says. "The going lesbian U-Haul rules state that it's either three confusing coffee meetings—where no one's sure if it's a date or not—or it's two discrete instances of kissing. I think we'll hit at least one of those metrics. But I would like to see the relationship agreement before I sign it."

"Whoa, girlfriends is not a state that requires signatures," I protest. As much as I adore Maze, this seems fast even for lesbians.

"I was speaking figuratively," she replies, grinning, still sitting on the floor in boxer briefs, with those too-obvious nipples— now hard probably from the cold more than anything—looking utterly, queerly resplendent. I want to put my hands under her layered shirts so badly that I twist my fingers together hard to keep from reaching out.

I tell her, "And I'm speaking metaphorically but I still mean it."

"Oh y'all are about to be girlfriends for sure," Char says. "Maze, good to meet you and I'm glad you speak Lys. Can I get your number for when I need a translator?"

"You assume I can translate our language into Earth human standard," she says, nearly deadpan except for a curve at the corners of her mouth.

"Wow, I am so leaving you two alone as soon as possible. I'll shower later. Just let me get dressed and no checking out my ass."

"She does have a nice ass," I tell Maze, to needle Char.

Maze sighs. "Not interested. No offense, but I'm not for straight girls."

"None taken?" Char's answer comes out as a question. She's probably wondering if she should be offended as she goes to her side of the closet and shoves a pile of my clothes out of the way with her foot. I need to get to those, but not right now.

Maze retrieves her phone from her jeans pocket and starts reading and texting. Mostly her moms, I guess, from how she's shaking her head but half smiling. I replay the last few minutes of the conversation, trying to figure out what's happening. Did Maze say we were going to have coffee dates or kiss?

"Bye, lovebirds," Char calls as she heads out the door. "If you're going to fuck, for the love of God put a sign on the door so I don't walk in on that."

She doesn't wait for any kind of answer, which is good since we're staring at each other. Maze's sleepy eyes have gone wide, eyebrows rising on her forehead.

"That seems really fast for her to expect," Maze says, voice low. "I didn't know if you meant me to come here to sleep or something else. When you moved my hand closer last night I figured something else, but probably not the whole thing where we verb the noun."

"What?" I laugh and clap a hand over my mouth to keep in other sounds of surprise.

She grins sideways up at me. She's still on the floor and I'm looming over her from the bed. Should she come up here or I go down there? She's practically in the laundry pile at this point.

She says, "You know: do the deed, butter the biscuit, feed the kitty, sweep the chimney—as I say these, I realize they're both heteronormative and, in some cases, awful."

Wow, so many sex euphemisms take the structure verb, plus "the," plus noun—and her euphemism is the meta structure "verb the noun"—and now my entire body is desperate to move closer to her entire body. Even if that means sitting in my laundry pile.

"Does it always work?" I ask and try a verb with a noun. "Maintain the wetlands? Actually that's not bad."

"Deliver the assignment?" she suggests with a low chuckle.

"Offer the poem?"

"Are you offering?" she asks. "Not the whole poem, maybe a few lines?"

"Yeah, if you mean—?"

She climbs into the bed and puts her mouth on mine. Maze kisses in great detail, like a painter going over the same square inch again and again to get the brushstrokes right. She's getting the brushstrokes very right.

As our mouths open to each other, the feeling of paintings slips away. Now each kiss is a miniature sculpture that needs to be built up, worn down, polished, admired before beginning the next. I want to pile my arms full of these kisses, for when they're not full of her.

We pause to catch our breath and Maze asks, "Does your roommate honestly think we're going to verb the whole noun this morning?"

"I have no idea. But I'm not planning to."

Her shoulders relax with a sigh. "Straight people, I guess. I mean, my roommate's been with her boyfriend for the last two years of high school so I don't know. Do they just jump into bed? Not judging, honestly, since I'm in yours and we sort of only met last night except I've seen you around and your responses to my posts and—if I'm being honest—I saw you on that panel that first week of class and have been thinking about whether we had enough in common to strike up a conversation but then I got caught up in other stuff. I'm sorry, I'm talking too much."

"I like you talking," I tell her. "You saw me on that panel? I thought the other first-years were touring during that."

"I know my way around. I've been here a bunch for events and stuff while I was in high school. So I skipped out. I wanted to see what folks were saying."

"About decolonizing the classroom?" I ask with some disbelief.

"Well, I came for the queer theory applied to grading and stayed for the decolonizing. Wow, I hear us and I get what your roommate was saying."

"So are we girlfriends or going to be?"

She raises her eyebrows and kisses me.

"How about provisional girlfriends? That way at a future time one of us can dramatically ask the other to be her girlfriend. And also because this seems so fast and I like you tremendously but I'm a little scared."

"So we're engaged to be girlfriends?" I ask. "Because that's…"

"Scarier?" she suggests. "How about time travel? We traveled back from a future in which we're girlfriends and have to play along with this timeline until we catch up to ourselves. And I am still afforded the space for a sweeping romantic gesture at some point between now and our future girlfriend selves."

"That…actually works. How much more kissing can we do before that's too much for people who kissed for the first time less than twenty-four hours ago?"

I lean into the woody gingerbread and balsamic smell of her.

"More," she says.

CHAPTER FIVE

Maze

How did I get through days without Lys? Can't honestly remember. After waking up with her Saturday morning, and a lot of kissing, I skip going home for the weekend—there are other weekends—and spend the rest of it with Lys. We walk over to my dorm room for my ADHD meds. Seeing that my roommate and her guy are out, we kiss more on my bed. Sunday we alternate homework and kissing—a perfect system.

Monday's hectic: I have so much homework and she has physical therapy for her knee. I've crashed by the time she's available. We manage dinner together Tuesday and Wednesday nights. Watching her next to me at a table in the food commons, I feel like I've been doing this for months.

She's fully talked me into the literary treasure hunt so Thursday evening I meet her at the student commons and we walk over to the kick-off meeting where we'll get the official rules, become an unbeatable team and begin a literary journey that I'm pretty sure I've already taken. I've been reading lesbian classics since I was twelve. My moms hid the sexy ones, but I found those around age fifteen.

Today was sunnier than the weekend and the slight warmth lingers into the evening. Lys's oversized jacket swings open as we walk across the campus, showing a white sweater that highlights the warm gold tones of her skin. I flash to Friday night, curling behind her in bed, the comfort of her body—and to last September when I saw her on the panel, the wild creative leaps she made, the connections of insight clear even when I wasn't sure what she was saying. That was my fault for not knowing the subject, not a flaw in her delivery. I want to stop her now and kiss her wide mouth set under broad cheekbones. I'd much rather be doing that than going to this meeting, but if it means I'll be on a team with her for the next few months, I'm willing.

"No brace," I say, pointing at her knee.

"Keeping up with the PT every day this week, in case I have to walk back and forth across campus a lot," she says with a grin. My dorm is on the far side of campus from hers.

We hold hands without gloves, despite the cold. Her fingers are sturdy and rough in spots. Weird to remember that a week ago I barely knew Lys. Even now it's like I've spilled a massive puzzle from the box onto a broad table and I'm excited to fit it all together. I had some of the outline and not enough of the middle. I knew she grew up in Lansing with three siblings and that her folks are still together—but I don't yet know how she feels about all her siblings. I'm an only, so sibling dynamics are endlessly fascinating.

In the Humanities Building, we take the elevator up to the top floor, a big room with huge dormered windows that must've been built back when people rode small flying dragons to meetings like this. Would a full dragon wingspan fit through those windows? I ask Lys, "Could dragons fit in here?"

"Eastern for sure, they're long and narrow," Lys says. She gestures. "Over there?"

We take two seats by an empty table at the side of the room so we can see the front and most of the audience. Also this is away from the weird popcorn, falafel, and mouthwash smell that always pervades this room, from the corner with the microwave.

Who's using mouthwash by the microwave? The room is filling up as we shuck our coats and settle. I wonder if the whole campus already knows that I spent a night in her room five days ago. How much does Char gossip?

I feel like secret queer elves have been watching me all year and trying to hook me up with anyone, but that might be pressure from Mom. I'd rather have matchmaking queer elves—and I'd rather be holding Lys's hand through this whole meeting, but since we're only time-displaced girlfriends and everyone will talk, I'm not sure that I want to in this precise room.

Lys waves at a group of girls across the room that includes Char. All rugby people? They look sturdy and fit. She knows way more people than I do, but maybe that's because I'm from here and I've already got people, but not on this campus. Also never been big on team sports. I like to move my body, biking and lifting the occasional weight, but I'm not coordinated when other people get involved. They're so distracting.

A third person joins us, sitting on Lys's other side, short and square, brown skin, green braids—ah yes, the night of the party, the debacle with Bas—this is Kai. She's wearing a T-shirt over a long-sleeved shirt. The T-shirt features a brown unicorn with a blue afro. I'm not sure how to say Hi because she and Lys are deep in conversation about something rugby related.

Glancing around the room, I spot Bas. She's standing by the clump of young gay guys, glaring at me. I raise eyebrows at her. As if she has justification to glare like that. I'm the one who got her home on Friday after...oh, wait, this makes sense: she's glaring because Kai is at my table.

She flounces her long coat and settles into seats with the gay guys. She fits with them in her skinny jeans and ankle boots and probably ironic frilly pink shirt under the pirate coat. She's rebuzzed her hair to its usual quarter inch, so her high cheekbones look extra sharp and her greenish eyes extra big—except when she squints to glare at me, which is half of each minute.

Lys sees me staring and then Kai follows both our gazes. I expect a snarky comment but she asks, "How's she doing?"

"Usual, I think," I say. This is not a lie; Bas's usual includes a whole lot of states and I don't want to admit that she's been sulking. She didn't return my texts until Tuesday and since then I've gotten one- and two-word answers. Last semester that would've made me run over to check on her, but time with Lys felt so precious this week that I figured I'd catch up with her at this meeting. Bad plan.

Kai asks, "Do you think she'd read some stuff if I sent it to her? About Professor Leland and his anti-accommodations position?"

"Not yet."

"How close are you two?" Lys asks me. "You could talk to her."

"I wouldn't know where to start," I say. "And, sorry, but why does it matter? If she quits the job, they'll get another student to do it."

"If a bunch of students refuse to take that job, it sends a message," Kai informs me.

"Would that actually happen?"

"Two have quit already."

I have no idea if that's enough for anyone to notice. I don't get financial aid, but judging by Bas's work assignments last semester, receiving it could get pretty random.

The room hushes and I turn forward to see which upper-class student is officiating. There's always a student organizer in addition to the professor who oversees the clues. Linc is standing in front of us all, waving his hands to call for order(ish). I wince. The bi guy who was trying to make out with Lys is not in my top ten. But Linc is a junior and nearly won this treasure hunt his first year, which I know because he has humblebragged about it in all the conversations I've had with him. He and his teammate got all the way to the combination, but couldn't find the lockbox. He officiated last year too. Probably staying close to the treasure hunt in case he can get to the lockbox first—assuming the combination hasn't changed.

He's wearing a jaunty purple fedora and a low-cut, skinny-strap, black tank top despite the freezing weather. The dark tones of his hat and top against his pale skin emphasize the scruffiness of the facial hair he's been working on since at least the start of the year. He's one of those guys who has big patches of skin on his lower cheeks that the scruff does not cover, but the chin part is coming in nicely.

"Thanks, everyone who signed up," Linc says. "We have some new rules this year, given what happened last year. Since some of you haven't met Professor Haille yet, let me introduce the queer beacon of the Education Department and good friend to our beloved Professor Stendatter, who founded this treasure hunt. Professor Haille was even Best Woman at her wedding."

"I wish I was in her class," Lys mutters. "I wonder if she'd be my advisor."

Professor Haille blurs the lines between soft butch, low femme and at least two other genders that have yet to be named. Her clothing, makeup and hair always contradict strict gender categories: if she's in jeans and boots, she'll have a frilly top, colorful scarf and dangly earrings—or the classic flannel shirt with flowing pants and ornate shoes. When her hair is loose, it hangs to midback. It's also dyed from the midpoint down so that when she wears it up, the messy top bun is a bright color over her usual blond—currently a faded teal.

She steps to the front of the room and Linc hands her a folded sheet of paper. "New rules from Professor Stendatter," he says. "In addition to what she already sent." His voice is low, but we're close enough to hear it. How many new rules are we getting and why?

Linc slides into his seat as Professor Haille tells us, "Because those of you eligible to sign up for this year's treasure hunt are first-year students and weren't here for last year's event, you may not know some of the goings-on. I won't go into all of the details—"

"Oh do! We love details!" Linc calls.

"All right, some details. Due to rumors about the value of the collection that's the treasure, some teams wildly ignored pandemic safety precautions. Two students got sick and missed weeks of class. One had to take a leave of absence. Additionally, teams who were already struggling in their classes did worse. We had to stop the treasure hunt in its fifth week. I know those details aren't as salacious as you hoped, but I think you can understand why we had to change the rules for this year. The first change is that you must keep your grades up. Because grade averages can vary student to student, we'll use your fall semester GPA as the standard you need to keep to. If your midterm grade is more than two levels away from your fall grade, you'll be asked to leave the treasure hunt."

Grumbling murmurs around me but I don't hear any real protests. Two grade levels means that I could go from an A- last semester to a B and stay in. That seems fair. If I'm below a B average, I'll need all the focus I can get, but I'm not worried. The part of school that's about going to classes and having answers comes easily to me. It's the part of school that's about being social in big groups that messes me up.

"As in past years, all the clues are on campus," Professor Haille says. "And you'll still work in teams of two, but this year the teams will be chosen randomly."

Loud groans rise from around the room. I turn toward the door, wondering if it's too late to leave. I don't want to be force-teamed with some random—or worse, some of the people in here that I actually know. Lys's fingers brush mine and I catch them, hold tight. I don't want to be doing this if I'm not doing it with her.

"Stay," she whispers to me. "We'll be a secret team."

I nod.

Professor Haille says, "All the rules are on the website. You can email me any time with questions or stop by my office hours. Linc, come on back up and do team selection."

From the table next to where he's been sitting, Linc retrieves a dark-green fedora and holds it up, saying, "I printed your names and put them in this literal hat. If you pick your own name, keep it and pick again. I'll draw our first contestant, to keep this random." He fishes in the hat, opens a scrap of paper and says, "Paisley, you're up."

A figure stands from the table surrounded by the first-year students who live in the trans/nonbinary student housing—and

I double-take. He's in another bright shirt with a paisley tie, dark red hair, heavy-cheeked serious face that I remember from the couch at the party. The person with the paisley neckties is actually named Paisley?

He steps up to the hat, wiggles his fingers and plunges a hand in. When he reads the slip, he starts bouncing on his toes. "Brantley!" he yelps.

The all-green person from his lap at the party is now in all purple and leaps up to meet him in the middle of the room for a hug. If they're both in the group of trans students, did I misgender Brantley at the party? I tap Lys's hand. "Do you know those two and their pronouns?"

She nods. "Brantley is on the team and Pais comes to all our games and some practices to cheer them on. I don't know why he doesn't join the team too. Those two are the cutest and most sickening couple adjacent to the team this year. Oh and Brantley's pronouns are they/she/he and I'm not sure when to use which, so I use they and so far that's been well-received."

"Does Brantley always dress in shades of the same color?" I ask.

"Oh yeah, but only green or purple. They're matching their aura."

I have so many questions and no idea where to start. Pretty sure Lys's aura is gold, but I could stare at her for a while to make sure.

Linc pulls another slip out of the hat and calls for Kai. She goes up and fishes around in the fedora. She reads the slip of paper, squints at it and says, "Sophi?"

"Here." A Black girl raises her hand on the side of the room where most of the BIPOC queer and trans students are clustered. Her dark brown braids, wound in a high bun, have strands of red-purple in them. She's wearing a maroon sweater that's shaped like a blazer, way more formal than anything I own. Her eyeshadow is wide and sweeps across her eyes with the colors from her hair and sweater, plus gold highlights.

"Wow, what are the odds?" Kai asks as she moves toward Sophi, loud enough for the whole room to hear.

From across the room, Char calls out, "One point five six percent."

"Thanks, Char," Kai hollers to her. "Seems lucky."

I turn to Lys who sees the question in my face and whispers, "Kai and Sophi are the only two first-year Black women who are also queer—or at least who are out and come to meetings. Not friends though. I guess they're into different things."

Kai drags a chair next to Sophi and sits, the two of them talking quietly as the next name is called. Kai hunches forward, very "all in," but Sophi sits back in her chair, upright.

"Balls," Lys whispers. "Kai was my backup if I didn't get you to sign up. She's fire in the scrum."

I don't know what that means, but from her tone of voice it's a good rugby thing. She's trying to teach me rugby but we're at the looks-like-chaos stage.

A student I don't know has paired up with another student I don't know. As they move to sit together, Bas pushes up from her seat and comes to the chair on my right. She settles in and crosses her arms.

"How are you doing?" I whisper as another student goes up to pick a name.

"Worse now that I see you're on Team Kai, traitor."

"I'm on Team Lys," I tell her.

"I noticed."

I shrug. I don't know a polite way to say: you were a real ass.

Linc calls, "Lys, you're up."

Lys draws a name, blinks at it and folds her lips inward. She has to be biting the hell out of the inside of her cheek from that sour grimace.

Finally she eyes her roommate and asks, "Char, you signed up for this?"

"Trans girls allowed," she says.

"You're straight!"

Char says, "I can *read* about lesbians."

"Do you *want* to?" Lys asks.

Char shrugs and Lys returns to her seat next to me. I miss the next teams in a furious cloud of whispering with Lys about how much this sucks not being on the same team and what we can do. Even though Char says she can read about lesbians, she's not known to be an avid fiction reader and Lys is worried she's going to be working solo. But this could be good in terms of us being a team no matter who I get paired with. I don't want to get an overly intense gay guy who wants me to pay attention to his every idea.

"Maze," Linc calls.

We only have two teams to go and I don't know who else's name is in the hat. Only first year students can sign up and Linc said there were eight teams, therefore sixteen students. From the two meetings I'd attended last spring, that's nearly the total out, queer, meeting-going population of the first-year class, though it's possible that someone who didn't go to the meeting had also tossed their name into the literal hat. Plenty of students, first year and otherwise, don't care about this event. The lure of a rumored treasure isn't enough to get them to add six books to their over-full reading lists. I wonder if that's a reason they don't tell us what the treasure is. Or maybe nobody on campus knows—maybe after she hid it, Professor Stendatter didn't tell anyone, to make it harder to find.

When I get to the front of the room, four slips of paper sit in the bottom of the hat. One has my name on it. Did it matter who I got? In my heart I was for sure on a team with Lys.

Opening the paper I read the name: *Bas (Sebastienne)*. She actually wrote out her full name, like anyone here doesn't know it, when it's impossible to meet her without getting "Sebastienne" in the first five minutes along with the amount of time she's spent in France.

I sigh and look at her, slumped elegantly in her seat. "Bas, it's you."

"Hah!" she laughs. "Fate is on my side. Suck it, other teams!"

Linc names the last team and returns to his seat. Professor Haille steps to the table in front of the room and opens the box that holds copies of our first books. Everyone in the contest gets their books for free, but you have to figure out what the next book is before you can ask for a copy.

"I'll give you the first book and clue," Professor Haille says. The title of the first book was on the website, but not the clue. "When you read the book and apply the clue, you will ideally figure out what the next book is. I'm not giving details about how to figure it out or what figuring it out looks like, so don't bother asking. All you get to know is that if you read this book and think about the clue and this campus, you *may* be able to find your way to the second book. And yes, the clues are vague and overly broad. You're meant to search in multiple places and explore the campus—and to think deeply about what you're reading."

She pauses and stares at each of us to make sure we are listening, then says, "When you know the title of the second book, you can come ask me for your copy. Do not try to run the names of dozens of lesbian classics by me in hopes of hacking the hunt that way—you get three asks for the next book and if they're all wrong, you're out of the hunt. And trust me, you will know when you've gotten the next book. You don't need to guess."

She opens the box and holds up the book: Audre Lorde's *Zami: A New Spelling of My Name*. "Here are your copies of *Zami*. The clue that goes with it is: *bridges and passages*."

More groans throughout the room. I guess I'm not alone in expecting more than a three-word clue. I need to go through *Zami* again specifically for bridge and passage references.

The room breaks into pairs and clumps of people. Char drags her chair over next to Lys. Kai and Sophi sit knee-to-knee now, whispering close. Even closer are Paisley and Brantley.

Lys sees me watching them steal kisses in between their whispering. "They're going to be tough competition. They work really well together. Sucks that they're a team and we're not."

"Sucks so much," I say. To Bas, I add, "No offense."

She shakes her head. "I know, you don't want to get thrown together with your lackluster antagonistic bestie when you could have your new girl take up all your time."

"What were you two even fighting about the other night?" Lys asks.

"Her jacket," I say.

At the same time Bas says, "Maze has been pissed at me since I kissed her ex last fall."

"What?" Lys's eyebrows rise significantly.

I cross my arms and glare at Bas. "You didn't only kiss her, you moved my feet off the couch like I wasn't even a person and then made out with her."

"I thought you were asleep," Bas counters with a return glare. "And I put your feet in my lap. I did not throw them off the couch. I cradled them on my thighs."

"You never even apologized for that, or leaving me at the party last weekend."

"I came back! Okay fine. Here you go: I'm sorry you got your feelings hurt because I kissed your ex—that you had broken up with months before—and that you've been having feelings about all of this ever since."

"I am not *having* feelings!" I retort. "I am made out of feelings and very few of them are about you." That's not the defense I wanted to make, I realize after I've said it.

"Feelings are important," Lys insists.

"You're on her side, got it," Bas says, taking an ostentatious step back from us, then addressing Lys. "Do you have any exes I should be careful around?"

Lys glances across the room, but I can't see who her eyes have focused on. She has an ex here? How do I not know this?

Lys says, "It's fine. Did you end up dating Maze's ex?"

"No, not at all. So why's she still mad, right?"

I protest, "You were making out with her on the same couch where I was sleeping, practically on top of me!"

Bas gives me a long stare, then says, "Some people would take that as an invitation."

"I…what?"

"Text me when you've read the book again and let's talk," she says and swooshes away in an enviable swirl of pirate mystique to find the gay boys. It's her second-best pirate coat. The first must still be missing a button. I wonder if she did go quest for it in the street the next morning. Does she care that much about her things?

Lys watches her go. "Is what she's wearing part of an actual vampire costume?"

"Historically accurate pirate," I say. "She likes two-hundred-year-old replica coats. It's a whole thing. Though I'm not convinced she's not also a vampire."

"Rough about your ex. Were you still into her?"

"No," I say. "It was the principle of the thing."

The real problem was that at the time I was into Bas. Hard to imagine now. So glad I'm not. Time to focus on Lys and *Zami* and treasure.

CHAPTER SIX

Lys

Maze and I spend Friday taking turns cheering the other one up about the fact that we're not on the same team. She bounces back faster than I do, so she does more of the cheering up. Now that she's in this treasure hunt, she wants to win for the bragging rights. I could really use the money that would come from selling the collection—whatever that is, it has to be worth something—but if I win that, Maze doesn't get her triumph. I feel trapped. There's no way for both of us to win now.

Realistically, on a team with Char who thinks lesbian sex is "ishy," I'm probably not going to win, so at least I can help Maze. Though Char has been talking about using some data science to analyze possible solutions, so who knows what she might come up with.

Maze goes home for the weekend. Her moms like to have her home one weekend a month and because she skipped last weekend, it's now been five weeks. I get it, my folks want to see my face on a video call every weekend given that this is my first year of college, first time away from home and there was that whole-ass pandemic. I spend the weekend while she's gone trying to catch up on class reading while also reading *Zami*.

I'm supposed to meet Maze for dinner Monday night and I'm super excited to see her—especially since it's Valentine's Day and I've never before had a person to be kissing on that holiday. But when Monday at five thirty rolls around I am in no shape to go out to eat with her, even to brave the student commons to get food. I am, instead, sitting on a cold bathroom floor in the Admin Building when Maze texts.

Hey, are we meeting for dinner?

I type back: *Be there in a bit.*

She asks: *Where are we meeting?*

My knee is driving knives of pain into my thigh and calf. It's burning and jabbing, so that there's no break where I can recover between the jabs, there's always baseline pain. I didn't move it enough the last few days and then today I sat in chairs with it bent and it locked in place so when I straightened it to stand up from the last meeting, the pain flared hard.

I limped into this bathroom to have a place to sit with it stretched out and so I could cry for a while without anyone seeing me. Now I'm not sure I can stand up.

And I'm so immensely pissed about this pain, especially today. I'd been doing my PT and it felt good. I was walking easily, not even lopsided by my efforts to baby this weak part of my body. Being pissed is probably making the pain worse. The next pain spike seems to jab from my knee up into my jaw, but that's probably from how hard I've clenched my teeth.

I don't know how to tell Maze any of that.

I text Kai: *pain episode in basement of admin, can you come?*

Then I text Maze: *Meet at the commons in a bit?*

Pain is so strange. It's the most real thing in the world when it's happening—and then later I can never remember the intensity, only the impact of it. I remember if I cried or curled into a ball or wanted to punch my knee for being such an asshole. I guess it's good we don't remember all the details of pain because then we'd be in pain again.

My physical therapist had me read part of a book about how

stress makes pain worse, so I've been trying to not freak out about it.

Kai replies: *20 min.*

She doesn't have to say more. We've done this before.

Then Maze asks: *Are you here? Do you want to meet somewhere else?*

Is she walking around the commons searching for me? Another pain spike jags up from my knee. I close my eyes and rest my head on the cool wall. This won't last, I remind myself. Feels like forever now, but I've never been in this kind of pain for more than an hour or two. An hour of it is the longest hour. I need this to not be that long so I can meet Maze.

I must've been in the pain for too long. She texts again: *I'll come walk you. I like walking in snow with you. Where are you? Are you okay?*

I make my fingers move, slowly hit the buttons to spell: *Not okay. Just pain tho.*

Where are you? Can I come meet you?

I type: *Admin basement. Bathroom.*

I hope she understands that my telling her where I am means yes, she should come meet me. I clench my teeth and unclench them as soon as I can, trying not to put more tension in my body. I rub at the tears with my sleeve, even though my coat fabric smears them around without drying them.

The pain is fading into a dull, steady state when Maze appears in the stall door. It's the big stall and I didn't bother to lock the door—didn't pause to do it because I was too eager to sit against a wall and stop trying to hold myself together. She's in her big outdoor coat but also wearing sneakers that are making puddles on the floor. Did she run through the snow to get here?

"Should I call someone?" she asks. Her dark eyebrows pinch close, wrinkling her forehead, the skin paler than usual. Her eyes show a contrast between the small dark pupils and the ring of warm brown that I can see fully because of how open they are.

"Kai is on her way," I tell her. "You can sit if you want. It's cold and hard and kind of terrible so if you want to go have dinner, that's cool."

"What can I do? Should I get ice?" She's half-pacing, tiny steps forward and backward in the stall door.

"Sit." Staring up at her is making me feel nauseous. When did I eat last? I'm going to need food to take my pain meds.

Maze sits next to me, reaches toward my hand and stops herself. She folds her hands in her lap. Maybe she's reaching out to comfort me, or herself—I don't have the ability to figure that out right now.

"What happened?" she asks.

I shake my head. "Do I have food in my bag?"

She drags my bag over to her and opens it, carefully pushing things to one side and the other, then taking them out and putting them in neat stacks.

"Dump it out," I tell her. "It's not organized."

She blinks at me. Peers into the bag. "I can organize it."

"Sure," I tell her. "That'd be great."

She needs to keep moving so she won't freak out and I've got no space for managing her feelings. At least she's not yelling or trying to make me go somewhere. I want to lie down on this cold floor and then fall through it into darkness.

The bathroom door swings open with a bang. Kai steps into the stall doorway. She's about five inches shorter than me but we're pretty close in weight and I swear most of the difference is in her leg muscles. I want calves like hers so badly. I've never seen her get pushed over on the rugby field.

She says, "I brought your—oh, hey, Maze."

"Hi, Kai," Maze says. "I'm organizing."

"I see that." Kai waves her hands in a big half circle that could mean a dozen things, probably does. She sits next to me and unzips her bag. "How bad?"

"Sevenish, plus pain spikes," I tell her.

"And the elevator's out again," Kai grumbles, waving in the direction of the building's ancient elevator. "I can text the team, see who's around to help you up the stairs. Or maybe someone's still in Disability Services down the hall."

As she talks, Kai digs into her bag and pulls out a small metal thermos, a protein bar, and an old prescription bottle of mine with two pills in it.

"You're a godsend," I say as she unwraps the top of the bar and hands it to me.

During fall semester as the pain worsened, Kai offered to carry a rescue kit for me in her bag. I'd had a pain spike in the Education Dept and managed to camouflage it by sitting in a study spot in a corner, but had to ask her to run to my room for my meds. I don't take them that often, not the heavy-duty ones, but they do help—especially when I need to get back to my room.

"I can help get Lys up the stairs," Maze says.

Kai shoots her the most dubious look. Maze is a bit taller than Kai but much smaller in build, not sturdy.

I eat two bites of the bar, wash them down with the stale water, and swallow a pill. Parts of my body start to relax, knowing that help is here. "I can do the stairs in a bit," I say.

Kai has her phone out. Not texting the team. She wouldn't after I said no. She's doing random phone things because she knows to give me space when I hurt. Maze doesn't. She's repacked my bag and is watching me, like I'm going to leap up into a jig or I should.

"What're you doing here?" she asks.

"Finding out there's *nothing* anyone can do about my design professor outing me," I say, harsher and faster than intended.

Maze's forehead wrinkles return with intensity. Probably because I have four different incredibly queer sweatshirts and she knows I don't mean "outed" in a gay way.

"What did she say?" she asks.

"She was giving a lecture about universal design online and used me as an example," I tell her. "That students like me with ADHD might need to get information in other ways. I like her and I don't want to have to talk to her about it but…it sucked."

Maze reaches for my hand and I nod, sliding my fingers into hers. "Are you going to talk to someone else about it?" she asks.

"Not worth it," I grumble.

I wish I had another project to give her, to occupy her focus.

I glance at Kai who peeks up from her phone in time to catch my look.

Kai sets her phone on her thigh and says, "The forwards are slacking off when you're not at practice. Coach asked me to see if you have any ideas."

Kai is so clever. I don't completely believe what she's saying about the forwards, we're pretty hardcore, but Kai knows this topic will distract me from the pain and might pull in Maze. "Are they doing weights and running?" I ask.

"Or swimming."

"Boring. We need to use our brains with our bodies more. Are there simulations for peeling off from the scrum and making tackles? Can you tie that to the exercises somehow?" To Maze I say, "The scrum is when all the forwards kind of crunch together and then the ball is tossed into play in the middle. We haven't been great about defending from the scrum."

"Are you saying the rest of the team isn't that smart?" Kai asks. She's part of the rest of the team.

"Hah, you said it," I tell her.

She snorts. "You want me to get out some paper, smarty-pants, so you can show me these simulations?"

"Can we try getting me out of here? This floor is inappropriately cold."

Kai scoots closer and waits for me to reach toward her. I feel wobbly from the meds, but I get my arm over her shoulder. With my other hand, I pick up the cane by my leg. Maze has my backpack reassembled and I trust her to bring it along. Kai stands up slowly, using the leverage of her body to support me pushing up on my good leg.

"Doors?" I ask Maze.

She darts ahead and holds the bathroom door open like a sentinel or queen's guard.

Leaning on Kai and using the cane for balance, I get into the hallway and face the stairs. I want to think I could've done them by myself before if not for the pain spikes, but all the stress of my professor outing me is piled on top of it. Plus I have to put weight on the bad knee to lift my other leg to the height of the first step—and now I can lean some of that weight on Kai.

The first two steps are doable, but the third causes a wave of pain that makes me gasp. Kai stands like a sun-warmed rock, letting me lean on her.

It's only six steps up. As if that's not a big deal when the elevator is out. As if there aren't people with more severe mobility issues than mine. Why don't people pay attention to this? How hard is it to understand that some people can't do stairs—that some people don't want their neurodivergence talked about in front of the class?

Three more to go. I think about my bed and how comfy it will be, especially if Maze is in it with me. I have to pause and catch my breath at the top—from the effort of moving through pain—but I make it. From here it's an easier journey. Even with my knee locked up, I can walk on flat surfaces and there's a good elevator in my dorm.

I tell Kai, "The pain is doable. I can get back to my dorm."

She glances at Maze and back at me, chuckling. "Oh, it's like that. Ten days of dating and you have plans, huh?"

"Valentine's Day," Maze says, inner corners of her eyebrows raised with hope or maybe doubt. Possibly both.

"Right. Have fun, kids. Lys, I'll tell Coach you won't be at practice tomorrow."

"I'll come if I can. Upper body is good for me."

"Don't stress, Monday is soon enough or Sunday if you get bored, I'll be lifting. Text me, though."

"Always."

I watch her walk across the campus, gesturing to herself over a conversation she's having in her mind. Should I have invited her to dinner with us? Feels awkward.

Turning, I walk carefully toward my dorm, Maze keeps getting ahead and jumping back to stay even with me.

"I'll get dinner," she says. "After we get to your dorm. I can bring it."

"This is not how I wanted tonight to go. Am I screwing this up? Going too fast and being a whole mess?"

"What mess?" she asks. "You can't control your knee thing.

What do you want to eat?"

"One of those mushroom burgers. I'm kind of fixated on them. Like I could eat one every day for a month. I'll get you my meal card when we get to my room."

"I can get it," Maze says.

"You got the Thai food I was going to split with you. I should be buying you dinner."

"Let's save that for a…" Maze pauses.

I finish the sentence for her. "More spectacular date night when you're not picking me up from the floor of a bathroom?"

When we make it back to my room, Maze heads out to get us dinner. I stick a shoe in the door so she'll know to come in when she gets back. I find the CBD balm, then shuffle to my bed with my water bottle. I kick the shoe off my painful leg and then bend the other so I can get that one off with my hands—and then I can snuggle back into the sweet softness of my bed.

I feel like I've ruined tonight after looking forward to it all weekend, but at least my knee is starting to tone itself down. Can we get a do-over on Valentine's Day? Is it that important? The pressure in my chest and behind my eyes says it is.

* * *

By the time Maze gets back with food, the ache in my knee is dull and ignorable and I'm spacey and loose from the meds. I want to salvage some part of tonight but my brain is like a rugby team in disarray, some players managing the pain, many more upset about today and tonight, a few completely focused on how great Maze looks. She's got her hair loose and has on a medium-blue V-neck sweater over two shirts: dark blue and sky blue. All that blue makes me feel that I could fall into her, sink and rise gently, like she's deep water and the sky at the same time.

"Where do you want me?" she asks, holding up the two bags of food. I raise my eyebrows at her.

"I have some ideas."

"Oh really?" Maze asks as she kicks off her boots, then slides into the bed next to me, careful of my leg. She sits against the heap of pillows at the head of the bed and opens her bag to take out a portobello burger. I guess she decided to try my same dinner.

"I've taken my stronger pain meds," I warn her. "I'm wobbly, conversationally and emotionally, and kind of needy but also flirty. If you're into that."

She chuckles. "That sounds great, honestly. I'm sorry about your shitty day."

"You know, I didn't even go to Disability Services about my professor. I was trying to ignore it. I went to see if Harper—she's one of the cool folks in DS—had something to make the chairs less awful. With my knee messed up, I have to sit kind of sideways so I don't bend my knee all the way and that's throwing off my hips and I'm getting backaches. I thought maybe she'd have a cushion. I don't know what students do if they have all-over pain. Suck it up, I guess. But then she was asking how my classes were going and I blurted out the thing about being outed and it got tense because there isn't anything that she can do after the fact except maybe talk to the professor. She offered to. And I'm supposed to file a complaint but I like that professor so I don't want to complain about her, which means I'd have to go tell her myself and I don't have the bandwidth for that at all. I mean, I kind of want to skip her class tomorrow and think about it."

"Kind of?" she asks.

"I like the class but I really got called out there. Now everyone thinks I'm a lazy spaz."

"You're so not," Maze says, head tilted as she squints at me like she can't figure out how I think this. The brown of her eyes is one shade warmer than her hair. I want to wrap myself up in her.

I sigh and lean my head back against the pillows. At least the tears aren't starting up again. I can get pretty emotional on the pain meds. And off them—but then it's different emotions.

"I know, I know," I say. "I'm a badass hunter or inventor. But some days it's so much and I see the looks, it's like I can hear what they think."

"I thought you were a flanker," Maze tells me with a little grin.

"Flankers are like hunters. We're always scanning for tackles and other opportunities on the field. Have you read the hunter/farmer stuff about ADHD?"

Maze shakes her head. Wow, do I get to tell her for the first time?

"It's the idea that our neurodivergent brains evolved because they were advantageous for most of human history and can be now—that we're always scanning our environment because that's what makes a great hunter. We didn't evolve to plant fields and do all the boring farmer stuff, we evolved to spot things and go after them, and it makes us highly creative."

I sit up taller against the pillows. She's watching me intensely, nodding. She says, "I notice movement a lot. It's why I have trouble studying in the food commons or the library. Every time someone walks by, I have to look. Cool if that's a hunter thing. But how much place is there for hunters today?"

"We're also great inventors and entrepreneurs," I say. "Well, except for the details of running a business, I guess. I'm not sure this is one-hundred percent science, but I like how it feels to think of myself as a hunter and inventor. My folks are always telling me I have a good brain—and it's so sensitive to food additives and environmental pollutants. They almost didn't want me to go to this college because it's in a big city, but I pointed out that it's actually farther from the downtown than our neighborhood at home. They think that if I have a hunter brain this also means it does less well with all the chemicals of modernity. And they're not wrong. But I believe that's not the whole story either."

Maze grins at me. "The metaphor I got with my Adderall was that I have a sports car brain with bicycle brakes. It's a whole boys-have-ADHD metaphor. What I do like about it is the idea that my brain has light brakes, maybe even that I take the brakes off my brain so it can do things other people's can't. What I hate about it is we can all see that a sports car with tiny brakes is a bad situation. Nobody wants someone driving that car in their neighborhood."

"It's still pathologizing," I say, agreeing. "It's still about you and your brain. It doesn't call out the culture. In the hunter/

farmer model, we're legit variants. We're not disordered or broken. We're stuck in systems not designed for people who are creative. They're designed for people who follow timelines and crap like that."

As we've been talking, she's been sorting the remains of her dinner for the parts that go into the organics bin and the ones for the trash can. She reaches for mine and I nod, letting her add my trash to her piles. She takes all of that out to the big hallway trash can, so food bits won't stink up the room.

"Do your meds make you feel more or less broken?" I ask. "Sorry, you don't have to answer that. It's the pain meds—they make me too open."

"You can't be too open," she says, flashing a grin that she quickly presses into a smile, like she's being proper.

I am very melty about this.

"Oh. Good. I was thinking, I take these because there's pain because something went wrong. I twisted this knee so badly a few times in high school and then the doctors who tried to fix it made it worse and now it gets inflamed and hurts easily and a lot. And maybe I'll get another surgery and fix it. I hope. But for me meds are something you have to take because part of your body went wrong. What does it feel like to do that for your brain?"

Maze crawls back into the bed. "My mom Joy suggested the meds are like the ones people take for high blood pressure or high cholesterol. We don't think people are broken because of that, just maybe there was a mismatch between how they've been eating and what their body is set up for."

I get what she's saying: she can be a person growing up in an environment that her brain didn't evolve for and uses medication to bridge that difference. Of course I'm asking because I wonder if I'd do better with meds—and if I can take them and still have this belief about being a hunter, inventor, creative person.

"Do you think there's a time when you won't take meds?" I ask.

"I don't know, they're pretty helpful. But...I worry that the meds change me. Not in a huge way. Then I wouldn't take them. Sometimes it feels like the change is good, like it's easier to focus on what I love. But it's also easier to shut up, even when maybe I shouldn't."

"You shouldn't," I mumble. "One more question while I'm spacey?"

"All the questions you want," she says.

"Is Maze a nickname or your given name? I figured if we're in this whole dating/Valentine's thing, I should probably know that."

"Given name," she says. "Though kind of a nickname from before I was born. My mom Kelly was on a big Greek mythology vision journey situation and kept wanting names for me like Britomartis, which at least would shorten to Brit, but then my mom Joy wisely pointed out that 'maze' is a synonym for 'labyrinth.' Both of my moms love labyrinths—and love me enough not to name me that. So: Maze."

"That's beautiful," I murmur. I've been sinking down among the pillows and I'm almost horizontal. "Lie down with me? But on my other side."

"Is there room?"

I scoot as close to the edge of the bed as I can get, which makes more room for Maze between me and the wall. She's laughing as she climbs over me and settles on her side, facing me. I touch the side of her face to tug her close enough to kiss.

"How long do we have until Char gets back and yells something ridiculous at me?" she asks.

"Poopsock," I mumble, because that was her most recent, as I text Char. I report to Maze, "She says she can stay gone another hour and she'll text before she comes back. And then knock really loud. She's included a lot of highly suggestive emojis. This may be putting me off broccoli for a while."

"Yeah but before we try to steam the broccoli, you're woozy on pain meds, can you even give consent? And I don't want to hurt your knee worse."

"We have exceptionally creative brains. And it's our maybe second date, if we're having dates, so we'll stay above the waist—and I can definitely consent to everything above the waist, even woozy. Hand me those pillows."

I put more pillows under and around my knee and then turn my face back to Maze. She kisses the side of my face along my jaw up to my ear. A tingle goes through me, making me gasp— but at the same time, I tense and send a fresh jab of pain up from my knee. "Ow, fuck."

Maze pulls back. "What?"

"I have to remember to tense only one leg."

"Can we be girlfriends?" she asks and puts a hand over her mouth, fisted and sideways, like she's going to blow into the space between her fingers and palm.

"Wait, what?"

"Is this our second date?" she asks. "Because I was counting last week, all the dinners, and it could be our fifth or sixth and I want us to be girlfriends officially but if it's too soon, I get that."

"You're asking me?"

"Oh shit, I'm doing this backward," she says and scrambles out over the foot of the bed.

She grabs her bag and zips it open, pulls out a big red heart-shaped box of candy and three cards and two silk roses with their stems entwined, one blue and one yellow. Slipping back into the bed she spills of all it into the area that would be my lap, but since I'm lying down it falls over my belly.

I lift the roses with one hand and touch the cards with the other. Tears are happening and I ignore them. "Why are there three?" I ask.

"I couldn't decide. One's funny and one's ridiculous and one's serious. Which one do you want to open first?"

"You. I want to climb into your brain first and then kiss you all night."

"Oh…Yes."

"We're definitely girlfriends," I tell her as she bends down to me and we crush a box of Valentine's chocolates between us.

CHAPTER SEVEN

Maze

I don't know how to tell Lys that I like her more now. It sounds weird, right? It's not that she's hurt, it's the way she is about it—how tough she wants to be and the soft, steady vulnerability that comes out instead and pulverizes my heart. After our Monday night date in her bed, she's been busy for a few days, balancing school with a trip to the doctor to get an update on her knee. It turns out that part of her knee was out of place and swollen and hitting a nerve, so she gets meds to reduce the swelling and then sees a bodyworker who's able to put everything in the right place again.

I use the time to finish *Zami* and obsess about it—and make sure I'm caught up on my classes. She texts me on Friday afternoon and comes over to keep me company while I'm attempting to fold laundry. She points at the copy of *Zami* on one of the dryers. "Did you finish it?"

"Yep. How far are you?" I toss my T-shirts into the basket. It's hard to want to fold them. They mainly go under other shirts, especially this time of year. Nobody will see the wrinkles.

"I finished it too," Lys says. "I had a bunch of waiting at the doctor's and to get another scan. Plus it's kind of amazing. I mean, I don't know if I like it or not, but I kind of love it. The first few chapters were a slog—due to the trauma, not the writing—but then I couldn't stop. I don't know how I want to say this, but I feel that Audre Lorde is kind of like me, except for all the ways that she isn't—born almost a century earlier, Black, immigrant parents—but like me she's poor and disabled and hella queer and I bet she's all kinds of neurodivergent. I was wondering if she was Autistic because she started talking so late as a kid, or maybe a combined type with some ADHD in there."

"Oh yeah," I agree as I fold an overshirt. "I'd like to think so."

"Did you figure out the clue?" Lys asks.

"Half," I tell her and pick up the book. "That part about bridges, check out this quote: 'I got this under the bridge' was a saying from time immemorial, giving an adequate explanation that whatever it was had come from as far back and as close to home—that is to say, was as authentic—as was possible. So it's about going back, close to home, authentic, I think. But I don't know about the passages."

"Maybe it's key passages in the book?"

"Like what?"

"Well that one where she gets her period. That's so much. Or maybe where she quotes herself. She's going back to her own passages."

"That's pretty genius," I say. I should go back to folding, but she looks so eager and hopeful that I'm paging through the book again. "She quotes herself a lot, though. The first one I'd call a passage, because it's not poetry—wait, is poetry a passage? Well, if it isn't then the first one is this quote: 'Things I never did with Genevieve: Let our bodies touch and tell the passions that we felt.'"

"That could represent any of the thousands of places on campus where people hook up," Lys points out.

I'm about to say that I don't think a professor would hide a clue in a place because people hook up there, but I see the brightness in her eyes. Flirting? I hope so!

My brain scans through all the places where people could hook up and comes up with a plausible place for a clue to be. I tell her, "Yeah, but the clue could point to a call number in the library so what if it's a place where people hook up in the library?"

"You mean those study rooms that are reserved all the time?"

"Exactly."

Lys protests, "If it's in a study room, someone would've found it already. Why are these clues so vague? Did she not understand she could give us GPS coordinates or something?"

"We're supposed to have to go to a bunch of places and explore the campus. That why it's only open to first year students," I remind her. "It's like she retired as a professor but can't stop trying to teach us things."

I toss the remaining clean clothes on top of the few I folded, heft my full laundry basket and grin. Have I memorized a few suggestive quotes from *Zami* for just this moment? Of course I have. "What if it's not that easy to find. Maybe as part of the search we should, 'Let our bodies touch and tell the passions that we felt' and that will give us the right angle to find the clue?"

"You are clearly the smartest person ever. How will we get in?"

She follows me down the hall to my room.

"I did a lot of research at the library last semester. I have connections. I traded one of the work-study students for dibs on a time they'd signed up for—and I haven't used it yet."

"What did you trade?"

"My virtue, absolutely," I say and wait a beat. "I'm kidding, I helped with a queer theory paper."

"Way to take one for the team," Lys tells me, smirking.

She knows that I love nerding out about theory. The way I talk about it makes her laugh. She told me she's used to "theory of…" but not people saying "theory" by itself—or even with "queer" attached—like we're talking about Chicago or someplace super modern like Singapore. She said I make it sound like theory is a place I visit so often that I can walk in and say "the usual," and everyone else in theory knows what I mean.

I loved that image and have been trying to figure out what my usual is.

"How long until this study room is ours?" she asks.

"If I text her now, I'll bet we can get one for tonight." I toss my laundry basket on my bed and send the text. I got about a third of it folded. That counts, right?

* * *

In the study rooms, students used to tape pieces of paper over the windows so people walking by couldn't look in and see them making out, or more. But that only alerted library staff and security to the rooms in which something untoward was happening. Now the thing to do is set books and laptop out on the desk so it appears that work is happening and then get busy on the floor near the door, out of line of sight for anyone checking through the tiny window, high on the door. If security is checking and knocks, one student stands up, waves, says they were stretching or napping and goes back to the desk.

I'm sure it doesn't always work, but it works enough. Probably because security doesn't want to see all our student antics and most of the time if they've knocked on a door that's enough for the students to quit what they were doing. I explain all this to Lys on the way to the library.

We find our room, set out my laptop, a copy of *Zami*, and my taking-notes-by-hand notebook that's mostly doodles. Then we sit with our backs against the door, wrap arms around each other and bring out mouths together.

I kiss Lys's neck and tease the curve of her breast with my fingertips while I scan the underside of the desk and the far wall. Could there be a clue written in glow-in-the-dark paint—too obvious—maybe we needed a black light? No, extra equipment would put a burden on our budgets. So far the contest has been pretty aware and kind to our budgets. Plus to be fair the clue would have to be painted in every study room.

Lys slips from sitting to reclining. I study her carefully shaped eyebrows and her completely incautious mouth. There's a wonderful symmetry to her face. Every time it changes I know she's feeling something, even if I can't always name what that is. Even if she weren't almost easy for me to read, I'd still trust her because she tells me what she's thinking and feeling.

I hope Audre felt this way with a lot of her lovers, especially after the rough go she had with some early on. I wonder if she gets to watch over us now, the patron saint of the Erotic.

I scoot down next to Lys. We're angled, I don't think our feet are visible through the little window in the door. Plus it's dinnertime, the library is almost empty. Her shirt rides up, making space for my hand on the soft, cool surface of her back. When I press there, she murmurs and leans into me, her breasts on mine. I shift half under her to feel them more fully and she gasps.

"You okay?" I ask. "Pain?"

"No, your thigh. Do that again."

I'd pulled my foot in and bent my leg up in hopes that I stayed out of view of the window—putting my thigh strongly between her legs. I bend my leg another inch and tense my quad. Her hips rock, the heat between her legs rubbing against me.

"Dear Diary," she gasps. "Today I developed a thing for muscles in a single second from Maze's thigh."

"I knew reading on the stationary bike would pay off someday," I tell her and flex my thigh again. In case she had any shyness about riding my thigh, I move a hand to her butt and encourage her. Forget heteronormative sex; feeling her molten heat moving up and down my thigh makes me wish for nothing else.

Not that this was sex. We'd been dating three weeks, that wasn't long enough for sex, right? Even if she saw me more clearly than anyone else I knew, even if I felt love radiating off her. I guess it depended on who you asked. Bas would've given it three days, and Char, with her love of romance shows that run to double-digit seasons, would say much longer. What would Audre say?

I hope she's telling me to go for it, because the way we're rocking together I want to keep going. We're lying on the floor now, diagonal from the base of the door to the wall so the desk itself covers the lower parts of our legs. My right leg is between Lys's and hers is bent slightly, weight on both my leg and the floor. On the walk over she didn't have her cane and wasn't limping so I trust, with the sliver of my brain available, that she'll let me know if this hurts her knee.

Lys's hand, which has been curled around my breast, trails down to my belly and finds the button on my jeans. She fiddles with the button until it comes open, tugs down my zipper, pauses.

"Yes?" she asks.

"Yeah."

There's lots she can do down there that isn't actual sex. Not that I don't want sex with her—I almost don't want anything else—but maybe not in a study room on the floor. There's a cool draft coming under the door across my ear. Every time I get a gust of it, I remember where we are—and every time her hand moves, I forget again.

We've been above the waist for a week and I'm running out of things I want her to do to my breasts—though not out of things I want to do to hers. Everything I knew about lesbian sex was from books, conceptual, distant, imagined but without the real knowledge to infuse that imagining. I knew so much historically about love between women, technically about how it should work. I knew viscerally that I wanted it—but not that feeling her bare breasts against mine would drop me into an entire other world.

I have the echo of that feeling now, even through winter layers, the yielding density of her breasts on mine. The berry scents of her hair mix with the citrus of mine and, rising through that, I get the deep ocean scent of our bodies. I hold her tighter and kiss her mouth, praying she can feel how invaluable, priceless, incomparable her body feels to me.

Her cheek presses mine, her breasts quickening with her breath. My free hand explores the side of her body, softer than fresh snow and much hotter. The knot of self-consciousness and fear in my chest catches fire in that heat and burns away. My legs open more to make room, to fit our bodies together.

Her skin is silky, firm, dry—Audre Lorde would compare her to a fruit, certainly, but I haven't eaten enough fruit recently to have a good repertoire, plus my brain is focused on the reality of her skin, how completely human, vulnerable, like mine. Meanwhile, her fingers find, to the surprise of no one, that I'm very wet and this makes her hips speed up. I keep her rocking with me as those fingers slip around, mapping that intimate geometry. I want to feel this rocking reach its peak, feel what happens to her body as she presses into me.

Those fingers trail from my clit to between my lips, my head tips back, my vision focusing on the edge of a ceiling tile, worn with age. Passages, bridges, "I got this under the bridge." Where *is* under the bridge? What bridge? Which passages? Names rise in my mind: Gennie…Ginger…Afrekete…all Black women that Audre loves in *Zami*.

"Should we…?" I can't find the end of the sentence. We obviously shouldn't stop. I ache from my armpits to my toes with how much I want her. And every time her fingers move up to my clit and down between my lips again, a shudder goes through me. I grab her shoulders, shift her weight more on top of me.

"In?" she asks.

"Yes."

Thick, strong fingers come into me, not far but curled up, hitting the spot that reverberates up into my jaw. I think: *Oh, this.*

And a long time after that: *This is why.*

The warm caramel of my thoughts slides down the inside of my body and wraps around her fingers.

This is why people do this.

I arch like a bridge, stars and galaxies in the corners of my vision until my eyes close themselves and leave me in a breathless darkness.

I keep my thigh tight against her, rocking with her while we shiver and gasp together.

When she pulls her hand out of my pants and rests it on my belly, I press my shirt over it and wipe the wet off her fingers.

"Well shit," she says. "This was not what I had in mind for our first time. But it's kind of epic."

"Saint Audre," I manage, still gasping.

"Bless us in our time of…eroticism? I think she did. I thought we'd have candles though, and an official date first, like at a restaurant."

She shifts back and up, so she's half-sitting against the wall. I roll forward as she moves, my cheek resting on her shoulder as she wraps her arms around me.

"My moms used to date," I tell her and immediately regret bringing them up in this moment. But I'm blissed and loose and rambling. "They still have date night sometimes. Oh, you know that because of the party. It's like Netflix and chill but without the sex."

"That is merely Netflix, since any regular chilling is implied," she points out. "So how does anyone know whether they're watching with a friend or on a date?"

"They never do. I've dated so many people by accident, it's astounding."

"Yeah me too," she says, but low, serious, like she actually has.

"Really?" I ask.

She shrugs. "I've only *really* dated two people."

"I've only dated one," I say, like this might make her feel better. "The ex that Bas…was into."

"I'll bet she never showed you fine times on the floor in the library."

"Never," I say. "But to be fair, we mostly dated remotely during lockdown."

She pushes up on her arms to stare at me.

"Maze, *where was* your first time?"

I turn my face to the side before it can give anything else away, but she presses fingers to my cheek and returns me to facing her. I raise my eyebrows, hopeful.

"Um, library. Floor."

The way her words curl around themselves tells me she doesn't quite believe what she's hearing or asking. "You own *The Whole Lesbian Sex Book*, haven't you been having The Whole Lesbian Sex?"

"My moms got it for me. I mean, I asked for it, but that's just so I'd know."

"You let me—" Her words collide into a choked sound. She rubs a hand across her face, though there aren't any tears. She looks upset, even I can make out the thunderstorm gathering between her eyebrows.

"I wouldn't have if I didn't want to. I'd have told you to stop. And I love the library. It's my second favorite place on campus after your room."

"Candles! Dinner! A date, like romance, like not me jumping you in a study room. And stop trying to make it better. You shouldn't have to comfort me."

"Where was yours?" I ask.

"A hotel room after junior prom," she says. "And yes, there were candles and sparkling cider and strawberries dipped in chocolate."

"Oh shit, I could've had those? Seriously, I like books more. Plus you know I own things. Toy things. The kind for sexy activities. It's not like that was the first time I've had a foreign body down there."

She snorts at *foreign body*.

I sigh and lean my head back against the floor, staring up at the ceiling with its one funky tile. Why that one tile? Was there a tiny leak above it? Maybe a pipe dripping a single slow drip. Or did someone accidentally squirt water up there—a water bottle incident gone awry? A flirty water fight?

"We'll have another first time," I say. "Though I'm already pretty sentimental about this one. I think we did Audre proud."

The tiles of the ceiling remind me of stones, paving stones, the underside of a bridge—and I feel it. Knowledge moves up through layers of my consciousness. I hold still, put my hand out to keep Lys from speaking. I feel the campus around me and all the kinds of bridges it holds—physical ones, community bridges, emotional, relational—they're all sorting themselves by type in the felt space around me.

I feel them with the surface of my skin, much faster and more complete than sight. I mentally push away the ones that don't have an "under." I push away the ones where we couldn't get something related to the book—something small but crucial—because we need to get something from under the bridge. I keep asking myself: why that one? Why would this bridge be different from the others? All the bridges fade except one.

I push up to sitting, Lys rolls to her side and then sits up too.

"I think I know where the clue is," I tell her. "We have to go before the food court in the commons closes."

"This worked? I thought you were trying to get us someplace where we could mess around for a while without roommates. I thought the whole 're-create the sex scenes' was a line."

"It was. But it worked," I say. "We have to go."

We zip and button, then run across the lawn to the student center. We're on the late side, some of the food counters starting to clean up, preparing to close down. Tables are mostly empty. A few have single students with the remnants of meals set to the side, books or tablets in front of them. One table has a group of students arguing, many broad gestures. I can't hear the topic.

I hurry to The Roti Shop. There's a guy at the counter, maybe a student. Nebulously older than me but still young—a patch of hair on his chin, the lean cheekbones of an active kid under sleepy brown eyes.

I thumb through my worn copy of the book to find the quotes I'm looking for, then ask, "Do you have red delicious pippins or green plantains?"

"Nope," he says. "There's some red apples over there. We've only got roti and cassava fries."

"We'll take those," I say, because their cassava fries are excellent. "But there has to be fruit that goes with it. Maybe ripe red finger bananas?"

"I don't even know what those are."

"Can you ask someone?"

He shrugs, looks at me like I'm thoroughly in the wrong

place. Then he goes into the kitchen. For a long time.

"What's next if this isn't it?" Lys asks.

"I don't know but I'll figure it out." The sense of the physicality of the campus hovers around me, waiting to open up again if I need it.

"What happens next in the book?" she asks.

I hand it to her and watch her read and then blush. "Is it safe to do that with fruit? I mean, wouldn't you get a wicked yeast infection?"

"I have no idea."

Lys hands me the book and types on her phone. "The Internet says no, we should not do that. I mean, unless you desperately want to."

I'm saved by the return of confused counter guy. Our roti-to-go bags show up in the window from the kitchen and he hands them to Lys as I tap my card to the reader. He doesn't say anything.

We go to a side table, me trying to squash a growing wave of disappointment. Lys sets down her bag and goes to get more napkins and some hot sauce. I open my bag to get a cassava fry while it's hot—and see the banana.

I shut the bag and grab Lys's, meet her by the napkins.

"Let's take this to your room," I tell her. "It's kind of cold here."

She raises her eyebrows but follows me back to her dorm, which is only half a block from where we are.

When we're inside the room, door shut and locked, roommate confirmed absent, me feeling as much like a spy as I ever will, I open the bag again and take out the notecard with the drawing of a red finger banana on it.

Inside, a looping script says: *congratulations!*

And then in print: urn:oclc:record:1029026704

Plus the words: *tried & true*

I show Lys.

"Oh wow! That's the clue for the next book. But that's not a call number. Let me see."

She types it into her phone and holds it where I can see. The page resolves to an Internet Archive page for the book *Curious Wine* by Katherine V. Forrest.

"Oh shit, my moms love that book," I say.

"You've read this one too?"

"Nope, seemed too weird. My moms actually quote from it on Valentine's Day and stuff. But I'll read it now."

Lys says, "I guess the clues are placed each year, otherwise how would they know that URL is up to date. But if they place them each year, how does that relate to the location of the treasure?"

"That's a super good question," I mutter while filing it away to ponder. It feels intensely important but not something that I can answer until I've seen more of this year's clues and read the books.

"How did you figure out where to get the clue?" Lys asks.

"To begin with, I had the best first time ever, for me at least," I say and am relieved that she's now grinning back. "And I've been thinking about how at the beginning of *Zami*, Audre's mother buys a lot of things under the bridge but the first mention is fruit, and then at the end, Audre loops back to that by telling us that she and Kitty go buy fruit 'under the bridge' and do sexy things with it. That's so many themes of the book all together and she's gone through all the passages, her life, people, time, quotes, so I figured that maybe the bridges at the beginning and end are themselves a bridge and…okay I ran out of words there, but my brain flashed on all the possible bridges on campus and places that are 'under.' There are only two buildings on campus that have bridges—if you think about skyways as a sort of bridge—and only one where you could maybe buy fruit under the bridge."

Lys's eyes light. "Because the Roti Shop is under one side of the second story walkway in the student center."

"Which is a kind of bridge," I say, grinning. "And they serve West Indian food so I figured if they had any of the kinds of fruit in the book, at least we'd get dinner."

"At this point I'm almost disappointed that we don't have to do anything else with it," Lys says, grinning back at me.

"Well, we could do something *without* fruit, to celebrate."

Our roti got very cold, which was a shame because cold roti is soggy roti and cold, soggy roti is nothing to write a biomythography about.

When Char texts that she's on her way to the room and we should put our damn pants on, I hand Lys the clue.

"Me?" she asks.

"I don't want Bas to know yet," I admit. "She's still acting like a jerk, maybe from Kai dumping her, maybe from our fight the night of the party. I'm worried she's working with someone else."

"So are you. So am I," Lys points out and I stick my tongue out at her. She asks, "Should I tell Char?"

"Give me two days to get it read so we have a head start and then tell her. It's not like she's going to put it at the top of her list—she's still getting over the sex in *Zami*, isn't she?"

"Not even getting over it," Lys says. "She would make a terrible lesbian. But there are gay guys who I'm sure aren't loving the sex scenes either, so why shouldn't a straight trans girl be in—except that I'm supposed to work with her and she's not making this easy. I know she wants the money but, shit, I need it more."

"Medical stuff?" I ask.

She hasn't brought up money head-on before, but I know her family has less than mine. A lot of her clothes are second-hand and when she wants something new, like a rugby shirt, she thinks about it for a long time. Plus I caught on after the third time she turned my suggestion of going out to eat into us going to the student food court that she eats all her meals on the prepaid meal plan. The food she keeps in the room is the kind that can be bought in bulk, inexpensive. I wish she'd let me pay for more stuff, but I'm contenting myself with not pressuring her to spend money and not being a jerk.

"Yeah, medical stuff, insurance doesn't cover all of it."

"And?"

Her jaw hardens, eyes narrow, looking across the room and

then at me—she seems to remember who I am and softens.

"My siblings all deserve to go to college, but it's a lot. The less my parents spend on me being here—and on me in general—the more my sibs have."

"That's a lot to have to carry," I say.

She nods. "Even if the amount the collection is worth isn't much, a few thousand, that makes a difference."

I stare at my fingers, twisting one of my rings. A few thousand doesn't make that much difference to me and the stab of that privilege gives me vertigo. I have such a safety net with my moms. They're not rich, but if I need something, they always have the money—and I never feel like I'm taking it from someone else who also needs it, though on the global scale, I guess I am.

How fake am I to be in this contest just for the reading, for the fun of it—and to have a project to share with Lys? I got the first clue, can I do that five more times? Can I find each answer and hand it to Lys so she worries less about her family—about her own future?

CHAPTER EIGHT

Lys

For the next few days, I remain super excited that Maze got the first clue. This feels like a fortunate omen, like if she can do this one, we can do all of them. The extra cloudy and cold February weather isn't getting me down as much as usual. I'm almost looking forward to my Monday morning class, "Education, Freedom and Personal Responsibility." A class I had such high hopes for until I actually started attending it.

It's in a room not quite big enough to hold all the students, the desks crammed close in three rows that leave small aisles at the sides of the room. A lot of education majors take this class. I signed up because it fit my schedule, I need the writing credit and it works as a prerequisite for a couple of psych classes I want to take.

Today I'm accidentally early, which gives me more choice of seats. The last few weeks I squeaked in barely on time and ended up sitting way to the left by the professor. Awkward. Now I duck into the back of the room where there's a spot by Sophi. I don't actually know her, just that Kai says she's intense about the treasure hunt—but in this class that's enough for me to want a spot near her.

She's wearing a headscarf with leaves in turquoise, yellow and green on a blue background—and her eye makeup picks up those colors and paints them around her eyes in curling fern fronds.

"Your makeup is always amazing," I tell her. "Does it take forever?"

She smiles without entirely looking up from her open textbook—a quick glance at me and back to the words. "It takes a while. Doesn't feel like it, though."

"How did you learn it?"

"Theater camp and then online."

"You act?"

Her smile moves sideways on her lips, lopsided smirky. "All the time," she says. "Not on stage much. I love making a play happen more than being on the stage. I do makeup and set design—and then get to watch it come together. Or not. Sometimes epically not."

I have a bunch more questions, but the room has filled up and Professor Leland is at the front getting his notes settled. Yes, *that* Professor Leland of the project that Kai opposes and I do too. I didn't know anything about him before this class. The first few days seemed interesting, but then Kai told me about his research. Now I don't want to talk to him about accommodations but I need to. I'm freaked out about the writing assignment deadlines and I'm missing parts of the lectures because I get distracted, and there are no notes or recordings. Disability Services sent him my list of accommodations, which includes transcripts or notes of the lectures, but he hasn't done anything about it.

Professor Leland has black-rimmed, rectangular glasses that look extra smart, which doesn't help with the intimidation factor. But he's also got graying dark-brown hair and a carrot-orange beard, or at least it looks orange with his pink complexion. It's like his beard and his head hair belong on two different people. I spent most of the first week of class thinking about what could've caused this and now if I feel too freaked out I stare at his beard for a while and everything feels silly enough to keep going.

"Small group work today," he announces. "Get into groups of three or four with the people you're sitting near."

I whisper to Sophi, "Group?" She nods.

The two students in front of us, a long-haired white guy who seems half asleep and a tiny dark-haired white girl, turn their desks around to complete a group of four. Professor Leland moves among the groups, handing out sheafs of paper, as he explains the assignment.

"Each group is getting a different sample accommodations letter," he says and I cringe. I hope "sample" means fake. He wouldn't use real letters, would he?

He continues, "Please read your group's letter thoroughly and then discuss how to deliver this class to a student who has this accommodation. Keep in mind ensuring that the class is fair for all of the students. You have thirty minutes and then each group will present their solutions."

I feel like we're doing his homework for him. He should be able to figure out how to deliver this class for students with accommodations, or go ask the Learning Center because they're great at this. Plus, looking at what he's given us, I feel like he printed out my accommodation letter and handed it to my group. It's not exactly the same, but it's a student asking for recordings of the lectures and notes, which I *have* asked for. It includes a note from the professor that the class material is proprietary. *Whyyyy?* I haven't learned anything yet that I couldn't get in a textbook or online.

"This is bullshit," I tell the group, pointing to the letter.

"But it's easy," sleepy guy says. He folds his arms on his desk and lays his head on them while talking. "Put the class online and let students stream it."

"That doesn't cover the written notes parts," I say.

Sophi chuckles, a short, dry sound. "Bet he doesn't know how to stream it."

The tiny girl looks up from her notes and says, "Plus he'll point out that a student could play it from their computer and record it on their phone."

"We could secretly record it in person too. What in this class is actually proprietary?" I scoff.

"His teaching style?" the napping guy asks without opening his eyes.

"His ego," Sophi says.

I flash her a grin. Not sure if she sees it because she's reading the letter again, but her half-smile has returned.

"What if you had an app read the textbook," the tiny girl suggests.

"He tells anecdotes in the lectures and one was in the test we had last week," I point out. "Our case study student would miss all that." I don't want to say I'm missing that content when it gets hard to concentrate in class because it's early or there's noise outside or inside the room or inside my brain.

"Does anyone listen to recorded lectures?" tiny girl asks. "And then why come to class?"

Sophi has drawn an eye on the letter and is making designs around it that turn into elongated letters as I stare at them. They spell h-e-l. "Some people learn better when they're alone," she says. "Or when they're moving. Alone and moving, even."

I want to support this point and add, "I learn really well when I'm working out."

Tiny girl says, "If he's afraid someone will steal his style, he could put his typed notes online and you could get your computer to read those to you. When he lectures he reads off notes, so they exist."

"Proprietary," I say, tapping that part of the pages he gave us.

"A lot of students are taking notes," Sophi says. She draws a calligraphic "p" down from the far corner of the eye, completing the word: *help*. "Put the student notes in a shared drive and have the computer read them."

"I like that solution," tiny girl says.

I kind of like it too—at least as a way to get through this class. And maybe if someone shares their notes, and I'm hoping that someone will be Sophi, I can skip some sessions of this slog and pass the tests.

I voice my reservation. "That puts the responsibility on the students. He's an education professor, he should be doing Universal Design for Learning."

The professor calls the class back and asks the small groups to present their solutions. He's standing to the side of the podium at the front of the room, one ankle casually crossed in front of the other.

The first two answers are straightforward: do what the accommodation letter says. For our group, tiny girl presents a list of all the ideas we'd discussed with pros and cons. As she talks, he steps behind the podium and shuffles through the papers on it.

When she's finished, he says, "That last solution is interesting." His gaze rises from the paper to sweep the room and settle on my group, one eyebrow quirked up as he asks, "Wouldn't it open up the possibility for the student with the accommodation to then blame their failures on the students taking the notes?"

Hair on the back of my neck stands up. I shouldn't take this personally except I totally should. My hand shoots up and he nods to me.

"A student seeking to blame others would find an excuse to do that anyway," I say. "And what if the student succeeds, doesn't that then empower other students in the class?"

"But the first student isn't learning to work on their own," he counters. "In the work world, you're not going to find someone to share their notes with you. Another solution might be for any student having trouble paying attention to cut down on fruitless extracurricular activities."

I sink down in my seat, arms crossed hard. He could've been dissing rugby, but I'll bet that was about the literary treasure hunt. Possibly he hates fiction or, more likely, thinks books about lesbians are frivolous. Screw him.

When the class ends, as students are leaving the room, I point at the letter that Sophi is folding into her notebook. "Is that a cry for help?" I ask, lightly.

She unfolds it and touches the corner of the eye. "I thought about adding a tear here to make that literal, but I prefer the ambiguity. Maybe she's from a world where people use makeup to show when they're available to help others."

"I'd appreciate that world," I say.

"Me too," she says and turns back to packing up.

There are so many things I want to say to that. I get stuck trying to sort them and before I have any concrete statements or questions, she's out the door.

* * *

I'm meeting Kai at the gym for a lunchtime workout. I'm so eager to talk to her that I'd run there if my knee wasn't giving me warning twinges. It's about three blocks from my class and the shortest route is over the pedestrian bridge that spans the highway north of the bulk of campus. I add an extra block to the walk to avoid all those stairs.

The gym is a long, low brick building, much wider than the ones around it. I swipe my card and hit the button to swing the door open automatically because it's super heavy. Maybe that's supposed to be part of our workouts.

I love gyms. I've been in sports since elementary school soccer. All the gyms I've known have a comforting blend of neatness and wear—weights stacked on their racks, but dings on the floor and walls from their use. The rooms smell of sweat and disinfectant, two kinds of work that make sense to me, even if I suck at cleaning. I wish my education class made the kind of sense to me that gyms and the rugby field do—or even that I could stand up and move around during class, but that's not on my official list of accommodations and I'm sure Professor Leland would call it disruptive.

After I've changed into workout clothes, Kai meets me in our usual spot by the weight machines. She's in sweatpants and a

T-shirt that says, *Stop Adulting, be a Mermaid*, with an image of a Black mermaid on it, her locs fanning out in the water. Kai took her braids out a few days ago and her hair is compressed from wearing a winter hat, the soft puff of her afro close to her head. She's in her regular cozy pants, or the workout version of those.

I'm in a college-themed T-shirt and shorts because it's easier to work out in the knee brace when the foam is against my skin.

"How's being on a team with Sophi?" I ask.

Kai's shrug turns into a sweeping, arms out gesture that's a multidimensional *who knows?* She says, "Fine, I guess. She's quiet. And has mindmaps for things, like our team. I don't do clues in mindmaps. She wants to list out all the possible clues. That's so many."

"I sat next to her in education and she's funny. I want to ask her if I can see her notes for the class. Do you think she'd be cool with that?"

"Cool?" Kai snorts. "She'd love it. Is that the Leland class? How is that going?"

"What's a metaphor for very shitty?"

"What did Char say the other day? A crapladle," she says. "So maybe sailing a crapladle up shit's creek without a paddle?"

I laugh. "Is that two metaphors or three?"

"We're rabbit-holing, what's he talking about in class? Do you have more info about this research study of his? I heard he's been interviewing the other professors who hate accommodations and that seems bad upon bad."

"He hasn't told us anything, which is unusual since he likes to talk up his projects, but maybe that's only the past ones."

"You'll tell me, though, right?" Kai asks.

"Of course! As soon as I hear anything."

We get into our lifting routine. I hate how much muscle I lost over winter break, being home and away from a gym where I can work my legs safely. Coach says the capacity is there and I'll have the strength back in no time. And I've been working on it with my physical therapy person.

Last fall, before I twisted my knee again, I ran most days, had practice often, and all that movement two or three times a day made it easy to get schoolwork done. Now I don't know what to do with myself sitting still all the time. Maybe make out with Maze more often? I hope that's the answer.

We move to the shoulder press and Kai steps into the spotter position, then makes an appreciative "uh-huh" when she sees how much weight I'm lifting. We started working out together back when we were sort of dating—we didn't call it dating, just hung out with some of our clothes off and our bodies mashed together, not so much with the going out to meals or movies and stuff—I guess there were movies, but we didn't watch them. Our dating-ish time spanned most of September and part of October, but then we got busy and out of sync and after midterms and fall break, we didn't have the same vibe anymore.

As I push the bar up, I ask, "Have you heard from Bas?"

"Not a word. I guess that's that."

"You did dump her in front of people."

"Yeah," Kai says with a sigh. "I didn't mean it to go that way. I thought she'd be pissed and agree to get another work-study job."

I finish my set and let go of the bar to shake out my arms lightly. I tell Kai, "We drove her home after the party and she slipped and got stuck under the car for a few minutes, not serious, just her jacket caught. She and Maze fought about something kind of heavy by the way they sounded and how quiet Maze got after. I wish I knew what Bas said to her."

Kai nods, lips compressed. "She has a real sharp tongue when she gets going. Maybe better not to have Maze repeat it. Hey, how are you guys doing with the new book? If you want to tell me."

I like that she's asking about me and Maze rather than me and Char, but that might be because she knows that the secret team is the one most likely to have the answers.

I exchange positions with Kai so she can do her shoulders. "We've got nothing. You?"

"Same. What worked for Maze getting the clue for *Zami*?"

I'm blushing and glad I'm behind Kai so she can't see the look on my face. But I'm quiet for too long and she says, "Spill it."

"We decided to, uh, enact some of it. The sexy parts."

She laughs with the bar extended and I have to tighten my grip on the bar because she can't hold it up and laugh at the same time. We get it into its rest and then she bends forward, laughing more.

"Which sex?" she asks, way too loudly for a shared gym. "Not the awkward white-girl sex?"

"No! I wouldn't dishonor the memory of Audre Lorde like that."

"So you're getting down like Audre and Ginger and suddenly Maze looks up and is all, 'sweet Jesus, I've got it!' like that?"

"I mean, she didn't invoke Jesus."

Kai finishes her next set, still chuckling. We move to back extensions.

She asks, "Have you tried the sex from *Curious Wine*? There's plenty of it."

"She started making a list. But then I had questions and her moms wanted her to go home for the weekend and help with the basement."

"That's so cool. 'Her moms.' My mom should get a girlfriend."

"Would she?"

"Who knows. Pretty sure she's straight but I can dream," Kai says. "You should go try more of the sex from the book tonight, unless Char's got someone we can talk her into trying with."

"You could date someone," I point out.

"Nah, I don't need any more complications this year. No offense."

"Oh, was that about me?" I ask playfully, knowing it wasn't. "I was soooo complicating."

I try to remember exactly what the characters did for sex in *Curious Wine*. How much of that have Maze and I done recently? Most of it, I'm pretty sure.

I tell Kai, "I think me and Maze have already done most of the stuff in the book and she didn't have a revelation. What if we're doing the wrong scenes? I love the one where they're smoking weed and doing all those questions, the 'encounter games.' I Googled it and it was a whole movement in the sixties—people got together and did deep psychological stuff, like in the book."

Kai pushes up and sits on the extension bench, facing me. Her grin bunches her already round cheeks. "How many people in that?"

"Six," I say.

"That's you and Maze and both of your teammates, plus me and—can you talk Sophi into this?"

"Sure. That's a great reason to text her and also ask about her notes. How bad are you two as a team if you don't want to ask her?"

Kai shrugs. "She's...not my vibe at all. After the whole mindmap thing, she got real quiet with me for wanting to do it all digital. It's been the twenty-first century for a minute now, but I get no points for not dissing her old-school style."

"Maybe she needs the maps."

"Then she can fill 'em in. You know I'm not for the paper and pen interface."

I nod. Kai has dysgraphia, which means her hands tend not to write everything her brain is thinking. That sounds super frustrating. Sometimes when I'm taking notes I have to write super fast, near illegible, to get it all out before my brain distracts itself to something else. I can't imagine what it would be like not to be able to do that, though I feel like I'd scream a lot. Kai is a wicked fast typist, though.

"Sorry," I say. "I thought she'd be more understanding."

"Me too," Kai says. "And that was merely the first fight."

"You want to tell me the second?" I ask.

"Food," Kai tells me.

Kai has particular tastes and procedures for what she eats and they are not to be critiqued. That makes it sound like she's super healthy and she isn't—there's a delicate balance between the percentage of fried foods in her diet (high) and the percentage of protein (also high). She insists that "crunchy" is both a flavor and an essential food group. She'll chug any kind of smoothie she needs to in order to get more crunch into her life: ideally chips or popcorn. In a pinch, fried chicken or fried fish. In dire circumstances, fried veggies. She's kind of converted me, if I'm being honest.

"Ouch," I tell Kai. "I'll text Sophi and see when she's free for this."

I'm eager to see the reenactment and also hang out with Sophi outside of the classroom. I need to make sure that sharing notes won't somehow get us in trouble with Professor Leland, but I need something to change in that class. There are a bunch of other education classes I want to take, so I need to survive this one.

CHAPTER NINE

Maze

I love Lys and Kai's plan to reenact the encounter games from *Curious Wine*. I don't know what it was about being in the library and sex and thinking about *Zami* that put the clues together in my mind, but I'm hoping the same magic shows up for us today. If it doesn't, I am entirely down to reenact more of the sex from the novel with Lys.

Plus I'm so curious about what a queer encounter group would be like. Having lesbian moms means I got a lot of queer history, but it's just enough that I want so much more. My moms were born in the seventies, so the idea of entire adult lesbians meeting in the seventies and having a romance feels like having cool grandmoms I haven't met yet. What would my moms be like if they'd had lesbian grandmoms or any kind of elders?

Lys and I decide we should take over half of the common room on her floor in the Hampton dorm, since Char's also in the competition and Kai's dorm, Rivera, is the next one over. This is an easy meeting point for half of us. We move six chairs together, which drives out some of the students who wanted quiet. The others have noise-canceling headphones and are sitting on the far side of the wide room.

Lys goes to her room to get us beverages, so I'm there alone when Bas arrives. She sweeps in, wearing a light gray frock coat over a coral-colored crop top and drops sideways into a chair, stretching her feet over the neighboring one. Her hair has grown out to a half-inch that she's gelled up on the top and back on the sides, so maybe she's growing it out. I don't ask. We haven't talked about anything other than the treasure hunt since the night of the party—and I don't particularly want to talk about anything else.

"Great party," she says. I ignore her and rearrange chairs until I hear her say, "Come on in."

Sophi stands inside the doorway, her coat folded over her arm. She's in loose gray pants and a cream-colored sweater with a thick cloth belt of gold, indigo and turquoise wrapped around her waist, outside of the too-small belt loops. Her eyeshadow matches the colors in her belt, with indigo over her eyes, swept through at the inner corners with gold and turquoise, colors vibrant on her brown skin.

"I wasn't sure this was the right floor," she says.

Bas straightens and jumps up from her chair. "Wow, your eyes! Did you pick the colors to match the belt?"

"I bought the belt to match colors I have," she says with a hint of a smile. "Your coat is lovely. What's it made from?"

"Denim, if you can believe that. Feel how flexible it is. I couldn't believe when I found a whole bolt of this on sale last summer."

Bas holds out an edge of her coat to where Sophi can rub it between her fingers.

"You *made* that?" Sophi asks, her voice expressing the awe I'm also feeling.

"Yeah. I make all my jackets. Otherwise the fit is wrong."

"That's amazing," I say.

Bas gives me a look—one eyebrow raised, lips twisted wryly—suggesting that I could've had this amazing information months ago. I'm not sure it would've been worth it, but her jackets seem less pretentious now.

Lys returns with Char. Lys is in her usual school sweatshirt and jeans while Char is sporting purple skinny jeans that almost match her hair, a pink sweater, and a small, blue shoulder bag that's also a cat plushie. Her earrings are bits of computer innards. She's carrying a six-pack of sparkling water and Lys has a two-liter bottle of pop with cups.

Kai joins us last, wearing a rugby hoodie and what looks to me like fuzzy pajama bottoms in a blue and green plaid. Her braids are gone and her hair is a soft, dark puff close to her head. She drops into the only open chair, next to Sophi, with a scowl. I make a note to ask Lys about that later. She's said they're not gelling as a team, but this seems beyond that. Still, I won't let it spoil our plans!

"I bet you're wondering why I've called you all here," I say, but nobody gets that I'm winding up my league of supervillains speech, so I keep going. "Thanks for reenacting this with us. Helps us get into the book. If you haven't read it yet, Diana goes to stay at a friend's cabin and there's this very hot woman Lane there. They end up rooming together and you can guess where that goes."

"More or less sex than *Zami*?" Bas asks.

"Both have more than I expected for books published in the eighties about the seventies and the fifties," I say.

"People always have sex," Kai says without turning toward Bas, who is resolutely not looking at her.

In the novel, the encounter group was not a peaceful exercise—and we're set up for even more drama. Bas is obviously still pissed about Kai dumping her. Sophi and Kai are icy toward each other. Char's mad at Lys about roommate things, but Lys won't give me specifics. The chance that we'll make it through these exercises without someone yelling or crying is fading.

Stopping now would be weird, so I bravely push on. "There are six characters in this scene: the two lesbian main characters and then a pair of sisters and two friends—"

"I call dibs on Lane," Sophi says. "I'm the right height."

"What and then I'm Diana? Hard no," Kai tells her.

"Oh so you want us to give up the main characters and be the mean sister and the racist sister?" Sophi shoots back.

"You want us to be the lovers?" Kai asks, crossing her arms hard across her chest.

Sophi gives her a level stare. "No but Char is *obviously* the good-natured married one and I thought Bas might not mind being the one who sleeps around, no offense."

"I'm cool with sleeping around," Bas agrees, to the surprise of no one. To Sophi she adds a flirty wink and says, "Thanks for thinking of me."

Char puffs up, right hand closing around the arm of her cat plushie bag. "Wait, why am I the married one? I could sleep around."

"I *have* literally heard you singing 'Someday My Prince Will Come' in the shower," Lys points out. "Unironically."

"Fine as long as I don't have to be a jerk."

I sigh and look at Lys. "Which one of us is the mean one?"

"You don't want to fight to be the heroes?" she asks.

"In my mind, we're always the heroes," I tell her and Bas makes a gagging sound. "I thought it would be fun to be side characters for this. So much of the story takes place with these six women in this winter cabin—I want to know more about all of them. Like are Lane and Diane the only lesbians? What if they all were? What if one of them is trans or nonbinary. I thought the others should get some space too. Maybe there's a redemption arc for the sisters."

Lys nods, sets her cup of pop on the side table, arms staying open, shoulders relaxing. I slip from reading her body to imagining curling against her and only return to the present when she says, "Yeah, we can be them."

"Great. So we're supposed to sit in a specific order which is…" I consult the book open in my lap. "Bas next to me and then on her other side, in this order: Sophi, Kai, Char, Lys."

This puts Lys next to me, even though we aren't cast as the book's romantic couple. Will Sophi and Kai regret their choice? Sophi has her legs crossed away from Kai, who's leaning forward over Char to talk to Lys.

"In the book everyone shakes hands to start, but given our last year, let's just elbow bump, okay?" I suggest.

There's bumping and jostling around the circle.

"Next we pair up, hold hands and look into each other's eyes for a minute with no talking and no phones. Kai and Char, Bas and Sophi. I'll time you and then you time me and Lys for a minute."

"We could set an alarm," Bas points out.

"Then no one's watching to make sure we're doing it right," I say. Because yeah, I want to watch the others do this and anyway this is how it went in the book.

Everyone shoves their phones into pockets or bags and joins hands in their assigned pairs. Bas slouches back in her chair, which makes Sophi come forward, elbows on knees, her elegant face looking more sculpted than usual. They stare at each other like wizards having a magic fight, but a sexy one. Pretty sure Sophi's going to win. Bas has a good front, but on her best day she's half as together as Sophi.

Kai cocks her head to the left, showing how unimpressed she is with this exercise, but after a few seconds she straightens up and leans forward, really looking at Char. Char draws back, corrects herself and smiles.

"Time," I say.

Bas turns away from Sophi first and then Sophi shifts her body enough to gaze down the long side of the room. Kai and Char have dropped hands but are staring at each other.

"Your eyes are six different colors," Kai says.

"For real?"

"Yeah, I thought blue was just, like, blue, but there's gold and brown flecks and some kind of green and maybe a little bit of mermaid teal."

Char beams. "You're beautiful too," she says. "Not only your grin, everyone knows that's great, but the shape of your eyes is so pretty."

Kai ducks her head, fishing in her pocket to get her phone. She flicks to the clock app.

"I'll time you guys," Kai tells me and Lys.

Lys's fingers slide into mine, warm and rough and perfect. I probably shouldn't spend this minute thinking about all the places those fingers have been on my body, but the first few seconds couldn't hurt. Will she see as many colors in my eyes as Kai had in Char's? I don't have mermaid teal, for sure, but dragon gold figures prominently in the brown near my pupils.

The muscles around Lys's eyes crease with tension. Hard to sit still? Her foot jiggles. I squeeze her hands and she squeezes back, foot settling for a moment. Her eyes don't ease, tension shows in all the tiny muscles around the edges, but in the center of that kaleidoscope blue is bare desire and an emotion that, though her eyes couldn't say it out loud, I can only name as love. I relax my face and beam that back at her, wanting her to see herself in my view of her. She smiles and leans toward me as I do the same, jerking back at the edge of the we're-about-to-kiss zone.

"Time," Kai says. "What's next?"

I take a long sip of tea and another. I'm getting what was cool about this kind of group in bygone decades. I share a lot of stuff online, but usually not attached to my name or my actual body—this feels like posting a whole bunch of revelatory info and reading other people's, but with our whole bodies.

I open the book with its distinctive green cover to peek at what's next. "We're supposed to look into the eyes of the person on the other side of us," I say and turn to see Bas raising an eyebrow at me. "I'll set my phone for this, now that we know how to do it."

Wanting to get through this as fast as possible makes it feel like an age is passing as I gaze into Bas's bright eyes under her arched and sculpted brows. I can't help thinking about her saying I should've joined her and my ex on that couch. She was joking, right?

When the alarm goes off, I grab my phone to silence it. Beyond Sophi's back, I see Kai's face: no smile, all sharpness for Sophi. How long will it be until those two drop out of the hunt?

"That didn't suck," Char says and Kai's snort sounds like partial agreement.

"Kinda makes me see that I'm not the only one freaked out about being a human being," Lys says. She takes the book from my lap and turns a page. "Oh fun, it's touching next."

"What kind of touching?" Bas asks, hopefully.

"Not that kind," Char says. "Right?"

"Right," Lys confirms. "Just the face, if folks are cool with that." She pauses and gets nods from around the room, half of the nods accompanied by shrugs. "Same pairs as last time and you decide who does the touching first—wow that sounds wrong, but you know what I mean."

Lys sets her phone for two minutes with a beep in the middle so folks will know when to switch and we face each other again.

"Who starts?" I ask, but she's already reaching for me so I try to stay in my chair as her fingertips brush my cheeks.

She traces my nose and jaw, my ears, which doesn't quite tickle, but reminds me of her lips on my ear a few nights ago. My face gets hot all over, not only where her fingers touch. She presses her thumb against my chin dimple and grins, then traces my eyebrows.

The phone pings and she folds her hands in her lap, her feet moving restlessly. I brush my thumbs over her cheeks and rub her temples, tucking my fingers into the thickness of her hair. I trace around her lips and let my fingers wander down the sides of her throat. She's blinking fast, mouth open. I think we feel the same deep tug toward each other. If this minute doesn't end, I'm going to fall into her and keep falling.

The alarm rings and we all face into the circle, silent. I wish I could've seen the others. This second session I'm paired with Bas and as she's touching my face, I watch over her shoulder. I can see the back and side of Sophi, plus Kai's face as she touches Sophi. Kai starts narrow-eyed—suspicious, maybe wary?

I watch her eyes widen, her mouth open. Sophi is so still someone could've carved her, but Kai is melting by the second. The phone dings and Kai pulls her hands back and shoves them into the big front pocket of her sweatshirt. I reach for Bas's face, trying to do a decent job while not actually looking at her. She's staring at the floor and doesn't protest.

Sophi's hands cup Kai's cheeks with such gentleness the back of my throat aches. Her fingertips paint invisible colors around Kai's eyes, swirling up from the back edges, under the brows, down the sides of her nose, softly across the lower lids.

So slowly and carefully her thumb sneaks down—does she even know she's doing that?—to brush Kai's lips. Kai smiles, her face luminous, and puts a hand over Sophi's.

"Tickles," she whispers, loud in the silent room. But she doesn't pull Sophi's hand away.

The phone alarm rescues me from having to brainstorm more nonsexual ways to touch Bas's face.

"Holy shit," Lys says. "That's intense. When does the book get to the part with weed?"

"After the trust falls," I tell her.

Bas says, "There is not enough weed in the world to get me to do a trust fall."

"And after the 'what animal is this person' question," I add.

"Hard no," Lys says, looking to Kai who backs her up with a nod.

Kai says, "Not doing that."

"Skip to the weed," Bas suggests.

"Let's take a break, like fifteen? And anyone who wants to smoke go for it," I say.

Lys, Kai and Bas bundle up and go outside. Char leaves too, but I get the impression she's not going with them.

Sophi sits upright in her chair with her hands curled around her phone in its heavy tactical case. "Any ideas about the clue?" she asks. "I heard you were the genius who figured out *Zami* and I'm pretty sore about that one."

I say, "I've learned that it's hard for me to think properly while touching people's faces, but that's it. You?"

"With the clue like 'tried and true'…yeah, nothing here either."

"We're definitely trying. How was doing all this with Kai?"

"Irritating. Do you mean the exercises or the contest? Actually she's irritating both ways, so never mind. I understand that we both think we're right about all the things, but she's so dense about some things I can't get through. She won't even brainstorm with me: either she knows the answer or she's not going to engage. She thinks she can intuit a solution to this clue and nothing I say changes her mind. How long have you and Lys been together?"

"Oh, you know? We've been trying to be chill."

"I'm good at reading vibes," she says. "You don't want people to know? Why?"

"Lys and Kai dated last fall and it seemed like a jerk move to rub Kai's face in it."

"They did?" If the intensity of her voice weren't enough, Sophi's thumb is chafing the thick, black rubber phone case like she could rub it right off the phone.

"Just in September," I say. "Anyway, we got together about a month ago, first weekend in February."

"You two need to be careful. Did you see the new guidelines for the competition this year? Linc sent out an email reminder. During the first half there can't be secret teams."

"Whoa what?"

She glances at the door and back at me. "I gather that last year a lot of the teams would get together—kind of like we're doing now—and share info, but they also shared some viral particles. I think what we're doing today isn't enough to get kicked out, otherwise I wouldn't be here, but we need to watch out. And you and Lys need to keep to yourselves until we're through book three."

I'm still staring at her in horror when everyone gets back from outside, bringing a faint skunky smell of weed to overlay the waxy apricot scent of this common room. Lys texts Char who answers by arriving a minute later.

Lys takes the book and says, "Next we go around and you say what you like about the person on your left. This is described as giving 'some strokes' so laugh it up, Bas—also you're first."

"So I'm stroking Maze?" Bas asks.

I suppress a sigh—unsuccessfully. "Yes. Verbally."

"You're smart as fuck. Though I don't know if that counts as what I like about you. You're weird in a cool way and you're always saying shit that makes me think."

"Thanks," I say. I like being weird in a cool way.

Lys is on my left and I turn to her with a million possible great things to say. Strands of hair are coming out of her messy bun and she's tucked them behind her ear. I make myself focus

away from that and try to find something that's appropriate—
with Sophi's warning about secret teams still in my brain canals.

"You're there for your people," I say. "Loyal and protective
and there's a wisdom about how you take care of people."

Lys breaks into a grin and almost grabs my hand. She twists
her fingers together and presses back into her chair.

"Char," she says. "I like that you keep things tidier than I do.
Hah! Not only that, though, you have a sweet heart. You worry
about people in a really generous way."

"Aww, thanks." Char turns to Kai. "I don't know you outside
of the team. But I know Lys trusts you deeply, so you must be
super trustworthy."

"Wow, appreciate that."

As Kai faces Sophi, the room silences, like we're all waiting
for lightning to strike, not sure what kind, heat or destruction?
Sophi lifts her chin and stares down at Kai. Sophi is the tallest
of us and Kai the shortest, so it's a long stare.

"You're clever," Kai says. "We're all smart. You don't get to
this school if you're not. But the way you apply your smarts, it's
clever. I've heard about how you solve problems in the Theater
Department, sometimes way before they get to the problem
stage. You're working upstream. I admire that."

Sophi's face brightens. "You—" She cuts herself off and
looks over her shoulder. With effort, she turns to face Bas. "I
like that you know what you want and you go for it. A lot of
people bullshit around, but you don't."

Bas grins. "Thanks. Do we go the other way with
compliments now?"

Lys shakes her head. Another strand of light brown hair is
working its way out of her bun, and I want to tuck it back in. Or
play with it.

She says, "Not quite. We go the other way, but you tell the
person who said something nice about you a thing you'd like
her to do differently, change, maybe an area for growth. Bas, do
you want to start?"

I'm super glad that Lys padded that one with some
psychological bits and is starting with a pair in the circle who

have almost no history together. In the novel, the characters get pretty critical of each other.

Bas tilts her head to the side, tongue peeking out to touch her upper lip before she tells Sophi, "You seem kind of hard to get to know and I want to get to know you better. Does that count?"

Bas's tone is soft, but Sophi stiffens, pulls back. She shrugs one shoulder. "Sure, that counts. I'll work on it." She turns to Kai. "You're missing the process of slowing down by not using paper. Everything doesn't have to be instant. You can take your time."

Kai's nose wrinkles, lips twisting to show the edge of her teeth. She turns away from Sophi to Char. "Crap, Char, I know you've got a hell sandwich in some areas of your life, but please check your privilege one of these days."

Char's head rocks back, eyes wide. "What?"

"You brought that basic straight white boy to meetings last November and he said some shit that you did not correct. I could go the rest of my time here without having that in my queer space again, right?"

"He was an asshole anyway," Char says, shaking her head and looking everywhere but at Kai. Both hands curl around her plushie backpack, pulling it into her lap.

"Maybe find that out *before* you bring someone into our safe spaces," Kai suggests.

"Yeah, fine." Char turns to Lys. "You know what I'm going to say. Your desk and clothes—and all that space in front of the closet, like basically the whole floor—it's a huge mess all the time. Could you keep that stuff from ending up in front of my bed and closet and desk? I get that you're messy, but don't put your mess in my space."

Lys turns away from Char, to me, and I see the tears gathered in her eyes.

"I'm trying," she whispers.

I grab her shoulders and pull her against me. I know that shame of my laundry taking three times longer than neurotypicals, the shame that there's always a pile of clothes in my dorm room, usually two piles: clean and dirty, but sometimes I can't tell what's what, the shame that I can't do these easy, little, tidying things that other people seem to do automatically.

My moms, Mom and Joy, both used to clean my room when I was younger, but very differently. Mom would just do it while telling me how ridiculous I was for not putting away a sock or a toy. Joy got me to work with her and sometimes we'd move a hamper or trash can if it wasn't in an easy place for me to use it. That's what should've stuck with me, but it's Mom's messages that stuck. I wonder what messages Lys is hearing right now.

"I'm not being an asshole. I have to live in that room too," Char says, fingers digging into the soft parts of her bag. With her face tipped down, eyes narrowed, it's hard to see that she's peeking sideways at Lys. "I don't care what's in your space as long as it's not stinky food, but I need space for my stuff and not to lose it under your stuff."

"Not helping," Kai says, leaning across Char to rest a hand on Lys's knee. Lys wraps her fingers around Kai's.

On Kai's other side, Sophi has her phone out, thumbing through screens. "There's probably an easy hack for this. What layout does your room have?"

"This is so not the time to talk to Lys about rearranging her whole room," Kai tells her without turning toward her.

Sophi expands a view on her phone, bringing it closer to her face. "Not the whole room. A system."

"I suck at systems," Lys grumbles into my shoulder.

"A good system is one you can't suck at," Sophi says. "That's how you know it's the right system for you."

"This is not the time for systems," Kai says loudly, lips tight and hard around the words. She leans further away from Sophi, angling half across Char, who is playing with the ears of her cat backpack and staring at the floor.

Sophi's head comes up, her face blank except a slight lift of her eyebrows and parting of her lips—like her question died on the back of her tongue. That look is one I've felt so often.

I tell her, "Sophi, we're drowning under course loads, still worrying that there's going to be another Covid variant or another pandemic. There's too much going on to add a new system. Plus our brains were made for creativity, not organizational systems. Lys doesn't have space to hear what you're offering."

"Oh, okay," she says and goes back to sifting through her phone.

Kai swivels toward Sophi, pulling away from Lys as she raises both hands in frustration. "So Maze says one thing and you're totally cool? That's it?"

"Yep," Sophi says. The hand without a phone is balled into a fist at her side. "All I have are systems that work. What're you bringing?"

Kai throws her hands up all the way. "I'll be the one helping sort it out."

"Good," Sophi says, unironically but with some force, even anger. She stands up. "I'll be back."

Lys pulls away from me and watches Sophi leave.

"I do not understand her," Kai grumbles after Sophi has left the room.

"I'll make sure she's okay," Bas says. She grabs her coat and scoots out through the doorway.

Bad idea to have Bas be the only one checking on Sophi, but I don't want to leave Lys. She sees me watching the empty doorway and says, "Go. I'm going to get tissues and wash my face."

I nod and head for the hall.

From behind I hear Char tell Lys, "I know you're drowning. But you're starting to pull me down with you. I don't know what to do. I'm not trying to hurt you."

"I know," Lys says. "We can talk about it."

Where would Sophi go to get away from us? She wouldn't leave completely, in case someone figures out the clue. There's a big first-floor lobby with a vending machine, so I head down the stairs.

At first, I don't see her. A group of people sit around a board game in the middle of the main part of the lobby, across from the vending machine. I turn slowly and spot her standing in a strip of the lobby without couches or chairs, half-hidden by a square white column, staring out of the big windows facing campus.

Bas isn't there. She must have peeked at the main part of the room and assumed Sophi went another way.

I move around the column so Sophi can see me, but don't step too close. She might want to be alone.

"Are you okay?" I ask.

"How much more is there?" She doesn't turn from the windows.

"We don't have to do it all."

"Did you figure it out?" she asks.

She hasn't told me to get lost, so I move up next to her to see if I can tell what she's staring at—maybe the tree in front of the dorm or the sky behind it.

I tell her, "Not yet. But I have more data now. I have to give it time in my brain, let it marinate."

"Your brain marinates?" Her voice has deepened with humor. "Does it also stew and cook and bake?"

"For sure all of that. It should have its own cooking show. Marinate is what my mom Joy says when she's being creative. But I guess it's more a weaving together and sorting. Like my brain recorded everything today but it can't access it all yet, not until I've had time alone for it to…I want to say 'parse the data' but that sounds too analytical and it's an organic process."

"What does it feel like?" she asks.

Utterly surprising question, but I like it. I want to answer.

"I don't know. I watch videos or listen to music or play games on my phone and I know that something's happening where I can't see it. It's like the big thoughts need a lot of time to sort themselves out."

She nods. "I call that sensory dumping. Some people have brains with more connections, more sensitivity than typical brains. That's how I can get so happily lost in colors and set design and costuming. But if we're like that, we go through the world picking up all this stuff we sense and notice. That gets stuck in our nervous systems and our bodies start to react to all that junk and we need to dump it out or it gets kind of toxic. Basically: more information goes in, more needs to be processed and dumped out."

This sounds like my process, or part of it. When I try to imagine it, I see the external brain of my room at home and my dorm room here, see all the items that help me orient back to my big thoughts, help me understand what's interference and needs to be cleared out of my mind. But it sounds like Sophi does this inside her body, not in the space around her.

I say, "I've been thinking about how I process ideas in the space around me—and other ways to say that. I'm playing with trees as a metaphor. Can you describe it in that context?"

Her eyes focus on the tree beyond the window, gazing down the trunk and then up to the branches. "Maybe sending energy along the branches to find what's alive and what isn't—to dump what isn't alive and to push away the excess, into the root system. Then what's alive can nourish me. There's space and movement to know what belongs in me and what doesn't—and to allow the parts that belong to fit together in new ways."

I map the tree onto my body and begin to understand how to do this internally. "You can move and do that?" I ask.

"Depends how I feel."

"What kind of movement?"

She turns to me and chuckles. "Sometimes real stimmy stuff." She snaps fingers on both hands simultaneously and then rhythmically back and forth. "Bits of dance, Pilates, other stuff from theater classes. Huge menu of options."

"Stimmy?" I ask.

"Stims, you know, stimulation, for when you're understimulated, or over, and the energy has to go somewhere." She pauses, her wide, dark eyes taking me in all at once. "I haven't seen you fidget."

"Because I do it on the inside or with ideas in the space around me," I admit. "I'm always moving in my mind."

She rocks onto her heels and forward, eyes shining. "I use my breathing when I'm not supposed to move, and leg muscle isolations if people can't see my legs. But I also try not to be in too many situations where I'm not supposed to move. Sitting for this group exercise is uncomfortable."

"Let's stop. Let's go tell the others or do you want me to?"

"I'll come back to say bye," she says.

Walking down the hall from the common room, I snap my fingers in counterpoint—and remember how much I used to do this as a kid—and how Mom would put her hands over mine to stop me. I stare at my palms then snap, feeling lightness expand through my chest. What is this magic? I want to know what other movement Sophi does. Can I ask her? Do I know her well enough?

When we get up to the common room, no one from our group is there except Lys, who is reading *Curious Wine* toward the end. She's sitting lengthwise on the couch, propped against the arm. Her face has returned to its usual light tan, no blotchy crying effects lingering. I hope that means she's feeling restored inside too.

Lys spots us as soon as we cross the threshold and closes the book. She tells Sophi, "Bas thought you might have gone to get food. She went to the commons with Char. Kai said we should text her if we're doing more book stuff. Are we?"

"We've done enough," Sophi says. "I'll head to the commons and let Bas and Char know we're done." She pulls on a black down coat that falls to her knees, shoulders her bag and heads out.

I sit on the end of the couch, but Lys bends her legs and waves me closer. When I scoot near, she stretches her legs over my lap. I rest my hands on her thigh and shin.

"I'm hoping that was enough," I tell her. "That my brain will blossom an answer sometime in the next day."

"Speaking of answers," she says. "I have a lot of questions. The one woman, Diana, runs away from the other woman, Lane, who's obviously great, and goes to a casino where she meets a guy who sexually assaults her. But later that same night she goes back to Lane and has sex with her. Do people actually do that?"

"Yeah, I think so in the seventies," I tell her. "And eighties and nineties, pretty sure."

"You're joking."

"I wish. I've heard things."

"Your moms?" Lys asks.

I nod. "Joy is solid, but Mom's a mess. Should've started therapy ages ago but she wanted to work through it by literally spending all her time at her job. And she's not half as bad as her parents. Like, my grandmother doesn't even have a personality; she agrees with everything my grandfather says. They refused to talk to Mom for most of her twenties after she came out. Joy and Mom don't talk about it when I'm around, but I've heard some of their friends talk about the violence that happened to lesbians even in the eighties and nineties—still happens in some places. So I get that Diana in the novel is freaking out realizing she's queer in the seventies and then not making the most healthy choices."

"Can I talk to your moms about all that sometime? I'm supposed to interview someone for a psych paper and that would be amazing. Unless it's too weird."

"They'd love it," I say. "I might not stick around for it. Depends on how Mom and I are doing."

"Is it hard that your relationship with your biological mom is the rough one?"

I shrug. "That's part of what makes it hard. She thinks I owe her because she gestated me. She doesn't get that parent-kid relationships are mutual. You don't host a person in your body for nine months and then have them owe you for the rest of their lives."

Lys leans toward me, one hand reaching to grip my arm. "Owe her what?"

I move my hand from her shin to rest over hers. "I'm supposed to be her revenge on her parents by being super successful in all the ways they measure success. When I was little, every time I did something ahead of the curve she'd be on the phone telling them how smart and great I was—like this proved she was great."

"Exhausting. But fascinating." She grins at me. "Thanks for letting your personal suffering fuel my psych degree."

"Someone should benefit. Are we going for food or…"

She sits up straight and looks toward the door. "Oh, Char is getting food. To my room! Quickly! While Char is out. Let's go."

CHAPTER TEN

Lys

Maze talks to her moms about me interviewing them and they agree, so that Friday we take a Lyft out to Eden Prairie. The place name fits: a bunch of white people with a lot of money wanted to create an Eden out here on the prairie. Maze says this is the discount Eden, south of the real high price property around the lakes, but it's still bigger houses than near our college and way bigger than back home.

The front door opens to an actual entryway with cream-colored walls and tile, not some narrow space crammed with outdoor clothes and spare tools like my folks' house in Michigan. Maze drops her bag—like this is okay on the shiny floor—so I lower mine until it rests next to hers.

"Mom, Joy?" Maze calls.

A voice comes from deep in the house, "We're in the basement!"

"There in a minute!" Maze yells back. To me she says, "Let's drop our stuff in my room first."

We lift our bags again and she pulls me toward the broad staircase. I see a formal dining room through an open doorway.

"You call your other mom by her first name?" I ask. "I thought all the times you said 'my mom Joy' that was for the benefit of the rest of us."

"Yeah. I mean, I also call her 'Mati' sometimes. But when I was little and I learned what the word 'joy' meant, I wanted to call her that. We have a thing we'd say a lot when I was little. Still do sometimes. I say 'My Joy!' and then she says, 'No, you're my joy.'"

"Oh wow, that is the darlingest."

Maze's room is a trove of books and notebooks, clothes, shoes, plushies, action figures. They're in bins that go halfway up two walls. If I had this much space in my dorm room, I wouldn't keep leaving stuff in front of Char's closet.

Her bed is neatly made, with fancy pillows and three plushies: a black bear, a unicorn and a hedgehog. Other than that and the bins holding action figures and other plushies, the room looks more grown-up than mine. Well, the one that used to be mine but got taken over by my brother. I hope he didn't toss all my sports stuff in the basement—that gear cost so much.

I'm startled when Maze grumbles, "She cleaned it up again. It's going to take me forever to remember how I had it set up. I should bring it to school, but then I'll have to move it back here this summer."

"What?"

"My external brain. The position of things in my room reminds me what I'm thinking about. But any time I'm gone for more than a few days, Mom comes in and cleans it up."

"That sucks."

Maze laughs ruefully. "Hah, yeah. At least this time I took photos. I keep telling her to leave it, but she can't. And on that note, you ready to meet them?"

"Nope. But let's do it. I'm not going to get less sweaty and anxious by waiting."

Maze pulls me close and presses her lips to the space in front of my ear. "They'll love you," she says and there's an implied *like I do*. She's not going to say outright that she loves me. I'm not either. It's only been a month, though we've spent most of those days together. That feels like too soon. I think we're supposed to wait until later in month two or maybe the middle of month three. I've been meaning to ask Char about this—she knows all the romance timing.

We go down the stairs, through a living room with a huge TV mounted on the wall, through a pristine kitchen with stone countertops and stainless-steel appliances, then down another set of stairs.

The basement is one huge room with columns and it is packed with things. There's a full-size pool table with boxes stacked on it, a washer and dryer against one wall with a table to fold clothes that's so covered in clothes there's no folding room. There are racks for drying sweaters with sweaters on them. There's a wall of shelving with plastic storage boxes in light blue, some of them labeled. Another wall has more of those boxes and the gray cardboard kind. Two bookshelves hold books and DVDs.

A woman is crossing the basement with an olive-green storage crate in her hands. She's shorter than Maze, curly dark brown hair barely covers the back of her neck, wispy bangs in front, bright blue eyes—even brighter when she sees Maze halfway down the stairs. Her straight-mouthed scowl turns into a full, sort of dorky smile. Her jacket is unzipped, showing a belly over the top of her jeans, and between that smile and her casual belly, I'm calming down about meeting her.

She rests the crate on a corner of the pool table. "This is your girl?" she asks.

"My Joy," Maze says. "This is Lys."

Joy gives me a thorough once over, nodding and smiling. "Welcome, wonderful to meet you. I'd offer to shake hands or bump shoulders, but I'm covered in dust. Mazey, you didn't get my texts?"

"I what?" Maze fumbles her phone out of her pocket and thumbs through her texts. "Oh shiiit no. Uncle Karl's coming *tonight*?"

"Tried to warn you. He'll be here any time now and you know he'll stay for dinner. You two want to run for it, eat someplace local?"

"Probably," Maze says. "You're the best. Don't tell my other mom."

A voice from someone I can't see—she must be kneeling or sitting on the floor on the other side of the pool table—calls, "I can hear you."

Joy heaves the crate from the pool table onto a stack of similar crates and the voice calls, "Careful! You know Karl."

"What's in them?" Joy asks.

The voice says, "He made me swear not to open them."

Joy snorts. "Probably porn. On VHS tapes. And the player, they're heavy as lead."

The voice cautions, "He wouldn't care enough to drive down here for porn. So those are probably guns."

A woman stands up on the far side of the pool table. She's taller than Joy, long hair, dyed blond, the roots growing out light brown. Her natural color is enough lighter than Maze's that I'm wondering what Maze's bio-dad looks like and trying not to wonder. Seems rude.

Maze's other mom is a tanner shade of white than Joy, but not by much. She and Maze have the same long, straight nose—and the same habit of not smiling all the way, reserving judgment. Honestly though, Maze looks more like Joy, at least in the eyes. They both seem like they're twenty-percent still figuring everything out.

"Lys, this is my mom Kelly, which is probably what you should call her. Unless you want her to call you something else, Mom."

Mom-Kelly crosses the room and offers her hand to shake. Super firm grip.

I eye the stack of four olive green crates. "That's a lot of guns," I say, not entirely convinced I haven't stepped onto the set of a horror film.

"Oh, if it is guns, and I'm half kidding about that, it's also all the gear that goes with them, including camping gear," Kelly says and releases my hand. "I think one of those has a tent in it. But knowing my brother we should be gentle about how we handle those. Can you two give us a hand taking some of this up to the garage?"

"Sure," I say, glad to have something to do. "As long as there's no live ammo."

Maze snorts. "Yeah, which boxes?"

"Everything along that wall can go up to Joy's parking space."

"Let me go change into something skungy. Come on," Maze says to me.

I follow Maze up that flight of stairs and the next, back to her bedroom. "Skungy?" I ask.

"Skunky plus grungy. Do you want a different shirt? I've got a bunch."

"Sure, thanks. What's the deal with your uncle?"

She opens drawers, tossing clothes onto her bed. "I don't know if I should bias you," Maze tells me. "Maybe he'll be on his best behavior. He does have a new boyfriend so he's probably in a great mood. The important family dynamic to understand is that he loaned Mom some cash to buy this house and even though she's paid him back, he still acts like he's a shareholder in this part of the family."

"What does that mean?" I ask as she hands me a big gray T-shirt that says: *Vulcan Science Academy*.

"Like he owns part of us. There's a lot of owing and owning in this family."

Maze digs into a bottom drawer and pulls out a faded blue sweatshirt that says *Dyke University* on the front, along with a double-headed axe and a women's symbol. While I'm changing shirts, she throws off her sweater and pulls on the sweatshirt. Then she rummages in a top drawer to find a lavender bandana that she ties around her head.

"You're a queer superhero," I say and kiss her.

"And you're perfect," she tells me.

We troop back down to the basement and start carefully conveying boxes up to the garage. By the time we have all the boxes full of maybe-guns and camping gear stacked at the front of the garage, I feel deeply imperfect. I'm the tallest of everyone here, though Mom-Kelly is close, and that has to highlight how sweaty I am and the fact that my hair will not stay in its bun.

Maze says we should wash up quickly and get out before Karl arrives with the new beau—but as she's explaining which bathroom I should use, a shiny blue BMW pulls into the driveway.

A man gets out of the driver's side and beelines for Mom-Kelly, to kiss her cheek in a way I've only seen in movies. He's wearing mint green pants, a lightweight navy down jacket and a blue button-down shirt with an ice blue scarf wrapped loosely around his neck, twice, and held in the open collar of the shirt. All the hair on his head is buzzed short, including his beard. Only his eyebrows are fully dark brown without any hint of gray, and they're a thicker copy of Maze's. Hard to tell with the salt-and-pepper scruff around his mouth, but his lips and the way he holds them are also the same as hers.

He turns toward the car and waves a "come here" gesture. From the passenger side, another man stands and gazes at both moms and Maze before fixing on me, eyes wide. My mouth is half open and I've forgotten how to shut it. I'd know that thatch of brown curls over a red beard anywhere—I've stared at it enough in class. The new boyfriend is my education professor, Mads Leland.

"We have to stay for dinner," I whisper to Maze. "That's Professor Leland."

"Oh shit," she says. "You really want to stay?"

"Want is a strong word. Have to, though. Can we?"

"Yeah, I'll tell them."

I want to text Kai right away and let her know I'm in position to get the scoop on Professor Leland's project, but I'm afraid he'll see my immediate texting as suspicious. Karl is introducing him to Maze's moms, but I see him glancing at me. He looks even less thrilled about me than I am about him.

CHAPTER ELEVEN

Maze

Mom sits at the head of the table—total power move about Uncle Karl—with Joy at her right, Karl at her left. I leap to the end of the table so that Lys won't get stuck sitting next to Professor Leland, but this puts her across from him. Maybe it won't get weird? Yeah it's going to get so weird. At least she's got me on one side and Joy on the other.

What are the chances that my uncle would end up dating Lys's professor? Pretty good, really. There are only a few exclusive groups for queer folks in the Twin Cities, and only one that's all gay men. Mom complains about it because she thinks they should be more inclusive—pretty funny for a group that costs a bomb in annual dues. I don't think professors make a ton of money, so any professor in that group has to also be bringing in cash other ways and therefore be high profile. The number of well-off, high-profile gay professors in the Cities who would get Uncle Karl's attention is probably…well, one.

They clearly share the same passion for expensive shirts. Uncle Karl's has a double collar—one collar folding over the other—and a strip of very light blue down the part where the buttons are, which matches the scarf he did not take off with this coat. Professor Leland's is a rust-colored shirt with rows of diamonds in three sizes, like a deconstructed, fancy plaid. They could be an ad for French cruises and, given Uncle Karl's hairline, that stuff that prevents balding.

As we pass plates around and serve ourselves, Joy asks Lys what she's studying, which should be an easy question, except it's so not. Bright side: Mom is trying to piss off Uncle Karl by serving an all-vegetarian dinner and has to explain in great detail what's in the meatless lasagna.

Lys takes a little of it. She tries to avoid dairy and wheat because they make her sleepy. At least there's a huge salad and a sweet potato mash. I'd assumed we'd order out, which is what we usually do the first night I'm home on a weekend, and that Lys could pick the place and her order. I want to run into the kitchen and find her other options, but that would cause Mom to ask me a whole lot of questions—and then ask Lys more questions. Not cool in front of this professor.

I space out the first part of the conversation, trying to eat and watch Lys while not looking like I'm watching her. I tune in when Mom says to Professor Leland, "Karl told me you're a professor at Maze's school. What are you teaching?"

Karl answers first. He and Mom have this forever competition between them. He's about a year older and Mom says he feels that her birth cheated him out of the sole focus of their parents—but they've always given him more money and support than they gave her. Mom came out as queer first and nearly got kicked out of the family and then when Uncle Karl came out, everyone said he was copying her, but they supported him way more than they supported her. Karl says this is because Mom trained them; Mom says it's because he always gets the best of everything in the family. They're each deeply bitter about the other one, but also super loyal to each other.

Karl says, "He's not only teaching. He got a grant to run a study over the next two years that's going to be huge."

He turns to Professor Leland with this shining, proud look that is only gross because of the situation, otherwise I'd be glad my gay uncle feels that way about someone. Except he's also competing with Mom by implying that his boyfriend is more amazing than Joy. I see everything they pull with each other and have since I was a kid, but learned real fast that blurting it out will bring both of them down on me. I space out a lot around them.

"Oh," Mom says. "A study?"

Professor Leland answers like Lys and I aren't at the table. Maybe he doesn't care that we're here. "I'm looking at the current rash of disability accommodations to figure out which ones make a difference and which don't, so we can phase out the ones that aren't working. Over the last decade, I've been approached more and more often by faculty in the sciences who feel that grades don't mean what they used to. That they're being watered down by departments who bend over backward to give students everything they ask for. It's especially relevant now that a year of remote learning has left so many students lagging. They need to know what's going to be expected of them in the real world."

"I'm missing something," Mom says. "Workplaces in the real world are legally required to provide disability accommodations."

Karl stage-whispers to Professor Leland, "She's a lawyer."

"What students want these days goes far beyond the legal requirements," Professor Leland says. "And it's putting pressure on professors who are already stretched thin from teaching during the pandemic. If we can figure out which accommodations work, then we can make useful recommendations."

"How?" Lys asks. "And will you talking about this in class? It seems relevant."

Both Uncle Karl and Mom double-take, but it's Joy who asks, "Lys is in a class of yours?"

"I can't say," he answers. "FERPA regulations prohibit me from talking about students."

"I can say," Lys says. "And I am. In his class. Education, Freedom and Personal Responsibility."

"How exciting," Uncle Karl says.

Right. Lys hates this class.

"It would be if I could get the lecture notes," Lys says and quickly takes a long gulp of water. I'm guessing she didn't mean to say that out loud.

Professor Leland is quick with his response. "Professors are engaged in many kinds of work beyond the classroom. Some of my material is proprietary. If it gets onto the Internet before I'm prepared to release it, other professors at other schools can leapfrog ahead of my research."

"It's probably already on the Internet," I say. "Just not searchable yet because of the way the search engines crawl sites."

Mom shoots me a look that I've seen often enough to make me close my mouth by reflex.

"Can you tell us anything about your research?" Joy asks.

"I'll give you the highlights," Professor Leland tells her. "We're looking at students with accommodations and matching them with demographically similar students without accommodations to see which group is doing better in terms of academic achievement. We've also been interviewing professors to get some of the qualitative classroom factors and to identify cases where one student's accommodation may be disruptive to other students. The classroom needs to be considered as a whole."

"Isn't that what Universal Design for Learning is for?" Lys asks.

Professor Leland turns to her, the picture of patience. "How much have you read about UDL?"

"What the Learning Center puts out," she says.

"Then you may not know it's still in its infancy. I'm not against inclusion, but I think we need to know what works and we need to standardize." He turns back to Mom and Joy, facing them diagonally across the meatless lasagna. "I'm not sure this generation knows what they need. They don't have the toughness of our generation."

"Damn right," Uncle Karl says and claps his hand on the back of Professor Leland's shoulder.

I want to support Lys and I'm not sure how. I turn to Joy who gives me a half nod, like she got way more info from my face than I thought I'd put there.

Joy says, "That's interesting. The girls came out this weekend to interview us about how tough our generation was expected to be—and all the damage that caused. I've been considering the women's perspective, but maybe you can tell us about the impact of the AIDS crisis. Especially with this pandemic, that seems quite relevant."

Karl shrugs and digs into his cooling lasagna with a gusto that shows how much even vegetarian fare wins over that topic.

Professor Leland answers, "It was terrifying. I was barely out of college and guys were getting sick, guys I was in school with. We didn't know the cause. They started calling it 'gay cancer.' I was afraid to date. But everyone pulled together. There was so much cutting-edge activism. It galvanized the movement like nothing else had."

Lys folds her napkin as he's talking, then unfolds it again and puts it back in her lap. She asks, "What's the difference between folks with HIV getting support and folks with disabilities? How is facing HIV/AIDS harder than facing Covid and climate change?"

"We learned what worked and what didn't with HIV and we need to do the same with disabilities in the classroom," Professor Leland says.

I get the impression he's willing to give way more resources to guys with HIV than to disabled students.

"Our generation is as badass as yours," I say. "We just don't value the same things you do."

"Like what?" Uncle Karl asks.

"Money being more important than anything. Pillaging the Earth. You know, you've seen the news."

"But you don't use accommodations, honey," Mom says in a too smooth, proud tone.

Honestly, I can't remember having had the option, but if I had, I wouldn't take it. Mom can't think I'm weak. Nor could anyone else. This generation needs its badass lesbians, like the ones in the books. I can be as tough as Audre Lorde...okay, realistically two thirds as tough, but that's enough.

I shrug. "Audre Lorde didn't need accommodations. I don't either."

Joy sighs and sets down her fork. "Audre Lorde died of cancer, you know, that she got from the jobs she had to work when she was young. If the world had been more accommodating, we'd have much more work from one of the brilliant minds of the last century. I don't understand why it's so hard for us, as humans, to take care of each other."

She picks up her plate and carries it into the kitchen, then comes back to see if she should start getting dessert ready.

* * *

My moms put Lys in the guest room, which is right next to my room, so as soon as the light is out under their door, I tap on her door. She opens it and I slip inside and into her arms. We hold onto each other for a while. With kissing. Then find the bed and snuggle into it together. It's more comfortable than my bed, which I'd be pretty mad about if I slept in my bed more than I do.

Lys says, "He's more of an asshole than he seems."

"He seemed like a whole lot of asshole all in one place."

"And if you ever have to take one of his classes, absolutely ask for all the accommodations you can."

I laugh. "I don't need them."

She sits up and looks down at me. "Really?"

She's in a dark tank top, hair loose, the lamplight turning her hair and shoulders two different tones of gold. I brush a lock of hair so the end rests on her shoulder and I can compare dark and light gold.

I tell her, "Yeah, I'm pretty good at school these days. Junior high sucked, but I got through. The Adderall helps a lot. Your folks should let you take it."

"Working on it," she says. "I'd still ask for accommodations, though."

"Even if you didn't need them?"

She stares around the room. I wonder how it looks to her. Mom keeps it super neat like every part of the house, except the basement. Neither Mom nor the cleaning service spend much time down there.

Lys asks, "What if I want them? What if I think professors should provide notes from their lectures and some recordings? If the point is me learning, I should be able to access that information a bunch of ways."

"Some things need to be standardized," I say.

"Do they?"

"Uh yeah. Otherwise, what did I do twelve years of school for? What am I doing college for?"

"Those first twelve years were to make you a productive cog in the capitalist machine," Lys says. "These four, I think that's up to us."

"Is that what you went to school for?"

I push up on my elbows so that my eyes are level with hers. Why am I more angry now than I was at dinner?

"I went for sports," she says. "Well, first I went because adults told me to. And then I liked some of the learning, but when I was excited to show up, it was the sports. I can learn on my own. What did you go to school for?"

Staring at her is too intense, so I end up staring at the stupid piece of wall art depicting a small town at the foot of a looming volcano. My moms did not think that through when they hung it up. Probably was a gift from Karl, by someone famous. How many houseguests have felt as alarmed by it as I do now—like lava is going to explode out of the painting onto the bed?

I went to school because I had to, because everyone did, because my moms had jobs and I couldn't stay home alone when I was young, and because I wanted to grow up and have a cool job. And yeah, at times I didn't see how school contributed because so much of it was about rules and deadlines, not about the information.

I went to school to make my moms proud. They hung my work and report cards on the fridge, the usual parent stuff. When a class was hard, Joy tutored me in it. Mom's perspective was to let me figure it out, but some stuff I didn't figure out. I did figure out by sixth grade that if I was super smart in one or two areas, I could convince the teachers that I was super smart in more areas and they'd let me slide if I didn't do a piece of homework. And, if I'm being honest, I cheated on some tests in junior high.

"Maze?" Lys asks.

I say, "I went to school for my moms. I still do. Not that I don't want to do college, I do, but I'm always aware of what they're going to think. Mom's not bad, she's just pretty fucked up for legit reasons. Early on when I started struggling in junior high she had a huge problem with it. She yelled at me a lot. And then I got diagnosed and she knew she couldn't, but I heard her talking to Joy one day—she had no idea I could hear, I'm sure she wouldn't have said it—she was for real asking if they should sue the fertility clinic because my ADHD must've come from my donor, so they'd gotten a defective product. And I know she meant the product to be the genetic material, but it sounded like she meant me."

Lys wraps me in a tight hug. "That's super fucked up. You didn't talk to Joy about it?"

I shake my head. "She and Mom love each other."

"Good parents want their kids to be okay."

"Yours won't even let you take meds," I point out.

"Yeah but they do everything else. That's their philosophy."

"Where's the line between philosophy and harm?" I ask. "You know you'd do better with meds."

"And you'd do better with accommodations and more support," she says, voice rising.

I shush her and we both look at the door to see if the hall light goes on, but it doesn't.

"You're afraid of appearing weak," she says.

"And you're afraid that…sometimes the system works."

"Fine. I'll talk to someone about meds and see if they're even possible with my insurance. What are you going to do?"

"Wait, what? I didn't come in here for a life problem-solving session with action items. What's happening?"

"Are you going to Disability Services?"

"No, that's not for me."

"Yeah, you've got it all together. But I saw you react to your mom moving your room around and wrecking your external brain. And what you overheard her say was truly awful. What if you stopped letting it be all on you?"

"You're the one freaking out that your class thinks you're lazy."

"They do," she says. "Some of them. You don't get that?"

"So prove them wrong."

"Maybe it's that easy for you, but it isn't for me."

I tell her, "It isn't. I own tests. I destroy them because of all the adrenaline and it's like a fight between me and the professors, even if I like them, and I'm good in a fight. I walk in and everything gets perfectly clear for an hour or two. It's the little things that pick and pick at me, especially when it's stupid busywork. I get it done, but I'm exhausted over and over—and then when I need something, when I ask for it, from Mom or even from some of my professors, they think I don't need it because my grades are so good. And what if they're right? What if it does make me weak?"

"Is that what you think about me?" she asks. "That I'm weak?"

Do I? I'm staring at her hands and trying to work out how I feel. I love her hands, her whole body. I love her, though I'm not ready to say that out loud yet. But also I do feel protective mentally. Like in the physical world, she's way beyond me, but when it comes to brain stuff, I'm the strong one. How do I put all that into words?

"Oh," she says.

"I didn't say anything."

"You're taking a really long time to answer, so I can guess what it's going to be."

"Not fair, I'm still thinking."

"Are you? About your answer or how to tell me that your answer is 'yes'?"

"I don't know."

"I want to go to sleep," she says.

"Oh should I...go back to my room?"

"Yeah."

She doesn't kiss me and I stumble across the gray room and patch of hall to my bedroom. I think we're fighting. I should go back and tell her she's not weak at all, but I don't know what to think or say.

I remember talking with Sophi, her idea of sensory dumping feels super relevant, but I don't know how to start. My nerves are slimed with toxicity. How do I get this out of me?

CHAPTER TWELVE

Lys

Sunday morning I get up as soon as I hear movement downstairs. I want to start the interview with Maze's moms before Maze is up. After Maze left my room last night, I slept shallowly, filled with fragmented dreams. Now I put on the too-pink robe I borrowed from Char, over a T-shirt and sweatpants, and head down to the kitchen.

Mom-Kelly is fully dressed, including a long black wool coat, with a thermos in hand. She says, "So sorry, I have to solve a work crisis. Can Joy give you enough for your paper?"

"Sure." I try not to show the relief that's bubbling up.

She waves, kisses Joy and leaves through the door to the garage.

"Coffee?" Joy asks me. Her curls are messier than the night before and she's in loose green pants and a brown work shirt over a lighter brown Henley over a green T-shirt—the same kinds of layers Maze wore the night of the party. So that's where she gets it from. And there's more resemblance between Maze and Joy, even though Maze's hair is straight and her eyes brown.

"Yes, so much coffee, thank you."

She chuckles and pours two mugs, pointing toward the cream and sugar if I want it. "We have gluten-free bagels and a lot of possible toppings," she says. "Maze told us you avoid dairy and wheat. I'm sorry about last night. We didn't expect that whole dinner party."

Unexpected tears prick my eyes so I gulp too-hot coffee and blink them back. I'm so angry at Maze but also I love that she was taking care of me setting up this visit. Now I want to see her—and also I don't.

We toast bagels and go into the den, a small room with a couch, two armchairs and lots of bookcases, my favorite that I've seen after Maze's bedroom. Joy sits in the armchair, giving me the choice of spots on the couch and the coffee table to put my papers and laptop on.

After a few minutes of us munching on the bagels, Joy smiles at me—a smile that's exactly Maze's. "Where do you want to start?" she asks.

I give myself a tiny shake and sift my stack of class notes until the info about the paper is on top. "My paper is about resilience factors. I'm supposed to interview someone and then detail the parts of the interview that reflect the resilience factors we're studying. Is it okay to record?"

She nods so I turn on my phone's recording app and say, "It was pretty hard to be queer decades ago but a bunch of people turned out okay. How did you do it?"

She laughs, a small laugh that gets bigger as she gets into it. "Kickboxing and therapy."

I consider my list of common resilience factors to see what's the best match. She holds out a hand and I pass it to her.

After reading, she says, "I'm kidding about the kickboxing. The head of our gay group at college could do the most flamboyant high kicks, so we all had him teach us and we'd laugh about dance moves that could be self-defense. I had a great group of friends in college. Coming out would've been so much harder without them. And I did get a lot of activity, so these points here about community and physical health. Plus

Next Chapter Booksellers

38 S. Snelling Ave
St. Paul, MN 55105
(651) 225-8989
www.nextchapterbooksellers.com

Cust: **Torzs, Emma**

20-Apr-23 7:20p   Clerk: Admin

Trns. #: 10382378   Reg: 1

9781642474497   *Curious Minds*

1 @ $18.95	-20.0%	$15.16

	Sub-total:	$18.95
	Tax @ 7.875%:	$1.19
	Discount:	$3.79
	Total:	**$16.35**

* *Non-Tax Items*

Items: 1   *Units: 1*

Payment Via:

VISA/MC/Discover	$16.35

VISA ***********0147
Approval: 01418D
TroutD: 0039

Thank you for shopping at Next Chapter
Booksellers!

You can return a book for a full refund for two
weeks after your purchase with this receipt.
Books must be in their original condition. After
two weeks we will give store credit.

my parents were supportive of me in general—pretty good parents."

"How did you come out?" I ask.

"I came out in 1988, to myself at least. My school had one girl who was rumored to be bisexual. Oh and she was so cute: punk girl with a big, bleached mohawk. Every chance I could, I'd hang out near her, reading whatever book I was into, those big fantasy epics mainly. She wasn't the one who helped me, though, it was this super straight-looking friend of hers who I heard one day talking about a report she was doing on 'homosexuality' and how she'd found some books on it at the public library. I went there that day after school and found Lillian Faderman's history book *Surpassing the Love of Men*. I'm not a history person, but I read the whole thing, a bit at a time, sitting in the back of the library because I didn't dare check it out.

"Faderman wrote about all these lesbian characters in the paperback books of the fifties and sixties. Like Claire Morgan's *The Price of Salt*, which I immediately found in the library and read. Oh and all the Ann Bannon books, *Odd Girl Out*, the whole Beebo Brinker Chronicles. I read them and started them over again. When I got to college, I began buying the lesbian books that weren't in the library because I could keep them hidden in my dorm room. And that's when I found that Jane Rule's *Desert of the Heart* had been made into a movie, *Desert Hearts*—our group watched that so many times. Well, the lesbians and bi girls did. I think the guys watched it once and then opted to go dancing. Do books count as community for resilience?"

"They must," I say, thinking about all the queer books I've read. "When did you come out to your parents?"

"Not until my midtwenties. I had relationships with women in college but I wasn't ready—and at the time the whole cultural environment was more threatening than now. Before the Internet it was so much harder to find each other. We went to bars a lot, sneaking in underage. And I'd hear stories there of the violence other people had experienced. They couldn't go to the police—they'd be laughed at or revictimized. They could lose their jobs. Still can in places, but now there's so much more cultural force against that kind of homophobia. Awful things happen but also many voices speak out against those actions. In my twenties, homophobia was in the water."

Maze comes in with the coffee pot and refills Joy's mug. She's in blue pajama bottoms and a school sweatshirt—one of the unfortunately mustard-colored ones—and looks extra pale under the sweep of her dark hair.

"More coffee?" she asks me.

I nod and hand her the mug. Joy's gaze moves back and forth between us, eyes squinting, but she doesn't ask why we're being weird. I return to the official interview to get details about where she grew up, her family, what jobs she had after college.

Maze gets herself a bagel and sits in the other armchair, across the coffee table from me. I ask questions by rote and try to hear enough of the answers to follow up. I'm glad I'm recording this.

When we stop the interview, I pack up my few things in the guest room. I text Kai to ask if she can meet me when I'm back on campus—because I have so much news about Professor Leland, but also I need a friend to talk to about the rest of the weekend. She replies with a big *Yes* and a lot of cheerful emojis. I want to be in that circle of cheerfulness so badly.

Joy drives us to campus, talking about the '93 March on Washington and all the radical changes she thought her generation was going to make. Maze directs her to my dorm. I hope that's because it's closer to a major road and not because Maze thinks I can't walk across campus from her dorm.

"We made a lot of those changes," Joy says as she pulls up by my building. "Still working on others."

"You've got our backing," I say and she beams at me.

We get out of the car. Maze has a big backpack and I've got my school backpack plus a small suitcase with wheels. Anger burns hot under my breastbone. I could easily walk across campus from Maze's dorm pulling this suitcase. I've been keeping up on PT and walking a lot. My knee feels good and I do not need to be coddled.

Maze strides ahead of me, presses her wallet to the card reader and holds the door open for me.

"I don't need your help," I tell her.

Her dark eyebrows pinch close. "I was being nice."

"I don't need you to baby me," I say and stomp through the door into the lobby. This is not at all what I want to say, but those are the only words I have.

"I'm not." Her voice sharpens. "What are you so mad about? You got the interview you needed. You even got the dirt on the Leland secret project. Is that why you're upset?"

"You're treating me like I can't do things for myself."

"I opened one door! When I did that before you didn't yell at me. And you needed this when you were stuck in the Admin Building bathroom. How am I supposed to know that things changed?"

"You're bringing *that* into it?" Now I'm definitely yelling. "That building has terrible design and the elevator barely works and I was not stuck. I was in a lot of pain."

Her jaw is set with anger, but her eyes crinkle with confusion. "You did need help for the stairs."

Plus I totally screwed up Valentine's Day, which she doesn't have to say for me to hear it in her words. Tears are so close in my throat and eyes that I can't talk.

Maze says, "I invited you home to meet my moms and outside of that interview you barely said a word this morning. And I know dinner was extremely messed up, but now I'm going to have to deal with Mom interrogating me about everything we talked about. Probably Uncle Karl's going to have a bunch of weird as fuck questions about your family connections—and I am trying to *help* you but you're not helping me at all."

The heat in my chest explodes past the tears. "Oh, did you need help? Last I heard, you could do everything on your own and never needed anyone to accommodate you because you're so fucking perfect all the time."

"I am not perfect! I hurt too but I don't sit around crying about it."

"Because your knee doesn't feel like it's full of broken glass and shredding nerves all the way up to your neck. I'm a hunter and a flanker and injured and getting screwed by this one-size-fits-all culture. I'm not defective!"

She rocks back on her heels, blinking slowly, raises one hand and presses it to her eyes. "And I am?" she hisses. "You act like I have to be all kinds of broken to get anything I need. Just like…" She stops and takes a ragged breath, eyes wide and glistening, then turns and stalks out of the building.

I take the stairs because I don't want anyone to see me crying in the elevator, even though my knee is grinding by halfway up. I want to get my phone out and see when Kai said she'd come over, but fishing it out of my pocket is too much effort. I limp down the hallway to my door, key it open and drag my baggage inside.

Kai is sprawled in the big chair, reading. I'm so relieved to see her familiar intense eyes, cheek-bunching smile and rugby sweatshirt.

"Char let me in," she says. "Then ran off to some volunteer thing with that guy she's into."

I sit on the edge of my bed and lean over to hug her. She pulls me toward her so it turns into a long hug with me half in her lap, fully crying.

"Maze's moms are that bad?" she asks, voice rising with alarm and surprise.

"We yelled at each other downstairs. I'm screwing everything up."

"Hard to believe," Kai says. "What happened?"

I tell her the things I remember saying and what Maze said. In the middle, my half-in-her-lap pose gets awkward and I slide to the floor. She comes with me, tipping the chair forward so its pillows support us, bolstered by my laundry pile.

Kai lets me cry on her until I feel wrung out.

After I've blown my nose a few times and gotten water, Kai asks, "Are you still up for organizing your room? Or do you want to talk more?"

"Room. But there's more news. Can we do both?"

"Of course! Walk around and pick up anything that's obviously trash and I'm going to collect all the clothes in the same place."

She drags over the basket full of clean laundry that I did a few days ago and haven't put away. Sitting forward, she starts pulling out items and sorting them into piles. Okay. Kai has a system—or half of a system or good habits—and I know that some of hers also end up in a pile on the floor, it's the reason I trust her.

I tell her, "The news is that Maze has a gay uncle and you'll never believe who his new boyfriend is…Professor Leland."

"The hell? I didn't even know he was gay. Dammit. I hate that he's gay and an asshole. That's worse."

"Yep. He said more about the project. Two years of study comparing students who have accommodations to 'comparable' students without."

"How would they do that comparison? How could they know which students are eligible for accommodations but not getting them? I bet they're comparing students who don't need accommodations to those that do."

I nod. "That's how it sounded to me."

"Of course the ones without are probably doing fantastically because they never needed accommodations in the first place—and he's going to use that to argue that students don't need accommodations."

I add, "Or he's going to cherry-pick so he can recommend only the accommodations that he doesn't hate. That way he'll look like he's being fair but he can still have solid sounding reasons not to record lectures or give us his notes."

I've gathered an armful of trash: empty boxes from protein bars and Pop-Tarts, soup-in-a-cup outer wrappers, a cereal box, the crumpled brown paper that pads shipped items, and a multicolored wad of lint that I imagine rode up from the laundry room on the bottom of a basket. Fueled by my anger at Professor Leland and, much as I hate to admit it, at Maze, I shove all of this into the mostly full trash can between my desk and Char's and stomp on it until it sort of fits.

Kai grins and tosses me an empty cracker box that I smash on top of the trash pile.

"I wonder if Bas would let someone look at the data," she says.

"Doubt it," I say.

"Hmm, do you want to brainstorm about how to get her to talk or look at these piles?" She gestures to the laundry.

"Piles," I tell her.

"Okay, you can fold stuff or not, depends on what works for you."

"Aren't I supposed to fold most of it?"

"Says who? Mess isn't a moral issue," she says. "It's functional."

I ask, "Are you sure? It feels like I'm a bad person for being this messy and Char is right to be aggravated about it."

"How's your self-talk?"

I love that she talks like that, and thinks like that. Should I be dating her instead of Maze? But Maze is breathtaking. Though Kai is too. The real issue with Kai and me is that we work each other up eventually. We both move a lot and social a lot. We don't rest well together.

"Hey self-care is radical, revolutionary," she says. "How about you talk to yourself the way you'd talk to me? Or Maze."

"If it were you two, I'd probably fold the laundry so you'd have nice stuff to wear."

"Don't bother. I fold almost nothing. Underwear, absolutely not. Socks, get all the same kind and you don't even have to match them, or if you like cute socks match 'em. Pants I fold because I don't want the wrinkles, and shirts I hang. Any shirt that's going under another shirt or sweater, I toss in the shirt bin. A key thing is to think about future-you and what she's going to want. Have a little conversation and see who needs the space more, does present-you need not-folding space or does future-you need some not-wrinkles space. The answer can change. Do you want to fold some stuff or not?"

"I can fold some," I say. "That's not the hard part for me. It's that I never put it away. Sometimes I fold it right out of the dryer, if I'm listening to music or a good podcast and it's not too late. And then it stays folded in the basket until I wear it."

"What do you hate about putting it away?"

I consider the movement of it, and that's annoying, but really it's the way the clothes vanish into the drawers and I can't remember where they are or what I have or what's clean or not. I tell that to Kai.

"Oh yeah, that's why I hang most of my T-shirts, so I can see them. But you've got less closet space here, that sucks. How do you remember stuff that isn't clothes?"

"Write notes to myself."

"So let's put notes on your drawers."

"That's going to look silly," I protest.

"Or genius," she says.

She grabs a pad of Post-it notes from my desk and hands it to me. I feel ridiculous but I make a note for "Socks" and stick it on the drawer. Part of me relaxes. Like I was clenching my spine about trying to remember the socks go there. This could work.

I label the other drawers, making some icons and smilies along with the words so the notes look intentional and friendly. Kai sits back in the chair and types on her phone.

"I'm not confident we can get Leland's data," she says. "Bas has no reason to risk it and we don't know the other students on the project. We can find some discrediting data based on what we know now. That's next. I wish we could run a study."

"That would be so cool," I say. "Show the ways accommodations are helping and what else is needed."

"Maybe we could survey students, but I think that's been done. I'll check with Disability Services. Harper will know what's been tried already and what we can do."

I sit on the floor and lean against Kai in the chair. She rests a hand on my shoulder. I sigh, looking at the labels on the drawers. That is going to be a lot easier. Now what's the label-the-drawers solution with Maze? How can Maze be so smart about some things and so clueless about others?

CHAPTER THIRTEEN

Maze

After the fight with Lys—it's a fight, isn't it? We raised our voices. I didn't mean to but all the pressure inside me kept bursting out. It's hard to remember all the points of that conversation now. They're mashed into a tight ball in the back of my skull. I never want Lys to be sad because of me. What am I supposed to do?

I text her to say good night and then I check in the next day. Nothing heavy. She sends back short answers, not bad ones, but not like us either. I don't know how bad this is. I need time to figure out what to do. I avoid the food court and spend a lot of time in my room and, when I get bored with that, the library. Tuesday evening I get an available beanbag chair on the second floor—well away from the study rooms. Wednesday I go midafternoon to make sure I get my same beanbag chair spot.

I've been there for about an hour when Bas says, "Yo, Beanbag," two inches from my ear.

I surge sideways, falling out of the beanbag, and pull out my earbuds. We've barely talked since the night Kai dumped her and she wanted me to scramble around under a car for her missing jacket button. Though, now that I know she makes her jackets, I kind of get it about the button. I probably should've apologized to her too. The list of folks I owe apologies is getting long.

"Do you have to do that?" I ask.

"Come with me," she says.

Maybe Bas knows things about relationships that I don't— maybe that's stored in the same place as the surprising revelation that she sews these historical replica jackets. I shove my book into my backpack and follow Bas out of the library. As we tromp across the snow, even her snow boots are cute. She's in her dark-gray pirate jacket and hat and her face still looks pristine: high cheekbones, mouth made for a teen heartthrob TV series, cosmetically exact eyebrows and eyeshadow. How does she manage all that in a shared bathroom?

"How's your romance?" she asks.

"I'm trying to figure out if I need to apologize for stuff I don't remember saying."

"You probably do need to apologize. If you're wondering that, it's a sign. What did you do?"

I close my mouth over a snarky query about how Bas can know so much about apologies when she's so bad at them. Instead I say, "I don't remember the whole fight. I think it started when I said I wouldn't ask for accommodations."

"Ooh yeah, I'll bet that made her so mad. You're supposed to agree with her on all that, you know," she says.

We've crossed the north side of campus and reached the pedestrian footbridge over the highway. I'm remembering parts of the fight, thinking about what I believe.

I tell Bas, "I think I do agree with her."

"Nope. You don't. You're like me, engineered to come out on top. Own it. You don't need or want anybody helping you out."

"I want Lys to have help. But when I say that, she thinks I'm saying she's weak."

Bas asks, "What's your definition of weak?"

Warm rush of memory from last fall. This is the Bas I stayed up late with talking about everything in the universe. I have to consider her question. I have been thinking that strong people are the ones who can do things on their own—but now that I hear the thought so plainly in my own brain, I can feel how out of step it is with everything I know about queer theory. Making people feel strongly individualistic is a great way to control us, because we're harder to control in groups. Part of that is suggesting that we should be able to do everything on our own and that my brain's differences are only about my brain, not about a society that's set up to turn a lot of people into cogs in a productivity machine.

I've been reading about Disability Studies—about how people are disabled not because of something within them, but because they live in a culture that doesn't have space for how they operate. A culture without accessible buildings and bathrooms, that expects all kids to learn the same way.

"I don't know," I tell Bas. "I've been rethinking my definition of weak. What's yours?"

"Rigidity," she says. "Because it's so easy to break."

Now I'll have to think about that for a while too. We've been walking toward French House, but we stop between Spanish and Russian in a stand of trees. I hadn't bothered changing my sneakers for snow boots and there's cold wet leaking in between my toes. This side street has ten houses for languages and other specialized subject areas—all built a century ago and bought by the college way before I was born.

"Why are we out here?" I ask.

"In case our rooms are bugged."

"Who would bug our rooms? And how?"

Bas shrugs. She unzips her coat and holds it open so I can see there's a book tucked against her abdomen: *The Gilda Stories*. Without pulling it away from her body, she opens the front cover so I can see the note inside that says: 1 + 2 = 8.

I'm pretty sure I know what the note means. I've read the book twice and I'd have made that clue too. I bite my cheek, swallow and ask, "You figured it out already. How?"

"Mad that I'm ahead?" she asks, quirking up an eyebrow and the corner of her mouth.

"Impressed," I say genuinely, hoping the admission covers over the legit anger that, yes, I am feeling.

"*Curious Wine*, at first I figured it had to be Emily Dickinson, since she's so important in bringing our girls together," Bas says. "But that would be way too obvious."

To everyone, I don't say out loud. "Uh-huh."

"And then, no thanks to you who'd rather get down with Lys than help your teammate, I got thinking about the gambling they do and that part about courage, so I played some online blackjack to get in the mood."

"Are you ahead?" I ask.

"Nah, lost twenty bucks. Running the numbers in the book didn't do anything either."

"It wouldn't. I'd expect it to be more literary."

"Not really," Bas says. "Lane's a lawyer, right? And that's pretty important, but it can't be only that. But if you crunch through all the data about everything legal at this school, there's one pre-law advisor who's in the English Department and teaches about law and literature and has been here long enough to be friends with the professor who set up the contest. I stopped by her office to ask if she could help me with a research project about Attorney Lane Christianson and that was it, she gave me the call numbers for this book and the clue."

"That's amazing!"

"You've read *The Gilda Stories*, right?"

"Twice."

"Great." She looks over her shoulder at French House and around us, like someone's going to leap up out of the snow. I'd say that she's being weirder than usual, but I've been the weird one of the two of us, so I can't judge.

"You okay?" I ask.

"Yeah, come on. I'm freezing."

She takes me across the front lawn. French House is a three-story rectangle barely rendered elegant by the white and blue paint of the French flag. The red of the flag is nearly absent except for the welcome mat. Last fall there were red plants and flowers in bloom. Arch-rival Russian House did not stint on the red, though it also features white and blue and a more stately pitch to its steepled roof. The lines of all the language houses are classic, but the exteriors get painted so often there's an uneven graffiti feel to them.

"They let me rearrange the first floor," Bas says as she opens the front door. "Because I've been working on the design of public spaces. The world is full of spaces that don't work for people. I want to make places like hospitals and government buildings that aren't shitty."

There's a place to sit and lots of hooks for coats next to that, above it, across from it, and there's a tree in a pot plus a picture of more trees.

"I feel preternaturally calm," I say.

"Cuts down on the bullshit," Bas remarks. "If people come in freaked out and stay that way, the problems multiply."

"You worry about other people's problems?"

"Don't you?" Bas asks—and for the first time I consider that I maybe worry less about other people than she does.

I like people. I find them fascinating because so much of the time they made no sense to me. Even my mom—how could she go to her office so many days of the week and want to stay? I'd seen the place and it wasn't any kind of thrill. I don't worry about her problems, not the way Lys worries about her parents. And she worries about the rugby team and folks she knows from her classes—I had a few of those too, but usually when people got my attention it was from working to figure them out, not from worry.

"I don't worry that much," I admit.

"Heartless," she says, deadpan, then grins. "Don't worry too hard over this clue. I need you sharp for the later books and the lockbox with the collection in it. Nothing's any good if we don't find that and we are going to find it."

Her bedroom is at the top of the stairs in the middle of the hall. Not the quietest or most private, but the best light. She's changed the arrangement of furniture since the fall—but how recently? When was I here last? Before the party, for sure.

"You moved your bed."

"Shared wall," she says and jerks her finger toward the wall that now holds her bookcase and desk.

"Are you making noise or are they?" I ask.

"Both, of course." She sits on her bed and pats the spot next to her.

I settle in, one knee bent, facing her.

"What's the clue about?" she asks.

"I'm guessing it's the chapters because there are eight in the book. In the first, the Girl gets discovered by Gilda and turned into a vampire, after she consents, of course. Much kinder and gentler vampires here."

"Gentler than the vegetarians in *Twilight*?"

"They ate animal blood," I say.

"You read *Twilight*?"

"And copious fan fiction, until I realized it was not giving me the useful life lessons I thought. Kristin Stewart is super crush-worthy from day one and in the right light Edward not only sparkles, he looks like a cute, butchy girl."

Bas shakes her head. "And you're into the cute, butchy girls, hence Lys?"

I shrug. I don't want to try justifying my feelings about Lys to a girl who can maintain a perfect manicure and still presumably rock lesbian sex. Plus in my secret *Twilight* fan-world, I was Edward.

In the silence, there's a tap on the door and Bas calls, "Come on in."

I'm expecting one of her housemates, but Sophi walks in. Her sweeping eyeshadow matches her green and gold paisley head wrap. She pauses two steps inside the door, dark eyes steady on us and unreadable.

"Oh hi," I say and regret how surprised and foolish that sounded.

"Did I get the time wrong?" she asks.

Bas's expression froze with her eyebrows raised and she forgets to lower them so her casual words come out anything but relaxed. "Nah, just still talking to Maze about the treasure hunt, but nothing top secret, or bottom secret. Hah. Do you want tea? Mint or green?"

My best guess is that Sophi is only part of what surprised Bas—that she didn't expect Sophi while I'm still here, is the main reason her face hasn't unfrozen.

"Yes, thanks, the mint. Can I look around?" Sophi asks.

"Oh please do, I'm very vain about my room."

Bas scoots off the bed and heads downstairs to make tea. Did she not offer me any on purpose? Should I be leaving?

Sophi moves around the room, looking at art on the walls, the little sculptures Bas has on her bookshelf, the spines of the books. "You and Bas are friends?"

"Since fall," I say. "Pretty early in the semester. She thought I was super stuck up and too good for everyone and told me so—and somehow that turned into us hanging out a bunch." I should ask something… "Did you come to any of the meetings before the treasure hunt? I only came to a few."

"Nah. Theater Department is very queer," she says. "And I don't love meetings mostly."

Bas returns with three mugs. She puts Sophi's on the desk and turns the chair out for her, gallant. Another mug she hands to me. Mint, because that's always what I drink when I'm here. Warmth from the mug flows up my arms and into my chest. She didn't forget.

"I'm glad you're both here," Bas says. She's had time to recover and her smile seems real.

"You invited me," Sophi says, a furrow between her eyebrows.

"Exactly."

Bas puts *The Gilda Stories* on the edge of the bed where Sophi can reach it. She makes an "oh" of approval and takes it, opening to the clue inside the cover. "Yes," she says, lips parted, curving up. "This is good."

Bas asks, "If the numbers are chapters, why do you think we only got three chapters? Is it mercy because we're coming up on midterms?"

I am so confused. She wouldn't talk about the book with me in her room but now that Sophi is here, she will? Though I notice that she didn't name it out loud. Does she seriously think someone would bug our rooms?

Quick calculations: this is book three of six. There are enough clues still to find that I can work with Sophi on this and then give the info to Lys so she has lead time as well. Did Bas make these same calculations? How closely is she working with Sophi? Is this some complicated flirting maneuver?

I say, "More likely it's part of the riddle of this one. She picked chapters that are far in the past and then out into the future—starting in the 1800s and then jumping all the way to 2050. Nothing close to the present time. If you think about it, she's disrupting the chronology in other ways. *Gilda* was published in the eighties, so it's published later than the setting of *Curious Wine*, but the times are way off. What do you think?"

"She's messing with us," Bas says. "It's definitely about vampires."

"Vampires as metaphor, sure," I agree. "But I don't know that there are a lot of vampire locations on campus."

"Russian House," Bas snipes.

There's a feud going on between French and Russian Houses, having to do with their shared alley and trash day. Bas would tell me all about it but I can't get myself to care.

Sitting in the desk chair, Sophi turns more toward us. "If we assume that *Zami* was about personal growth and reflection—and *Curious Wine* was about two people being extraordinarily loving to each other—then wouldn't it follow, given the clue, that the core of *Gilda* is about community?"

I turn and look at her full on. "That's—"

Sophi keeps talking. "I read it a few years ago so I need to check this, but I think at the end the main character is fighting to get back to her community. So we're getting the parts at the beginning, the key chapters where Gilda is welcomed into community and learns to be part of it—and then at the end where it's all that's left to fight for."

"Great," Bas says. "Now if we can figure out a location on campus that's about vampire community and isn't the Russian House, we'll have this locked down."

"The clue isn't about vampires," Sophi tells Bas and she actually settles, smiles into her cup of tea. Does Sophi like Bas too?

"I've got to go meet people about things," I say, because my brain is working independently from my mouth.

Neither of them is paying much attention to me anyway as I grab my coat off the foot of Bas's bed and head for the door. Bas is persuading Sophi to tell her the entire history of queer Black vampire stories. When I glance back, Sophi is leaning toward Bas, her hands drawing a timeline in the air.

Did Sophi show up early to a date and blow Bas's attempts at secrecy? And, if so, how is Bas's romantic life more functional than mine right now?

CHAPTER FOURTEEN

Lys

On Thursday, Kai texts me to meet her at the disability office after my last class. She has an appointment set up with Harper to talk about whether we can survey students who are getting accommodations—so we can amass data about what's working, to counteract Professor Leland's work.

I haven't been to the Disability Services office since Valentine's Day, over a month ago. The elevator is working, but I don't need it today. Glad it's there for the folks who do need it. I walk down the stairs slowly, resenting them and this building and the way Maze talks about me needing help. I haven't said much to her this week and I hate not talking. But I don't want to yell at her again.

Kai waits for me in the chairs outside of the office. The waiting area is in the hall because the office isn't soundproofed. She pats the chair next to her and I sit. She's in her extra fuzzy dark-green sweatshirt today with her white-and-green plaid pants. I want to cuddle into that sweatshirt.

"How was Education for the Able?" she asks. She's been making up snarky names for my class and I love it.

"Skipped it," I say. "Not up for another accommodations group assignment, or looking at his face while he's acting reasonable and smart and saying ignorant things. And Sophi has been putting notes online for me, so I hardly need to be there. Her notes are great."

"How's your pain, physical or otherwise?"

"Knee's fine. But Maze and I are not saying anything important to each other and it's driving me crazy. She's texting. I'm texting back. Everything feels so surface. We haven't talked about that whole thing at her moms' house."

"Why not? You're obviously upset."

"She avoids the topic and when we met in the commons for dinner last night, she only talked about our classes. I don't know if I even want to go to the queer group meeting tonight because it's going to be awkward."

"But you're still together, right?"

I nod.

Kai raises her hands, palms up, then circles them in front of her face in a swirl of pantomimed confusion. "Talk to her," she says. "Sit her entire self down and talk it out. You're really into her and you're not a human who thrives on low communication."

"What if I'd rather be in a sort-of relationship with her than risk her saying something else that hurts?"

Kai puts her palm over the back of my hand. "Send her to me. I'll sort it out."

I snort. But I don't hate the idea.

I'm still thinking about it when Harper opens the door and waves us inside. She's in a black V-neck sweater that brings out the brightness of her golden hair, plus flowing light blue pants. Her face looks like a set of friendly curves and planes: soft eyebrows, broad smile, high cheekbones, long nose. I hadn't noticed it last time I was here, but her square glasses almost resemble Maze's—except that Harper's are smaller and a semitransparent tan, while Maze's are dark. Still I like the comparison. There's a lifted feeling in my chest, a sense that Harper can and will help us.

Plus she's an alum. She graduated from here about five years ago so she's not that much older than us.

We sit in the mismatched chairs across from her desk. She has three, plus a folding chair against the wall. They look like they came from three different garage sales. Two are dining room chairs with thickly padded seats and radically different upholstery: shades of brown and orange on one clashing with deep purple on the other. The last is a skinny tan recliner. I get that one and lean it back so my legs can stretch out.

"Can we do it?" Kai asks as soon as we're both settled.

"You can," Harper says. "But is it going to be effective in the way you want?"

I appreciate that Harper gets right to the point. Kai sent her a long email days ago that detailed what we know about Professor Leland's project and asked if we could survey students for counter-evidence—and Harper isn't asking us to tell her that info again. I like that she actually reads our emails.

"Why wouldn't it be?" I ask.

A text buzzes my phone and I peek at it. Maze asks: *Are you going to the meeting? Linc is telling us about past years.*

I want to text back so many things and to ask why she doesn't want to talk to me about our conversation...our fight. But not now.

I tune back into the conversation as Harper is saying, "Plus students are in the middle of everything. They don't know how much accommodations are helping."

"Yeah they do," Kai says. "I know exactly how much mine help."

Harper holds up her hands, palms out. "I generalized. Some students don't know and won't until they've been out of college for a few years. What if you survey alumni?"

"Can we do that?" I ask. That sounds amazing to me—and I have to trust that if there are downsides, Kai is going to spot them. She's better at finding the negatives. Claims that I'm positivity on top of optimism and she's not wrong. She wins at enthusiasm, but it's a neutral kind of enthusiasm—pure energy.

"I asked Helen over in alumni relations and she's interested in helping," Harper says. "Same basic questions, but with a more reflective focus. Where are they now and how did accommodations help them get there?"

"What if no one takes the survey?" Kai asks.

Harper smiles. "You're no worse off than you are now."

"But if we only get a few people, it's not going to be enough data," Kai contends.

I sit up, lean toward her. "Individual stories are impactful. That's why charitable organizations always send you pictures of specific people and tell you what's up with them before they ask for money."

She turns to face me. "Could we do that? Individual stories. Show people's faces. Make it hit home with the faculty board that we're talking about real humans, real students who will go on to live the rest of their lives with or without the help they got here?"

Harper knocks on her desk. "Now you're talking! Do you want longer questions on the survey? Or do you want to give them an option to be interviewed."

"The second one," Kai says. "Or send us video. It's better if they're talking right to the faculty board. I'll update the survey doc."

I'm grateful that Kai is so fluent in online documents of many kinds. I wish it didn't make professors forget that she still has dysgraphia. Last semester she had to get the disability office deeply involved when a professor accused her of plagiarism because her typed papers were so much more fluent than her handwritten test answers. I heard a whole lot of yelling about that and did some of it myself. I don't know why they don't believe us when we say we need things or talk about how our brains work. Are there that many students trying to cheat? Maybe some schools have students like that, but I haven't met any here.

Kai and Harper go on talking, sorting out the details, while I space out about Kai—and my brain circles back around to worry about Maze.

When Linc opens the door, Maze not far behind him, it's like she stepped out of my worries into this three-dimensional space. Linc is wearing the dark-green fedora that we drew names out of for the contest with a strappy black tank top under his open jacket. Over his shoulder I see Maze's blue-gray bandana, the edge of her glasses, one shoulder of her high-tech winter jacket.

"Sorry," Linc says. "I thought the office would be empty by now. Do you need us to come back?"

"No, we're chatting. How're you doing?"

Linc gives her a chipper double thumbs-up. "Appreciate your help with the group scheduling and snacks, as always. Do you want me to do my spiel in the hall?"

"I want to hear it," Harper says. She's on the mailing list for the queer/trans student group and got invited to this campus tour of past treasure hunt locations like the rest of us.

Linc sashays into the room, followed by all the students still in the treasure hunt. I think he's in theater too and I wonder if Sophi knows him. He throws his arms wide and projects his voice.

"We begin our tour in the very office where our beloved Professor Stendatter met and courted her wife, who twenty years ago worked in this glamorous basement office. Rumor has it that when marriage became legal, the professor even proposed here. If you'll follow me…"

He goes back into the hall, other students trailing. I get up and join the group.

"You coming with us?" Kai asks Harper.

"Far too many emails to answer," she says. "I wanted to hear Linc's intro. Have fun."

We form a trailing semicircle around Linc as he crosses the main lawn of the campus, still orating.

"Two years ago, in a winter that seemed to defy global warming while actually proving it, we were tasked with the same seemingly impossible treasure hunt you find yourselves on today. Our first book, nay, *tome*, was the little-known but often-assigned feminist, queer classic published in 1799, *Ormond; or, The Secret Witness*. Friends, count yourselves lucky that you did not have to start with a text written over two hundred years ago. To call it slow going would be a kindness in the extreme. We slogged and ploughed and waded through a story that goes into great depths about household finances during the time of Yellow Fever."

"Was that the clue?" Sophi asks. Her braids are loose, falling past her shoulders, and her makeup is only silver and gold.

"Not at all. We finally figured out—well it wasn't our team, to be honest. But we all heard about the clue, which came from the fact that the entire novel is, ostensibly, a letter written by Constantia's girlfriend, Sophia, to a possible future husband, who none of us buy the existence of. Basically the book is a three-hundred-page letter. The clue turned out to be in the library's collection of historical letters where there was a series written by women in the 1800s."

"Okay but *how*?" Maze asks. "A clue about letters is super broad. There are all sorts of letters all over campus. And I get narrowing it down to women, but still, didn't that send you to a ton of different places?"

"Yes and be glad this tour isn't taking you to all those places!" he says. He opens the doors to the library and we all crowd into the entryway where we don't have to be quiet.

"We've all been to the library," Kai tells him. "Was it something special in the historical letters?"

Linc's shoulders slump. "No. Just talking to the work-study student there. I guess we don't have to go up. All the clues are this kind of hazy, imaginative business. That's what the professor was into."

"What was the next book?" Maze asks.

"*The Color Purple*, which was set in the early 1900s. We watched the movie first, which might have been a mistake because then we couldn't see the characters exactly the way Walker set them on the page."

"Yeah it was," Kai agrees.

Linc sweeps his arm to indicate the stacks of the library and intones, "You'll note that there's another letter theme in this book." He pauses and deflates, arm dropping. "We didn't get that clue either—neither the clue to the next book nor whether there was a meta-theme involving letters. I thought of that last year. Woke me right out of a nap."

Maze waves a hand to interrupt. "Wait, did you figure *any* of it out?"

Linc scoffs—actually takes an entire beat for scoffing—before he says, "We figured out the last two, which were, obviously, the most important. Fine, I'll tell you the middle two books without the drama: *Last Night at the Telegraph Club*, which had recently come out and we all wanted to read anyway, and *Rubyfruit Jungle*. Follow me and I'll show you where we found the clues."

We huddle back out into the cold, across the north side of campus to the Theater Building. When we get inside Sophi asks, "When are they set?"

"*Last Night* is the midfifties and *Rubyfruit* the early seventies."

"So it's all in chronological order?" she asks.

"It's always in chronological order," Linc says. "And until this year it always started with *Ormond*."

"Was the clue for *Ormond* always the same?" Maze asks.

She's standing near me but has barely glanced my way—and I'm resolutely not freaking out about that. The blue-gray bandana around her head matches part of her coat and reminds me of the night we officially met. I don't want to rewind that far, but could we go back maybe a week or two?

Linc shakes his head and tells her, "The *Ormond* clue was different each year. I guess she wanted to keep us on our toes."

"Was the solution to *Rubyfruit Jungle* 'grapefruit'?" Maze asks, smirking now.

Kai asks, "Why?"

"The protagonist throws grapefruits at a guy's dick for money."

"Damn, was it enough money for the therapy she'd need afterward?" Kai asks.

"Probably not," Maze retorts. "Was that the clue?"

"No," Linc admits. "But the clue was in this building." He raises his arm overhead to draw our attention to the two-story height of the Theater Building's lobby.

"And you guys didn't get that one either," Maze says.

"We *did* get the solutions to Dorothy Allison's *Trash* and *Godmother Night*, but I'm not sure you deserve to hear those," Linc tells her, words growing heated.

Maze straightens up. "Wow, *Godmother Night*? Props to Professor Stendatter, that's a cool book. It's about two young women in love who meet Godmother Night, who turns out to be Death—and she helps the women but also makes things complicated. They have a kid. It's hard to explain. It's really mystical. Lesbian and trans author too. What was the answer to that one?"

"My teammate got it," Linc admits. "Our clue was something about Tarot. The author, Rachel Pollack, is a huge Tarot expert and wrote guides for a bunch of different decks, but there's one she drew herself, *The Shining Tribe*. My teammate got a copy of it. He might've actually figured it out through a Tarot reading—something about the Ace of Birds in the position of what was needed. That card is an owl and there was an owl symbol in the WGSS Department lounge, a replica of a burial urn from a Greek island. But it also looked kind of like that lesbian double-sided axe, you know?"

He asks it generally, but Kai answers, "Hey, I'm a sword lesbian."

"Labrys," Sophi says.

Maze looks at her with impressed surprise.

"That was the last one?" I ask. "When is it set?"

"Alternate world, fantasy," Maze says. "So maybe it's happening now, you know. Somewhere. That puts the books all chronological. What did you find at the burial urn replica?"

"The combination," Linc says. "Come on and I'll show you."

We trek back the way we came because WGSS is in the building across from the library. At least this building has a good elevator. We don't all fit in it so Linc waits until we're all on the top floor, clustered around a black glazed urn on a pedestal featuring a big, reddish double-bladed axe on the front.

Linc picks up the urn and tips it toward us. "There were folded slips of paper in the bottom and when we opened one, there it was. We thought we just had to bring the combination to Professor Haille, but it turns out, nope. She said she didn't know where the lockbox is either."

"Do you believe her?" I ask.

"Did she ask to see the combination?" Kai asks.

"No, why?"

"If she had a photographic memory or even a good one, she could've remembered it and unlocked the lockbox herself, if she had it."

"I don't think her memory is that good. I've seen her forget a point she was making in the middle of it," Linc says. "Maybe she once knew where the lockbox was and then forgot."

Kai interrupts, "And we don't know that the lockbox wasn't somehow lost or destroyed. We shouldn't get too caught up in this." She's probably talking to herself because she's super caught up in it. I am too.

"I really wanted us to meet Professor Stendatter," Maze says. "I thought maybe when we got to the end, that would happen."

Linc shakes his head. "Unlikely. After she and her wife retired, they moved to somewhere in Europe. I'm not sure folks even know where or have their contact info. She said she was done with doing."

"Oh…" Maze breathes in the syllable. "That's a Le Guin quote. Damn. Now I really wish we got to meet her."

"Cash prize will take the sting out of it," Bas tells her. "Whatever she hid six years ago has to be worth more now."

* * *

At the end of the tour, I stand next to Maze as the room clears out. "Do you want to do something?" I ask.

She peeks at me, then stares down at her fingers that are twisting together. "Yeah, like a food?"

"I could food."

"I don't know how to talk about what happened," she says. It's one of those moments where she says what she's thinking without overthinking it and I love it. I move closer to her.

"We can figure it out. Char's going back to our room. Where's your roommate?"

"With the incomparable Steve, I think. I'll text to confirm. Are we picking up something on the way?"

"Yeah."

She texts as we take the elevator down.

"No answer," she says on the ground floor. "I think that's a good sign."

On the way to the commons to get food, she says, "Bas found the third book."

"Wow, go you guys."

"I want to tell you what it is. She already told Sophi. This seems fair. I mean, I'd tell you anyway, but now it's fair."

I look around, like we're in a spy movie, and admit, "I already know. Char got it yesterday evening. How'd Bas figure it out?" The more info I have about how the clues work, the more likely it is I'll work one out myself.

"She said she crunched a lot of data, which actually sounds weird for her."

"Yeah it does," I say. "And it sounds like exactly how Char got it. She wrote some program…can I text her about this?"

Maze shrugs and holds open the door to the commons. We head for our favorite food counters and I text Char while I'm waiting in line.

She texts back right away: *when can you get here?*

I tell her: *ten minutes? I'm bringing Maze.*

She answers with a bunch of exploding and sparkly emojis that don't seem to mean "No."

Bags in hand, we hurry to my room. There's no way we're going to talk about anything relationship-wise with Char here. Maybe we can talk to Char, eat and then scoot over to Maze's room.

Char is pacing when I open the door. Her hair is frizzed out in the back—she's been playing with it—and she's clutching her gray, fuzzy sloth warming pillow to her chest.

"Bas got the third book?" she asks Maze.

"Yeah," Maze confirms. "She showed it to me yesterday afternoon."

"What time?"

"Four-ish."

"And she actually said that, about the data?" Char asks.

"Yeah, something about all the legal-related data at this school."

Char spins on her heel and paces the other way. "Bas didn't crunch data, I did. That lit professor said I was the second one in her office yesterday and I got there a bit after five. How the fuck did she get my data?"

Char almost never swears without extra silly words, so she is deeply pissed.

"Could she hack your stuff?" I ask.

"With what?" Char shoots back. "Bas couldn't hack her way into a paper bag that's already open. I guess she could've hired someone."

She drops into her desk chair and types feverishly on her laptop.

Maze says, "She made us meet outside in case there were bugs."

"Ohh," I say. "And if she knows there are bugs in place in some rooms, that would make her paranoid that she's not the only one doing it. Classic projection. Char, has she been in our room?"

"Nope," Char says over her shoulder. "And so far my laptop's clean."

"Did you talk about the answer somewhere else?" I ask.

Char thinks for a minute. "I was in the library, first-floor study cubes between my classes and I texted you to see if you had time to run over to that professor's office, but you didn't. It'd be hard to hack phones, though. Oh no, she wouldn't have to if she hacked the Wi-Fi in the library. Not hacked, actually, spoofed it. You don't care. Forget the details."

"You're saying there is a way she could get the information from your text message?" Maze asks.

Char thumbs through screens on her phones. "Yep. Here's the text: 'Lys, got the treasure hunt clue from *Curious Wine*. If you have time, run by Professor Williams's office. I think she has the next book.' That's got a bunch of keywords in it. My bet is that Bas hired someone to set up a dummy Wi-Fi network that looks like the school's network so it can read all the messages.

They couldn't do the whole campus, so it's probably the library. Then they'd need a program to cull through it all and highlight keywords and phrases like 'treasure hunt,' but that's not hard to write. I mean, I spelled out the entire book name. That's so obvious."

"Is that legal?" I ask.

"Not at all. She'd get in serious trouble if we could prove it, but we probably can't."

"Plus Maze would get disqualified," I point out. If I didn't already hate Maze being on a team with Bas, now I really did. "How do we keep our info safe?"

"Keep important conversations to voice and if you have to text about the contest, turn off the Wi-Fi on your phone—if you connect through the cell network, the data is much more secure."

"And I'll tell you the next book if we get it first," Maze says. "It's only fair. I wouldn't have the book if Bas didn't spy on your data. Oh and that clue, I'm pretty sure it's the chapters: 1, 2 and 8. They circle around thematically like the bridge in *Zami*."

"Thanks. You're solid," Char says.

"Why would Bas risk so much?" Maze asks. "It doesn't seem like her. I know she tries to act all cavalier, but she actually cares a lot about school."

"If it's a coin collection, that could be worth a whole lot," Char says. "I heard that's what it is and it makes sense. It would be small and easy to hide. Professor Stendatter retired seven years ago, so that puts her in her early seventies, probably born in the fifties. I figured she might've gotten some coins as a gift when she was a kid, so I searched the forties through the sixties to see what's valuable from then. There are some rare pennies worth over a hundred thousand."

"Why would she leave something that valuable?" Maze asks.

Char shrugs. "I'm not saying the collection has one of those, only that coin collections can be worth something, so I figure it's at least a few thousand. But now I'm wondering if Bas knows more than we do—if she'd be willing to risk so much. She has to be working with someone. What if she didn't hire someone—they hired her to get in the contest and split the winnings?"

"She'd be splitting half," Maze says.

I point out, "A quarter of a hundred thousand is still a lot. And what if it's more than that? If Bas isn't the one who got Char's info, if she'd followed instructions from someone else, then she didn't risk her standing at school and she stands to gain a whole lot." I add, "I want to tell Kai. She should know to keep her info safe."

"Our food's getting cold," Maze says.

"I'll text and see if she's in her room and if we can come over in twenty minutes," I suggest. "And if she wants to invite Sophi."

Maze pauses in opening her bag of food. "Sophi might tell Bas things. They're spending time together. Of course that also means she might have good intel about Bas."

I nod. "I'll tell Kai all that and let her decide."

Char shrugs one shoulder, which is close enough to a yes. She's back at her computer, typing quickly. If she finds info that incriminates Bas, what happens to Maze?

CHAPTER FIFTEEN

Maze

After a hasty dinner, we hurry to Kai's room in the next dorm over from Lys and Char's. They all live on the north side of campus, closer to the gym. My dorm is southeast and nearer the artsy buildings.

Is Bas working with other folks? Would she take ill-gotten info? And, if so, is it right for me to use it?

Kai is in a big rugby sweatshirt and fuzzy blue-and-white plaid pajama pants, her eyes heavy-lidded, tired or confused or both. "What's the emergency?" she asks.

Lys tells her, "The treasure hunt."

"Well get in here." Kai ushers us through the door and shuts it. "And be careful. Did you see Linc's latest emails? The skinny gay guys got disqualified for getting information from the previous year's team."

"So weird," I mutter. "I'd think they'd want us to work together."

"Covid rules," Kai says.

Kai and her roommate put both of their bunks into loft mode so there's a ton of sitting room on the floor under and between them, which they've strewn with massive pillows. She goes to a pile of pillows and flops into it, half sitting, half lying down.

Sophi is already here. She's ignored the pillows, sitting with her back against one of the bed struts. Her hair is swept up and back by a black-and-gold scarf, her eyes outlined in black with gold at the inner corners. She has a thick, square notebook perched on her bent leg and is doodling.

Lys settles next to Kai with Char on the other side. Team Rugby. I want to sit near Lys, but I'm not sure how I feel about the pillows and the weirdness, so I take the other bed slat on the side with Sophi. I can kind of see what she's drawing. Not the usual eyes and doodles, but a tree made of big and small spirals in the branches and roots.

Lys explains that Bas got the next book, likely by stealing Char's results—and that sets Char off again about spoofing and Wi-Fis and all the tech ways there are to steal info. I watch Sophi's face for any changes that could indicate feelings about Bas and these suspicions, but her expression remains calm and even.

When Char stops to drink from her thermos, I say, "And we'd tell you the next book except you already have it."

"*The Gilda Stories*," Sophi says softly.

"And you're a good human," Kai adds. "We agree that the clue is about the chapters and the way they loop back thematically."

Sophi's head comes up, but she's not looking at anyone. I recognize that expression from the inside. She's seeing some set of ideas, maybe not arranged the same way that mine are, but all connected similarly. How does she sort her ideas? If I ask, will she tell me?

"Add in the characters," she says. "At the beginning we meet the Girl, who chooses to become a vampire, the new Gilda, so that's one becoming two. I haven't yet figured how it adds to eight, but I think by the end her vampire family is at least eight people. I'm pretty sure."

"There are basically eight important characters in *Curious Wine* too," I say. "The six women who go to the cabin plus Diana's gambling friend Vivian and her ex, Jack. I wonder if that's coincidence."

Sophi sounds tired but compelled as she says, "It's all connected, I just can't see how."

I laugh. "I know that feeling."

"That's a lot to think about," Kai says. "I call dibs on the relationships."

Lys grins and fake-punches her on the shoulder. Kai makes a face at her. I can't read the meaning of that face, but Lys brightens more. They're pretty cute together. Am I jealous? More worried that someday Lys will get sick of me spacing out on her. Though I know she feels the same way about the times she talks all in a rush to me about what she loves—she's said it—and I don't think I will ever feel that way about her.

"That's not the only thing we have to figure out," Sophi says. Her voice is always cool and smooth, even now when her maybe-future-girlfriend Bas has been revealed to probably be involved in some sketchy shit. "It violates the rules to work outside of our team, which we have all now done quite completely so we'd better keep this under wraps. Who is Bas working with? If we know that, we'll have leverage on her."

"You're asking us?" Kai's voice rises with disbelief. "You're the one hanging out with her."

"I like her aesthetic," Sophi tells her, giving a one-shouldered shrug. "She has not read me in on any super-secret spy plans."

I say, "She has a class with either Paisley or Brantley, not sure which. She's been hanging out with them more."

"That would be super obvious," Lys says.

"They don't code," Char adds.

"But you know Pais and Brantley are working with their whole crew," I point out. "Someone in there probably knows how."

"We need to follow Bas," Kai declares. "Unless you can bug her phone."

"I probably can," Char tells her. "But following is a good plan until I figure out how and whether I can get kicked out for bugging another student."

Sophi sets down her square notebook and opens her bag. "I don't think we need to follow her. Let me get bigger paper. This campus isn't huge. We already know a lot about her movements. Kai, do you have loose paper that everyone can write on?"

Kai scowls but digs in a desk drawer and pulls out sheets of paper, handing them around to us. She goes back into the drawer and gets a box of Pop-Tarts. Not a single box of one flavor, but a plain cardboard box into which multiple foil packets have been dumped. She starts that around the circle.

"Good choice," Sophi says about my selecting the cinnamon and brown sugar flavor.

"It's my favorite," I tell her.

"It's the only decent flavor," Kai says. "You should toast it, though."

"It's perfect raw," Sophi argues.

"You're wrong and stubborn and someday when I'm near a toaster I will prove that."

Sophi rolls her eyes, opens the Pop-Tart package and slips a raw corner of sugary pastry into her mouth as she continues to make a grid on a page of her notebook.

"Everyone write on your page the last times and days you saw Bas, where and who she was with."

"I didn't—" Kai starts and cuts herself off. "Oh yeah, in the commons...what day was that?"

I write down seeing Bas yesterday from the library to French House, even though Sophi was there for the second half of that. Peeking over at her page, I see a bunch of times, dates and notes. She's been seeing Bas a lot and yet she's still willing to do this. I'd do the same, though, especially if it was someone I'd only recently started dating.

Well, maybe. Would I do it about Lys? Probably not. I trust her way more than anyone else—and we haven't been able to talk about what happened at my house and when we got back to campus. Definitely need to apologize, even if I'm not sure how.

My page only has the one entry. Even Lys's has more because she saw Bas in the library a few times and walking across campus. Bas has been wearing a pirate hat some of the time and is easy to spot. I push my page over to Sophi, who is making a vast, multicolored map of Bas's movements over the last ten days.

She adds my entry to the map and then adds the ones from Lys. Kai brings hers over and stares at all Sophi's entries. A glance full of furrowed-brow worry goes from her to Lys to me.

Sophi makes arrows and notes on the spread pages. She says, "The names coming up a lot are Brantley, Paisley a bit, but also Linc."

"He almost won it two years ago. I'll bet he really wants to win. Makes sense," Kai says.

I let the words on the page blur and feel into the knowledge Sophi is revealing about Bas's patterns. I feel the information in the space around me: Bas's movement patterns from last fall and what I know about this spring. I can feel the gaps between the two, like a cold wind.

I say, "Bas is hanging out over by Takahashi, Brantley's dorm, and she didn't last fall. Plus Brantley is in one of my classes that gets out around the time Lys has seen Bas leave the library on Tuesdays and Thursdays."

"I saw them working out together." Kai taps her page. "And I've never seen Bas work out before that."

"They could be friends," I say, thinly.

"Yeah or they're hooking up," Kai says, which is an ungenerous read on Bas's intentions and capabilities, but I can't refute it.

Lys shakes her head. "Paisley and Brantley are on top of each other all the time. Do you think there's any way something could develop between Brantley and Bas without Paisley knowing?"

"That would be a whole disaster," Char adds.

I peek at Sophi. She doesn't look upset—at least not to me—but with Sophi I'm not sure that I'd know. The eye makeup tends to mask her expressions.

I say, "More likely Bas is spending more time with both Brantley and Paisley in case they drop info about book clues."

Sophi shifts through the pile of papers on the floor. "Char, you said Paisley and Brantley don't code—could they know someone who does?"

"Brantley's in data science, but only for the science credit," Char says. "Yeah, they know people."

Kai adds, "But Linc knows some coding, at least knows enough to update websites. He and Harper were talking about some work he did for her on the queer alumni site. I think Maze is right, Bas is hanging out with P and B for intel—and she's probably working with Linc."

Lys says, "We can't prove it—and if we could, that would get Bas kicked out of the contest and therefore Maze. So we have to be careful around all of them."

"Or feed them false information," Sophi says quietly.

Kai's head turns, not so far that she's looking at Sophi, but definitely in her direction. "I respect that."

"Who's going to pass what info?" I ask.

"Let's wait another book or two," Sophi suggests. "We don't need that much of an edge yet, but we will."

* * *

It's late and Lys has a morning class she wants to attend, therefore an earlier than usual bedtime. As we say good-bye, my chest sinks but my shoulders lift. We need to talk and I want to talk, but I don't know what to say. More time might help and I'll take it.

It's dark out and Sophi's in the Hicks-Anderson dorm, same as me, so we walk back together. The air isn't as cold as it has been and there's a haze from melting snow. Bits of ice crackle under our boots.

"Are you dating Bas?" I blurt after we've gone a few steps, because I can't find a non-blurty way to ask.

"No," Sophi says.

"Are you going to?"

"Probably not."

"Does she know that? You're spending a lot of time together. She might expect that you are. Or think you are."

She turns her face and grins at me, a wryly off-center, deep grin. "Wisdom," she says. "But I don't think Bas thinks we're dating. There's been minimal physical contact and my flat affect confuses her."

"What's flat affect?" I ask.

"You know how some people's voices change a lot and some are more monotone? I say what I need to say without changing my voice about it—same with my face usually. Flat affect is monotone for facial expressions."

Paradoxically, her face is the least flat I've ever seen as she explains this. The curve of her smile is reflected in the shape of her eyes and softness of her eyebrows. A host of tiny muscles are engaged, giving her face more contours.

"Same," I tell her. "Sometimes with Lys, I think she doesn't realize I mean what I'm saying because my face isn't doing the right thing about it. She jokes that I have three facial expressions and she's really asking what I feel when she says that."

"How many do you think you have?" Sophi asks.

"I don't know. I'm not usually paying attention to my face around her. I wonder if I should. How many do you have?"

"Three," she says, the grin drifting onto her lips again. "That's all we need, right? Usually, at least. I am working on a graph about extraordinary situations."

"Can I see it?"

"You want to?"

"I'd love to."

We've reached our dorm, one of the newer ones in the southeast part of campus, lots of metal and glass everywhere. We stop in the common room to sit on a tweed couch by a big, dark window. Sophi pulls a notebook out of her bag. Most of the stickers on the front are designs, but one says, "Cure Ableism."

I point at it. "At least you and Kai can bond over this."

"She hasn't seen this notebook," Sophi says. "She's still being defensive. She gets very reactive to my flat affect, I think, more voice than face from what I can tell. I was going to tell her that

I'm Autistic but she pissed me off so now I'm going to let her work it out for herself."

"Wait, what?"

"Which part?"

"You're Autistic?"

"Yes. I thought you knew and that's why you were talking to me about neurodivergence. Are all your Autistic models white boys?"

I nod. "Yeah, though to be fair, those are my ADHD models too."

"What makes you think you're not also Autistic?" she asks.

"I got tested."

"By someone who tests for both?"

"I don't think so…" I trail off because I don't have a particular question to ask—there are too many and they're not cohering.

"The overlap is huge," Sophi says. "Some people use the term AuDHD now because so many of us have traits of both."

She opens her notebook to a page with a quadrant graph that ascends to artistic swirls in its open right corner. "Here's what I've been thinking: trust level on this axis, energy level on this. High-trust, high-energy is here." She points to the swirls. "That's where I check into my face and voice fully. Here's where I'm not fully connecting when the environment doesn't feel safe or when I'm in a place that's taking too much of my energy to counter the sensory inputs."

Her finger taps the midpoint of the axis. "If I had a third dimension, it would be about how much sensory data I'm dealing with. How much do you know about Autism?"

"Not nearly enough," I tell her.

"We have over-connected brains," she says. "More connections than neurotypical people. Which means we take in more information, sometimes way too much. Plus we tend to want to process all the details—to start from the details and work our way up, instead of starting with assumptions and generalizations. So in this part of the chart, if I'm in a low-trust space, there's usually way more for me to process and I don't process it quickly, so I have to shut down a lot of my responses and feelings from my body just to have the bandwidth to cope. If people want me to show up in a low-trust space that's new for me, that's strongly mask only."

I stare at the chart-drawing for a while, then say, "I feel like this too. The more complicated the situation I'm in, the less connected I can be. Like I can either manage what's going on around me or inside me, but not both at the same time. Ohhh, that's why when things get emotional with Lys it takes me so long to answer her questions. Can I draw a bad copy of this to think about?"

"No," she says. "I'll draw you a good one."

"How did you even start to figure this out?"

"An older sibling who's a genius."

Watching her draw feels too intimate, so I stare at the window. With the light in here and the dark out there, I'm staring at our reflections. I thought Sophi was super into academics, the learning part but also the system of winning, the grades. Like me, I guess. And now she feels even more like me than that.

"When did you find out you're Autistic?" I ask.

She answers without pausing in her drawing. The tiny muscles of her face have relaxed so her only expression is intense concentration.

"My oldest sibling figured it out and went to our parents to get tested, but they said, 'we don't believe in that.' So my sib did all the research on their own and kept talking about it with their friends and me—and everything started making sense."

"Are you going to get a diagnosis?"

"I already know who I am." She hands the finished page back to me. "I don't know what else the diagnosis would get me. I'm good at masking and if I'm being honest the racism at this college is a lot harder than being Autistic. Not that those operate separately. But racism is exhausting all the time. Some days moving through the neurotypical world feels like an interesting puzzle."

I don't know where to begin asking questions about that and I really wish I did. My brain is still spinning with the revelation that of course there are Black Autistic people in the world—and sad about the reasons I've never thought about that before.

"Can we talk about this more?" I ask Sophi. "I have a lot of questions but I don't want to be obnoxious about it."

She smiles. "I'd like another neurodivergent friend. It sucks how much Kai doesn't get me."

"I thought Kai was...more like Lys," I say.

"She hasn't said anything. She gets mad a lot and I figure it's because I'm thinking too slowly for her or pissing her off with all the details I get into—seems like neurotypical reactions to me. We don't need to be friends to win this thing." She shrugs and closes her bag. "Are you still going to want to be friends when we win?"

We grin at each other over a space of unspoken teasing and knowledge. I tell her, "If you can beat me at this, I'll be your friend for life."

CHAPTER SIXTEEN

Maze

After our classes the next day, I text Lys and go over to her room. As soon as I get in the door, I say, "I'm here to apologize more. I need to say that before I get distracted. Because I was going to apologize yesterday, but wasn't sure how, and then Char said all that stuff about hacking. And anyway now I have a better idea about how to apologize."

Her face is bright: cheeks and eyes shining. Unsure, I check her body. She's in bed reading and has shifted to make space for me while also turning toward me, arms open and relaxed at her sides.

I sit next to her and put the page Sophi drew me in her lap.

"This is what happens," I tell her. "I'm supposed to be up here in the pretty part where I can feel stuff and talk about it. But the more that's going on outside of me, the more complicated it all feels, the more I end up over here in the low-trust, low-energy spot. It's not that I don't trust you, it's that in places like my moms' house I'm not trusting the environment. Does that make sense?"

She nods so I keep explaining. "When I don't trust, then I need a lot of time alone to work out what I'm thinking and feeling. I don't know how to do that in front of you. At my moms' house I didn't have anything to say yet. I hadn't worked it out. But maybe you thought I was coming up with arguments or trying not to say something negative. I wasn't. I don't think you're weak at all. What I worked out eventually is that I wouldn't ask for accommodations for me because it would be such a huge thing with Mom and I have a ton of scary feelings about it. I wouldn't even know how to ask for help and I'd be scared to and that's not about you. I think you're a badass and I'm smitten."

She stares at the drawing and traces the outside of the square with her finger. "I did think you were judging me."

"Wasn't," I say. "I was judging me and also trying to understand all these emotions happening all at once. That doesn't happen to you?"

She shakes her head. "I get one emotion really loud a lot of the time. Sometimes there's a second or third, but they're in the context of that loud one and the challenge is not to yell or cry or jump up and down."

"I'd be cool with any of that," I tell her. "Though I guess if you yell at me we should assume I'll get flat about it. I just shut my face down when I'm startled."

"How about we don't yell at each other," she says. "I'm sorry I did."

"I get it. I'm not mad. And I don't want to us to be distant like we've been this week."

Lys leans close and hugs me, which turns into a kiss and then more kisses, until Char's key turns in the lock.

"Want to come on an adventure with me?" Lys whispers as we untangle.

"Of course. Does that mean apology accepted?"

"Very," she says.

She grabs a big backpack, her travel one not her school one, and we set out across campus to the Language Arts Building.

Lys pulls me past the elevator to the stairs. We go down a flight to a door that's usually locked, but today there's a piece of cardboard in the lock. She opens the door and puts the cardboard into her pocket.

"We're going to get locked in and have to call for help, aren't we?" I ask.

"Hardly. That door only locks from the outside, there's a push bar, see?"

There is a push bar on the door to the stairwell and also on the door to my left. Through the window of that door, I see a lower-level hallway, longer than the one we're in. I remember being on the other side of that door once when I came to a meeting for a club I never joined. From the elevator side, the door to this bit of hallway is always locked. That longer hall by the elevator leads to two small classrooms that never get used for classes now that there's so much more space in the new Arts Building. Clubs use them. They're dingy and during winter, when the sun sets at five o'clock, being there feels like being in the absolute bowels of the Earth.

I figured that this little bit of hallway led to the usual weird building stuff: electrical, elevator, etc. But Lys takes me to the far end and unlocks a door into the kind of storeroom from TV shows about people reclaiming magical artifacts that mere mortals should never again come into contact with. We step into an open space with piles of boxes and some freestanding art pieces. Maybe not all art, some look like geography projects, teaching aids, cross-sections of Earth, models of caves—I expect to see dinosaur bones. The scents of rosin and wood come from a sad collection of broken musical instruments, most visibly a guitar and cello. Beyond are tall, crowded, industrial shelves going as far back as I can see.

"What is this?" I ask Lys.

"Storage from when they started remodeling the fine arts center. They tore down the walls between a few different unused classrooms so they could put all the arts stuff here while they worked and then a bunch of it wasn't reclaimed and more got added."

"How do you know this?"

"Rugby, of course. We meet down here in the winter and spring. Not in this room, in one of the little classrooms, but we got curious and found this door and then one of my teammates, and I'm not saying who, figured out how to get a copy of the key."

"And gave it to you?"

"Loaned it because I explained that my girlfriend and I were having severe roommate issues. And then I didn't know if we should come down here because everything got so weird. I'm sorry too. I shouldn't jump on you when you're working out your own stuff. I felt shitty about all of it."

"Our reward for apologizing to each other is that we get to make out in a storage room?"

Lys says, "There's a mattress in the back corner."

"That sounds so unsanitary."

"I brought a blanket."

"Which corner?"

She leads me between massive shelves piled with boxes. There's another open space here with boxes on one side and a mattress on top of wooden pallets.

"It's foam," Lys warns me. "No springs. You'll sink into it, so brace yourself. It was a prop in the Theater Department until they got a better one."

She pulls a thin blanket out of her backpack and spreads it over the mattress. I sit gently.

It leaves a lot to be desired, but it's soft and private. That last part is crucial. My roommate has been fighting with the incomparable Steven and has been in our room having feelings every single night for the last ten days. At the same time, Char is behind on her homework and has been confining herself to *her* room because she gets too chatty around people.

Down here in the weird storage basement, I'm not worried about being interrupted. Lys sits next to me, wobbling backward from the lack of support in the mattress and then righting herself. She's in an oversized tan corduroy jacket, looking even more sturdy than usual, and I want to curl into her.

She kisses me. Her hair smells like honeysuckle and the jacket like coffee, the blend deep and sweet like her kisses. It's cool in this storage room, but I am heating up.

"Wait," she says after too few minutes. "I have homework."

"I'm having trouble imagining that you brought me down here for homework?"

"I was hoping you could be the reward for me getting it done."

"Absolutely! And you can be mine."

Lys scoots to the edge of the mattress that's against the wall and leans back. That looks uncomfortable, so I grab a piece of foam that might once have been a prop mountain and put it behind her. There's enough of it that I can also sit against the mountain.

"I'll set a timer," she says and taps her phone.

I open my laptop and find some class reading I can get through without giving it my full attention, because I like watching Lys work. She has a cute face that gets cuter when she's concentrating, especially if she scrunches up her eyes and wrinkles her nose.

"What's the assignment?" I ask. I am not the least distractable study buddy.

"Write a response to this article about using mindfulness to treat ADHD."

I can't believe that topic was random. I ask, "Did you pick that?"

"From a group of four articles. It felt relevant."

I snort-laugh. "What are you going to say?"

"It seems like a good idea but also there's something off about it. Like sure, mindfulness is good for everything, but how does that help when I'm behind in three classes and one professor won't acknowledge that I have accommodations and I'm so freaked out about my financial aid and the grades I need that it's hard to think about any one thing. I used to go for a run or practice with Kai, but now she's super busy and I'm not supposed to run far right now. Weights are good, but they get boring. I wonder if I could learn to box while sitting down."

"I'm sure you could. If anyone could, it's you."

"What do you think?" she asks me.

"It's hard to argue with mindfulness."

"Actually it isn't," she says. "I could argue if I wanted to. Because the network of the brain that you use when you're being mindful is not the one you use to think about the past or future, or to daydream, or to be compassionate and empathic. Being in the now can actually cut people off and make them less generous."

I almost hop off the mattress. "So say that. That's great!"

"I could. The daydreaming network is very active in ADHD brains. I guess that's why we tend to be sweet people, when we can focus."

I laugh. "Yeah, when we're jerks it's not a failure of imagination, it's an abundance of it."

"What do you think?" she asks and tilts her screen toward me so I can see the start of the article.

I scan the first page, reach over to scroll down and read more.

"That's pretty pathologizing," I say. "I prefer the folks who say we should remove 'disorder' from the name or rename it entirely. I've been reading some of the hunter or inventor info that you told me about and I really like when folks say we're the energetic, creative kids. Also there's one 'variable attention trait' name that sounded pretty good to me."

This storage room has that forgotten feeling that makes it easy to talk about internal things. We're in the trust-plus-energy part of Sophi's chart. For sure nobody in the world can hear us down here and nobody knows we're here, so all the secrets are safe. We're probably surrounded by thousands of other people's secrets that we know nothing about.

"What are we supposed to do mindfully?" I ask.

"We could breathe for a minute," she says.

"Are you going to set another timer?"

She laughs and does so.

We sit and breathe and it's for sure not a minute before she leans over and kisses me. I kiss back.

The timer goes off and while she's turning that off, the other timer goes off.

"Hah, break time anyway," I say.

"I was kissing mindfully. It should count."

"Are you putting that in your response?" I ask.

"We'll find out when break is over."

"You'd better set a timer."

She does and then I push her sideways and down to the mattress. When the timer goes off, it's underneath her and we both reach for it, which means it goes off for a full minute as we're cuddle-wrestling.

"Back to work?" I ask.

"Another minute," she says.

A lot more than a minute passes.

"When is this due?" I ask as she helps me with the button on her jeans. They're super stretchy and as soon as she gets the zipper down, my fingers slip lower.

She gasps and grabs my shoulders. The word "tomorrow" comes out amid her panting breath.

"I should let you finish," I say, though I'm constitutionally incapable of taking my hand out of her jeans now.

She groans and looks at her laptop.

"If I do this," she says. "If I work for the next twenty minutes, will you leave your hand right there?"

"While you work?"

She nods, looking bashful.

"It makes the reward more obvious," she says. "And sexy things release dopamine."

"Right here?" I ask and move my fingers against some very sensitive parts.

Her hips jerk, rubbing the sensitive parts back against my fingers. She grabs her laptop and plants it on top of one thigh. I'm laughing a little but I can't argue with her—I'm feeling extremely attentive right now.

I straighten up as best I can with a hand in her pants and drag my laptop into view.

"This feels silly," she says.

"Shh, I'm concentrating. Don't mess with my dopamine supply."

Her fingers move on the keyboard. Sentences are happening as breathlessly as I feel. I rub my hand against her and she makes quiet, happy noises, but her typing doesn't stop.

I make slow progress through the text for my 18th century lit class, but for once I understand it—not only understand, but I'm enjoying the language. I'm starting to see why my professor is into this. Language is a way to code consciousness and this book is a time machine into the consciousness of the 1700s. With my left hand, I type that into a comment box next to the text.

Then to celebrate, I move my right hand against Lys. It slides easily in the endless wet accumulating down there. She murmurs and presses against me.

"Not yet," she whispers.

I decide that I can rub against her after each paragraph because they are long paragraphs. The timer goes off and she shuts off the sound with barely a sideways look. Her fingers dance over the keys. Sentences happen—and paragraphs.

I reach the end of the assigned session and type another one-handed comment about the inherent queerness of the unmarried brother. I don't want to interrupt Lys's flow. I'm staring at her cleavage where the big jacket has fallen open and the V-neck of her sweater is deep, thinking about how she looks with her top off, about getting her top off. Her hips are rocking lightly, continuously rubbing her against my fingers, and I'm not sure she's aware. Her eyes are locked onto the page.

I switch to next week's reading assignment and make my eyes focus on it as my free hand strays between my legs, over my jeans. I'm so needy right now I could probably get off like this, but I don't want to. My hand is there mainly to hold the situation together.

Finally Lys says, "Okay," and shuts her laptop. She grabs me and drags me on top of her.

* * *

When we're recovering from all the homework we did, I ask, "Did you get it done?"

"I even submitted it," she says. "And I started the next assignment so I won't have a blank page staring at me."

"Wow, we've discovered something powerful! I got mine done too."

She laughs. "I don't think they'll let me take tests this way."

"Is it really a disorder if we can solve it with sex?" I ask.

"Variable attention sex deficiency?" she suggests, still chuckling. "Though just because sex solves it for a time doesn't mean that's the core issue, or even dopamine. Like when you have pain and you take something for it and it goes away doesn't mean your body had a painkiller deficiency. Still, we're on to something. Maybe this can be the topic of my final paper in psych."

"What's your thesis?" I ask as I move back down between her breasts.

She cups the back of my head, encouraging me. "Brain-to-world mismatch," she says. "Do you think our ancient ancestors had a lot of sex?"

"I hope so."

We're kissing again when footsteps sound in the hallway and someone opens the door. The room is dark except for the always-on red emergency lights—and then the overhead lights go on. We freeze and silently zip and button our clothes, shoving laptops and thermoses into our packs.

"I'll look," I breathe into her ear. She might be stronger, but with her knee, she's not good at sneaking.

I creep to the edge of the shelving units and peer around. An adult I don't recognize. A guy somewhere in the mystery of midlife: brown work shirt over a belly and jeans. Maybe a cleaning crew person or someone putting finishing touches on the theater space? He moves deeper into the shelves, looking for something. Could be a theater professor or the husband of one, sent down here to find a long-lost prop. If we move along the back of the room, we should be able to cut across the open side and jet out the door. I'm working on a cover story in case he catches us.

I scoot back and motion to Lys, making circular gestures that I hope she understands to mean: let's go around the outside. She nods and follows me to the back wall.

He's wearing heavy work boots and his steps echo against the ceiling as he moves down a row of shelves and over to the next one. He's muttering—I can't discern words, but the tone is low complaint—the husband theory looks increasingly likely.

We get past the shelves without being seen, coming to the open section by the door. This area is filled with old props, art pieces and that whole geology section. Behind the model cave system is a six-foot-tall geological cross-section of Earth in glass, showing layers of dirt and stone. If we get behind that, we'll be out of sight almost all the way to the door.

The steps return toward us. I beckon to Lys and we hurry behind the geology display. The steps come closer, pause, retreat toward the back of the room.

We dash for the door and slip through it, shutting it silently. As we move down the hall toward the doors, Lys is limping.

"Okay?" I whisper.

She nods and points to the door that leads to the main hallway. I push it open, the grinding of the push bar sounds massively loud in the space, but now we're back in an area where students are allowed and near the elevator. I hit the button and Lys leans against the wall.

"Should've brought my cane," she mutters.

"You can lean on me."

She smirks and puts an arm over my shoulders. I try to be helpful and not think too much about getting under her clothes again or, better yet, getting them off.

We ride to the first floor and head out into the snow. "That was close," I say.

"I should've listened to the warning. The team member who loaned me the key said it's best to avoid times when theater classes and groups are working because they go down there pretty often for props. Good thing it was one person and not a whole class. I'll look up what classes are running in case we need a good story."

"Oh so we're going down there again?" I ask.

"Unless your roommate is staying with her guy this weekend." Lys sounds hopeful.

"She's not planning on it. Her midterms have been rough and she's fighting with him a bunch. But maybe I can persuade her to study in the library for a while. Eventually we'll get my bed again. What about Char?"

"She's still in the room all the time and is driving me bonkers. And every time I suggest she go somewhere else, she acts like she's hardcore reading for the treasure hunt and I'm messing with our future."

"Storage room it is," I say. "We need a cover story and a thicker blanket. And more homework."

"I've never been so glad to have homework in my life. And you know, I think I've figured out my new workouts."

CHAPTER SEVENTEEN

Lys

The remaining teams are: me and Char, Maze and Bas, Kai and Sophi, Paisley and Brantley—half the number that started. For fairness or something like it, the powers that be of the treasure hunt have decided we're allowed to work outside our teams if it's an official queer group meeting and everyone is invited. We're meeting to talk about *The Gilda Stories*, because we're all stumped.

I get to the fourth-floor meeting room early because I love how cozy it feels and Kai's going to meet me here with dinner. I should work on homework. But when I sit on the warm side of the room and snuggle into a big chair, with my knee stretched out over the seat of a small chair, all I want to do is read Kai's Batwoman fanfic. It's PG-13 and profoundly cute.

Kai arrives with our food and drops into the chair next to me. "What are you reading?"

"New chapter of your Batwoman fic. I love the humor."

She snorts. "I keep thinking of jokes when I'm running. There's a lot of breathless dictation on my phone."

She opens the bag and pulls out two paper-wrapped cardboard trays, one with a burger for her and the portobello burger for me, fries with both. After setting her tray in her lap, she carefully squeezes ketchup out of two packets and asks, "What do you think should happen next? I'm kind of stuck."

I don't know what to say, but luckily I have a portobello burger to put in my mouth. "Build more tension," I mumble around the edge of the giant grilled mushroom cap.

"At what point is it unbelievably way too much? They start out hating each other, fighting at least, but once they start to like each other it's hard to keep coming up with reasons for them to be apart."

I shrug and we eat in thoughtful silence for a few minutes. Paisley and Brantley arrive, wrapped up in their own conversation, and sit on the far side of the room. Paisley turns a chair sideways and stretches his legs over Brantley's lap. Paisley is wearing a plaid that would be very lumberjack if it weren't indigo and fuchsia. No necktie today except for the green-on-green one that Brantley has tied loosely around their neck and draped down the front of a green sweater. It's almost more scarf than necktie. When they're alone, do they still sit like they're a lesbian fashion meme?

This is my envy talking. Also "lesbian" is probably not the right term. Every time I see them, something jabs at me about Brantley having both green and purple Doc Martens and both pairs always looking pristine. Is it the shininess or the fact that my second-hand Docs are too heavy to wear when my knee hurts? Both.

Sophi arrives while I'm staring at them. She has her braids swept back with a shimmering blue headband, matching the blue and silver over her eyelids and around her eyes. She spots me and Kai and drags a chair closer to join us.

"Have you started talking about the book?" she asks as soon as she sits.

"No, fanfic," I say and shut my mouth because I realize the recommendations I recently shared with Sophi included one of Kai's fics. "But we were switching to the book."

"We were?" Kai asks. "Because I was about to hold forth about the lack of disability rep in superhero fics."

I sit up straighter, drop my burger into its cardboard tray and grab Kai's arm. I'm trying with my eyes and the grip of my fingers to compel her to stop talking.

"I haven't read a lot of them," Sophi says. "Only what Lys recommended. One of those made some excellent points about trauma in the Batwoman characters. Lys, did you share that one with Kai?"

I try to convey to Sophi—with my eyes and eyebrows and mouth and hands and shoulders—that we need to avoid this topic. She does not get the signal.

Sophi says, "I also enjoyed the creativity of seeing those characters in real-life situations, but funny, like when a dressing room door gets stuck. You'd think Batwoman would be able to get that open, but the author really made it work. That whole bit of dropping the utility belt and accidentally kicking it into the next dressing room stall—I was laughing."

Kai waves a hand in front of my face so I turn to look at her. Then she glares at me. "You shared my fic with Sophi?"

"She didn't know it was yours," I point out. "Until now."

Kai's face darkens, mouth tight, as she realizes she's outed herself.

"I'm so sorry," I tell her. "Sophi saw me reading it and we got talking about fanfic and how great it can be. I didn't say anything about the author. I didn't think you'd ever talk about it the way you two have been arguing."

"We don't argue that much," Sophi inserts. "I guess if that's what Kai's telling you maybe we do."

"I'm just frustrated!" Kai makes wide arcs with her arms. "And pissed now because you're going to tell me everything I should've done differently in that fic—and don't you even dare, that's my safe space."

"I wouldn't," Sophi protests. A long pause and then she asks, "Am I doing that? To you about other things?"

"You want me to write everything down. You hand me gorgeous notebooks with these fucking incredibly beautiful notes in them and doodles…"

Kai's eyes narrow, mouth turning down in a way I've never seen on her before. A mix of the expression she gets when she's trying not to cry and wounded anger.

I glance at Sophi and back to Kai. A thought that's way too simple occurs and I voice it. "Kai, have you told Sophi you have dysgraphia?"

"Everybody knows that about me. I say it all the time. I'm sure I said it."

Most of Sophi's face is unreadable, but I see how wide her eyes become. She says, "That's something I'd remember. But if you said it during that big meeting with all the rules, I might not have heard it. A lot was going on."

"Well it's a fucking important thing to have missed," Kai says loudly, shoulders jerking with tension.

"I know. I'm sorry. We can do everything online."

"I already asked for that," Kai snaps.

"I…can get rigid sometimes." Sophi's voice is quiet, face turned down.

I put my fingers back on Kai's arm. "She's apologizing," I murmur.

Kai heaves a deep breath into her lungs and blows it out. "What the fuck is with all the paper?"

Sophi's fingers rub together, like she's feeling pages. "The textures calm me down, help me think. The slowness of the pens, the soft way the ink comes out and sinks into the page, that's the speed of my thoughts usually. Plus I know paper and colors and inks, they're good friends."

"The keyboard is mine," Kai offers. "That's how I learned to really write."

Sophi says, "Your story is beautiful. I liked it a lot."

I feel like I should back away, but I can't without being super obvious because I am sitting in a chair and would have to get up and walk by Sophi.

"You're just saying that," Kai grumbles.

"Stories aren't one of the things I've practiced lying about," Sophi tells her.

I catch the moment when these words make it all the way to Kai's brain because her hands twitch and she laces her fingers together loosely. Her shoulders lower and broaden. Now all the other words are landing as she thinks back about what Sophi has been telling her. Sophi might think at the speed of handwriting, but Kai and I think at the speed of rugby players sprinting down the field—until we pause and all the other ideas catch up to us.

"What *have* you practiced?" Kai asks.

"When to talk but mostly how to shut up. What to talk about. How to listen to subjects I don't care about. How to calm people down, which doesn't work so well on you but I'm starting to see why."

"You've been trying to calm me down," Kai says. Statement, not question.

"So I can listen. Facts are easier for me when there isn't a lot of other information that my brain thinks it needs to pay attention to. Emotional information takes me a long time to process. I've been talking to Maze about that."

She looks to me. I nod and say, "Maze told me. Super helpful." I circle a finger to include myself, Sophi, Kai, and Maze, even though she isn't here. "We're all neurodivergent but in different ways—and the way we adapt is different. Kai, you've adapted by becoming big, taking up space, controlling the room to be safe. Sophi, I think you go into yourself."

"And I mask," she says. "Literally. But no one gets the joke."

Kai's gaze sweeps over the graceful lines of Sophi's makeup, which does strongly resemble a small domino mask. Kai rubs her fingers across her own eyelids and next to her eyes, like she's tracing Sophi's design on her own face.

She tells Sophi, "I'm sorry. I should've…I don't know how I missed that."

"We missed each other," Sophi says with a gentle smile. She asks me, "What about you and Maze—how have you adapted?"

"I think Maze goes away to figure things out, either away physically or away in her mind. If she can't get away, she says smart things so no one will realize that she's not present. And I try to keep everyone okay, take care of needs, be indispensable."

"They should give you your psych degree right now," Kai says with a grin.

"Are you worried that you're not indispensable?" Sophi asks. "Because the way Maze is about you, maybe you could worry less." To Kai she says, "I won't read any more of your story if you don't want me to."

Kai shrugs and shakes her head, still grinning. "I guess you can read it. But there's going to be sex, so if that's weird then probably don't. I've also been thinking maybe next I want to do a *Gilda* crossover."

"Oh my God—with who?" I ask.

"Maybe Audre Lorde. She hung out with the *Gilda* author, Jewelle Gomez, in real life. If we pretend Jewelle is the vampire Gilda, she could've shared blood with Audre."

"That's amazing."

I peer around because I don't want Maze to miss this discussion. She's arrived but is standing by the microwave talking to Harper, who's opening boxes on the table. Harper's chin-length blond hair is caught back with a barrette that's the same pinkish-cream color as her sweater. The color warms her pale skin and golden glasses frames.

I wave and Maze comes over to our table. She's holding a mug of tea and a plate of donut holes that she sets in the middle. "Harper brought donuts," she tells us.

"Thanks." I grab a frosted chocolate donut hole.

"What are we talking about?" Maze asks.

"Fanfic Gilda crossovers," I say. "Who does Gilda bite and turn?"

Smiling, Maze offers, "She bites Laura from Ann Bannon's Beebo Brinker series in the fifties and then Laura bites Beebo and we get five more books that are so different from the first five as lesbian vampires take over New York City."

That gets Kai going with more ideas and the two of them brainstorm until Bas arrives and calls the meeting to order. She was the last to arrive, but it seems like she also thinks she's the logical leader. She asks for all current ideas about the clue and writes them on the whiteboard. This is only book three of the contest, so if we all figure it out together, there's still plenty of time for one team to surge ahead.

Then we all stare at the whiteboard in dreary silence.

Kai suggests, "Maybe we need to reenact a scene from *Gilda* like we did with *Curious Wine*."

"You just want to be *Gilda*," Bas says, rolling her eyes.

"Me or Sophi, obviously," Kai shoots back.

"We'll be the audience," Paisley says. He now has Brantley sitting in his lap and is playing with the tip of their necktie. That would be cute if it weren't so cloying.

"What scene?" Maze asks. "Something out of chapter two, I think."

She turns to Sophi who suggests, "That one where the bad vampire is trying to get Gilda to kill the worse one. If chapter two is the key chapter, that's the climax of that chapter."

Maze says, "I thought Eleanor was the worse vampire."

Bas snarks, "Of course you pick the manipulative one. Samuel is clearly worse. He has no refinement, just a brute and not even a smart one."

Maze glances around the room, catches a few vacant expressions, explains, "Eleanor is the one who's manipulating Gilda—manipulating everyone—and kisses her to piss off Samuel. Then he attacks Gilda but he's not that strong, remember?"

"Who's kissing Sophi or Kai, then?" Bas asks. "It's quite a kiss in the text. Gilda's first, I believe." She opens her copy of the book and reads: "'The kiss bruised her mouth. Yet Gilda matched its power, feeding a need inside her like no other she had experienced before. Her hand became entangled in the mass of red curls, and she pulled at it while pressing Eleanor's mouth tighter to her own.'" Bas stares at Sophi. "Do you have a need inside like no other?"

I expect Sophi to dispute that, but she smiles slowly. "We'll only know if I get kissed by a vampire, won't we?"

"Okay then, if you're volunteering to be Gilda I call dibs on Eleanor," Bas says.

"I wasn't volunteering," Sophi replies. "But I can."

Bas strides across the front of the room and turns. "Nobody wants to be Samuel. He's the real weenie in all this. Harper, how would you feel about stepping in as an attacking vampire?"

Harper has been leaning against the back wall by the snack table. She steps into the center of the room. "What kind of attacking? I'm not much for violence."

"I thought you'd read *Gilda*," I say. I could've sworn I heard her and Linc talking about it in the library last week. I remember being tempted to lurk and eavesdrop.

"Oh years ago," Harper says. "I peeked at the first chapter again but I'm swamped with work, to be honest. What kind of attack am I supposed to do?"

"Here." Maze holds the open book toward her.

Harper scans the page. "Can I use a pillow for the pipe?"

"Of course!" Maze says.

Sophi adds, "You'd better. And no hitting in the face."

Are we actually doing this? Is Sophi going to kiss Bas in front of everyone? She looks like she kind of wants to and I can't tell if the hesitancy is about Bas or because we're all here.

Harper gets a round bolster from the couch at the back of the room and gives it a practice swing. Bas holds out her elbow for Sophi to take—because at the start of the scene: Gilda is walking with the other vampire.

They take a few ceremonial steps before Bas spins Sophi to face her. In the book, this happens in an alley, against a wall. My breath catches, unable to come all the way in, so I force it out. Bas steps close to Sophi—close enough to kiss her.

"Yearghhh!" Harper yells, running across the room and bopping the pillow against Sophi's shoulder.

Sophi spins and grabs it. They fake struggle over the pillow as Bas watches, more surprised than I've ever seen her.

Maze whispers the line to her, "'Kill him.'"

Bas shakes herself. "Kill him! Kill him, I beg you!"

Sophi and Harper have stopped struggling and stare at each other over the pillow they're both gripping. Harper's cheeks bunch with tension, like she's trying not to laugh, but Sophi's eyes have narrowed with intensity.

"I won't," Sophi says, the words sounding resonant and true.

"You must!" Bas insists.

Sophi drops her end of the pillow and spins to face Bas, who flinches away from the look Sophi is giving her. I know Sophi's in theater, but I didn't know she was this good at acting. She turns from Bas toward all of us, real anguish on her face.

When she says, "'I hold a grief inside of me that will not give way,'" she sounds on the verge of tears.

Bas and Harper both stand with their arms at their sides, glancing at each other. That wasn't the next line in the scene. I page forward in my copy and spot it in the next scene. Kai pulls the book out of my hands.

Then she walks to the front of the room, grabs an empty chair from one of the tables and settles into it. Sophi draws a chair close and sits facing her. This is the scene where Gilda goes back to the gay guys who are her mentors after refusing to kill the one vampire and leaving the other. Kai must be taking the role of one of the mentors.

Kai's finger trails down the page of the open book until she finds the quote she's looking for. "'You have time,'" she says. "'To learn when it is safe to love. We may...We may learn this lesson together'"

Sophi gives her a smile, full of hope and quiet joy.

Maze claps and we all join in. I'm grateful she knew where the scene ended because I'd have stared at Kai and Sophi all evening. As we applaud, Bas holds her elbow out to Harper, who takes it and promenades with her to the back of the room. Bas turns and gives a bow, while Harper holds up the half-empty box of donut holes as an invitation to the rest of us to finish it off. We get up for food and tea and bathroom breaks—and to move out of that heaviness.

Kai and Sophi stay in their chairs, leaning close. Kai draws big shapes in the air with one hand as Sophi nods.

Bas settles into the empty chair next to Brantley and there are capital-L Looks passing between them. I can't read their vibe other than its secrecy. Could be treasure hunt info, could be romance.

I want to get close and eavesdrop, but there's no place to sit that isn't obvious. I do see that Bas left her phone on the table. Will Maze hate me for this? I walk to the table and stack a couple of empty plates and crumpled napkins, putting my body between Bas and her phone. Quickly I flip the phone and swipe up to show notifications on the lock screen. There are two recent messages from Linc:

great info

text me later

And there are a whole bunch from Brantley that are stickers and emojis. These seem less suspicious than the few words from Linc. Did he help Bas hack the library Wi-Fi and steal Char's information? And if Bas did that, what else is she willing to do?

CHAPTER EIGHTEEN

Maze

A week has passed since our reenactment of *The Gilda Stories* and no one has figured out the clue. The remaining teams are watching each other like lion cubs learning to hunt. It's almost impossible not to. It's like trying not to think about a red truck and then seeing red trucks on every block.

I can now spot Bas, Brantley or Sophi in the furthest reaches of my peripheral vision: Bas's hats, Sophi's height and Brantley's monochrome green or purple outfits. Paisley and Kai are harder because they're shorter than the average on campus. I don't worry about Char; Lys will tell me if their team finds the next book. And of course I can sense Lys even when she's behind me, but that's because she might be looking at me and I want to catch the gooey expression in her eyes.

We've been in this treasure hunt for two months now and we only have six weeks to the end of the semester—that's including finals week. With three books read and three to discover, we all feel the pressure to pick up the pace.

Saturday afternoon, Lys and I are studying in my room because my roommate has finally made up with her boyfriend and is at his place this weekend. We're revisiting what we learned in the big storage room about sex and dopamine and focus—alternating sexy times with homework.

After a few rounds of homework, Lys asks, "Do you want to see some of the videos that Kai and I got for our project about alumni who had accommodations? I need to do more editing and it'll be more fun if you're excited about it too."

I'm afraid I won't be excited and worry that I'll say the wrong thing. This is still a scary topic. But I'm curious and want to support Lys so I nod.

We're in my bed, naked, blankets pulled up. She reaches over the side and gets her battered laptop, most of its dents and scrapes covered by pride stickers. We prop pillows against the headboard and she rolls the two videos they've finished editing.

The first shows a political aide standing on the steps of the Capitol—identifiable by her navy blazer and official name badge. She talks about being blind and how much extra time it took to do all the reading assignments because she had to either get them read to her or find them in Braille. Visually reading, there's other information coming in from the page—the sentences around the one being read, the place in the chapter or book—all of that goes away when text is being read, so she had to stop a lot, take notes, go back through her notes.

She says, "I was burning out sophomore year. I got accommodations for more time on assignments and that helped a lot. Plus one of the professors I talked to about the accommodations took the time to help me think through strategies to get information efficiently. I still use those strategies today and my office has adopted some because they help everyone process information better. I hope the faculty board will consider how accommodations and creativity about learning styles have a positive ripple effect throughout the community."

The next video is a guy in his midtwenties recording himself while biking. We can see the trees zooming past him. He has ADHD and intense dyslexia and starts out talking about how embarrassing it was to need test questions read aloud to him.

"My friends and the other guys on the soccer team really had my back. When they were in classes with me, we'd get permission for them to read me the questions. Plus I got extra time on tests because I felt so anxious about being singled out, the only one getting the questions read aloud. Various classrooms felt so different to me. In some I could settle down—as much as I ever settle down—and do well. In others my body felt keyed up, on edge all the time. That started my passion for somatic work. Now I help athletes understand how to improve by relaxing, getting more fully into their bodies. I'm starting an advanced program in somatic physical therapy so I can work with trauma survivors. Giving people the space and support they need makes us all healthier."

I tell Lys, "These are amazing!"

She says, "That second one has me thinking about work where I could combine therapy with physicality, help people be in their bodies while they work on their minds and hearts and lives."

"I'm an absolute yes to that," I say and emphasize this with a kiss or twelve.

Her phone buzzes repeatedly. We ignore it. It rings. She stretches out her arm, grumbling, and squints at the screen. Then she answers, "Kai, what?"

I can hear the excitement in Kai's voice but not the words, so I play with Lys's collarbones while Kai explains something that's taking way too long. Lys asks a series of short questions, "Now?...Where?...For how long?" She finishes by saying, "Fine, but you'd better share. Ten minutes."

She tosses her much battered phone onto the pile of clothes next to the bed—half mine, half hers. The laundry pile in front of her closet is a third the size it used to be and there are cute Post-it notes on all her drawers. I've been meaning to sneak an extra Post-it in with a sweet message on it, but I don't trust myself not to write, "I love you," on the back, so I should maybe wait a little longer.

Lys says, "Kai thinks they have the location. But also that Paisley is low-key following them. She wants me to go make a ruckus near Brantley and see if that'll draw Paisley off so Kai and Sophi can go look. Brantley's in the commons with Char and some other players."

I've been half on top of her so I slip to one side as she wriggles to the edge of the bed and snags her sports bra and T-shirt.

"I shouldn't come with you," I say, thinking aloud. "If it's you getting Char, it's obviously a treasure hunt thing since you're a team. But I could come to the commons and watch to make sure that both Paisley and Brantley follow you two."

She makes a short laugh. "I like this chain of following. Let's do it. Where should I take Char? What's believable?"

I've been studying the campus map in great detail and it's become a living entity in my map of the world. Consulting that map in my mind, I say, "The arts center. Tons of places to hide a clue."

"And it's on the other side of campus from the commons," Lys says, nodding.

This does mean we have to go the two blocks from my dorm to the commons and then turn around and come two and a half blocks back in this direction, but at least Lys's knee hasn't been bothering her much. The weather's been in the forties the last few weeks and that's better for her than below freezing.

We hurry across campus, Lys texting Char as we go. I figure everyone else in the treasure hunt is as aware of me as I am of them, so I let Lys get well ahead and then take a side door into the commons. Today the whole eating area smells like an explosion of chocolate brownies and burnt paprika. I cannot imagine what happened to cause this. I arrive in time to see Char get up from a table of rugby players and follow Lys out the main doors.

Brantley is already packing their bag. They're out the doors maybe fifteen feet behind the other two. I duck out the side door and stride around the side of the building—not too fast, since I know where Lys and Char are headed.

Lys texts me: *let me know when Pais joins.*

On it, I tell her.

I'm glad to be following Brantley, who's in all green again. Their aura seems to be more green than purple based on recent clothing choices. I wonder if their wardrobe is slanted toward green. Brantley is slightly shorter than me and could disappear into crowds of students if not for the deep pistachio of their jacket.

I scan for Paisley, who is even shorter than Brantley. Despite all his bright shirts and ties, I remember a dark winter coat. He's going to be hard to spot—and that is *not* the person moving between Lys's dorm and the next one over to join Brantley. Despite the extremely normal knit hat and non-historical jacket, that is clearly Bas. In disguise.

I text this news to Lys and she replies with a long string of exploding emojis followed by exclamation points. Should I be upset that my teammate is now confirmed to be working with another team? Or are Bas and Brantley together romantically now? I lengthen the space between us because Bas can definitely recognize me peripherally and she's looking around a lot.

Lys and Char reach the Arts Building and go inside, Brantley and Bas following. I wait in a doorway of the nearby Language Arts Building and text Lys: *should I come in?*

Wait, she sends back.

I zip my coat tighter against the wet cold. We've had cloudy skies for days but no rain, just dingy dead grass now that snow has melted so the ground is gray-brown and the sky gray-blue. I spend the next minutes testing different angles to hold my phone so I look like I'm reading its screen when I'm really scanning the area.

The big glass double doors that I'm pretending not to watch swing open and Brantley steps out, followed by Bas, both of them talking intensely, Bas gesturing in tight circles with jabs. I push back into the shelter of the doorway as they pass. I don't think they saw me. Bas would certainly say something snarky if she did.

Lys has texted: *Char stopped for coffee and I guess they realized we were faking them out. They left.*

I silence my phone and grip it in my hand as I follow Bas. She and Brantley go past the science center, then turn between that and the first of the north dorms. They act like they're heading for the science annex but Bas is glancing around a lot.

I duck behind a tree and get a dubious look from a passing student. I offer a lackluster wave. When I peek out, my quarry has made an abrupt right and Brantley is holding open the door to the Math Building. What could they need in there?

I text Lys: *did Kai check in?*

She replies: *Wasn't where they thought.*

I'm risking it. I hurry across the sidewalk and into the Math Building. I don't see Bas or Brantley, but the elevator is at the third floor. I don't want to run into them coming down, so I take the stairs.

The third floor smells like chalk and fresh paper with a top note of the virtuous sweat of many people focusing. On the wall across from the stairs are posters about number theory. What even is that? I know a lot of theory and none of it is about numbers.

Bas got the third book from a professor in the English Department, so I walk down the hall until I find the Math Department. Luck strikes! The student at the front desk is one of the gay guys from Queer Club: skinny, mop of brown hair, scoop neck shirt with a multicolored scarf wrapped around his neck and hanging down on both sides.

I don't remember his name, but I'm willing to pretend when he says, "Hey, Maze."

"Hi, you work here?" That's an obvious enough answer that I don't wait for it and add, "Were Bas and Brantley in here?"

"Yeah they were looking for the Fibonacci Club."

"The what?"

"You know, it's for fans of that number sequence from adding the previous digits: one, two, three, five, eight. And other great numbers, of course."

I hold up a hand because I just heard a number that included the one, two and eight from the Gilda clue. "What do I have to do to get into that club?" I ask.

He sighs but pushes up from his chair and walks down the long hall behind his desk. Near the end, he steps through an open doorway. He returns with a thick manila envelope. "This should really be about math," he says. "But I guess they were running out of places to hide these."

I tear the envelope open and slide a graphic novel out. The cover is very pink with the title: *Laura Dean Keeps Breaking Up With Me.*

I've seen this on Lys's bookshelf. I take a photo of the cover and send it to her. Then I open it and see the written clue: *Seek-her reversed.* I don't photograph that because I'm still a little paranoid about our phones.

Lys's text back has more exclamation points than the previous, followed by: *that's it? The next one? I love that book. How?!?!?!*

I reply: *my room?*

She says: *on my way!*

She and Char are waiting in the hall when I arrive. Lys is pink-cheeked from the cold and Char is playing with one of the pom-poms of her winter hat. I unlock the door and wave them in. Lys and I sit on the edge of my bed and Char takes my desk chair.

I start telling them about following Bas and Brantley, but Char interrupts, "Wait, *Bas* met Brantley?"

"In disguise too," I say. "I didn't think she owned a normal coat. Might've borrowed it."

Lys rubs her chin, working her lips like she's tasting her thoughts. "So Brantley saw us and assumed we were after a clue—especially after Char about-shouted the word 'clue,'—and instead of texting Paisley to meet them, they texted Bas. Which could mean that Paisley was supposed to keep following Kai and Sophi, or that Brantley is more loyal to Bas now. Do we think that?"

"Is Bas loyal to anyone?" Char asks. "Sounds like Brantley is teaming with her, though. I guess the Linc theory is shot."

I say, "Could be they're all working together."

Lys wrinkles her nose, shaking her head. "Or Bas is teaming up separately with Linc and with Brantley. Maybe she's playing everyone."

She turns to me and I shrug. Just because I don't want to believe that doesn't mean it's impossible.

Lys doesn't push it. She asks, "I guess they realized we were the decoy, but then how did they figure out the actual location so fast?"

"Is Fibonacci Club a real thing?" I ask Char.

Her mouth opens and closes a few times before she manages to say, "I know what they saw. The fliers. Next to the coffee cart. I hung those last week. How did I not think of that?"

"Fibonacci Club is real enough to have fliers?" I ask.

"Yeah, and the fliers have a whole design that's tiles the sizes of the numbers. My math prof gave me that to put on the… oh wow, he's in on it. I wonder if he made it to help us out—by plastering this clue all over campus." She tears open her bag and grabs a blue flier with a rectangle on it that holds smaller rectangles of various sizes and the numbers 1, 2, 3, 5, 8, 13.

I reach for it and turn it sideways, tapping the 8. "If you put that over the middle of campus, that's where the Math Building is. He literally gave us a map."

"How many professors are involved?" Lys wonders.

I say, "Professor Stendatter worked here for a lot of years, I'll bet she still has a bunch of friends on campus. Do you think they tell her what we're up to? Maybe that we've been struggling?"

Lys shakes her head with wonder. "So those two come in following us and one of them realizes that the design…"

"Matches the clue, that is one plus two and then there's a big space before the equals eight," Char says. "So on the original clue, she left room for the three and the five."

Lys picks up the story again. "They were waiting for us to order because of the afternoon line and have time to ponder it and realize the numbers fit—and that they could mean the Math Building. And that if we're getting coffee, we probably faked them out or realized they're following us."

"Bas has a better map of campus in her mind than I do," I say. "She thinks about buildings all the time. It's one of her things. As soon as they realize it's connected, I'll bet she figured out it mapped to the Math Building."

"You're a genius for following them," Char tells me.

I want to feel like a genius, but all I have is a sick worry about how deep Bas's plots run and all the people she might be toying with. I didn't think she'd be this devious, but maybe her accusations that I don't know her that well are too accurate.

CHAPTER NINETEEN

Lys

I'm so excited that *Laura Dean Keeps Breaking Up With Me* is a book I've read. I thought everything would be old classics. Isn't that the definition of "classic"? And I guess I thought there wouldn't be comics, but I did see *Dykes to Watch Out For* on one of the previous lists. *Dykes to Watch Out For* is the first queer comic I ever read. I found a used copy of one of the collected comic strips and slept with it next to my bed for the last two years of high school.

I read *Laura Dean Keeps Breaking Up With Me* in high school too. Then I read it again last semester when it was recommended by the sexual health peer-counseling group I've been thinking about joining. The idea of the group is that it might be easier for students to get information about sex from other students. So far that's been the case in the two meetings I attended—and not only about sex but about what healthy queer relationships look like and about how to take care of ourselves.

I go through the graphic novel for a third time over the weekend and keep thinking about how unhealthy the main relationship is. Our treasure hunt clue is "Seek-her reversed," which refers to a character in the book who does a Tarot reading for our hero, Freddie. "Reversed" is probably about Tarot cards. In the graphic novel, the Seek-her tells Freddie she has to break up with Laura Dean—but Freddie can't figure out how to do that because Laura Dean already broke up with her, more than once!

If the Seek-her's advice is to break up with someone who already broke up with you, what's that reversed? Not breaking up with someone who hasn't broken up with you, that would be too straightforward. Maybe how do you get together with someone you're already together with?

That's a great question. How would I do that?

If I need to get together with Maze, who I'm already with, what works? Better communication, for sure.

But there are far too many locations on campus about communication: the Communication Department, the Slam Poetry Club, the Debate Club, the folks who do the daily and weekly campus newspapers. I can't go around to all of them.

How could I shortcut that process? Last clue we got fliers. Professor Stendatter still has a bunch of friends on campus who tell her what's going on. Would she know that the peer counseling group reads this graphic novel every fall? Would she have picked something easy for late in the hunt?

I text one of the student leaders of the peer counseling group and ask what they read before this book came out.

She texts back: *boring stuff, bunch of non-fiction.*

Then, minutes later, she texts again: *you know there's a secret bible of our group right?*

I do not know this. I ask: *how secret is it? Does the counseling center staff know?*

She replies with a laughing emoji and: *they bought it for us.*

Could the professor have a friend in the counseling center? It feels like a longshot, but so did all the other clues. I text that I'd love to see this secret bible.

We meet in the library. Not in a study room, though. I'm grateful because my neck still gets hot when I walk past those.

We're in a far corner of the second floor with long tables and uncomfortable chairs. People only study here when all the other parts of the library fill up.

My contact is tall, lanky with frizzy hair in a high ponytail. She scans the area like she's about to hand off stolen jewels, then pulls a heavy book from her bag and hands it to me. The scarred and battered cover says: *Girl Sex 101*. I gently open it and peruse the table of contents. I am so about to read this whole book. But also, chapter two says "Communication & Consent."

"Can I borrow this?" I ask.

"Yeah, text when you're done. I'll note that you've got it."

She shoulders her bag, waves and walks off between the rows of books.

I flip to chapter two. There's no secret envelope. Dang. I wanted it to be that easy. I'm about to start reading but the margin doodles catch my attention. The first doodle resembles two big apostrophes on their sides making out, with a Roman numeral two underneath them. That's Cancer and Gemini in astrology. Below that is the word "hum" and further down the page the number 217.

Professor Haille did say we could have up to three wrong guesses with her before getting kicked out—and I know that room 217 in humanities is her office. I shove the book in my bag and run-walk out of the library.

Should I be careful? What if I'm being followed? But it's the middle of the day and most of the treasure hunt team members are in class. Plus Professor Haille agreed to be my advisor and I met with her last week about what classes to take next year. As long as I slow down and look a little bored, no one should suspect anything.

She's at her desk. I stand in the open doorway and knock. Professor Haille turns and waves me in. Her hair is in a loose braid today, falling to midback, the teal color at the ends almost completely faded. She's in a plain blue button-down shirt with a navy vest featuring vibrant purple butterflies.

Her office has a wall of shelves covered in books stacked every which way, facing a wall of framed photos. She appears in some of them, but not all. In addition to her desk and its chair, there's a round table with three chairs and a stack of card games on it. I slide into one of those chairs and she rolls her desk chair close.

I'm so caught up in the treasure hunt fervor that I snatch the book out of my bag before thinking about it. Then I realize I'm holding the world's most-read copy of *Girl Sex 101* in front of a professor whose classes I really want to take. I open it super quickly and point to the symbols on the "Communication & Consent" page.

"Yes?" she asks, expressionless.

"Cancer and Gemini. Is this a clue? Is the next book connected to astrology?"

A grin breaks over her face. She rolls back to her desk and opens her bottom desk drawer. The drawer has two sections. The one way in the back contains a sweater, but she reaches under that and pulls out the book: *The Stars and the Blackness Between Them.*

"You found it," she tells me.

I yelp and jump out of the chair, then sit so I can turn the book over and read the back. This looks amazing and Kai is going to be super excited to read it. How long do I wait until I tell her and Sophi? Until I tell Maze?

I should definitely tell Char first. I text her to meet me at the room but don't get a reply so I detour to the student commons. If anyone did see me coming out of Professor Haille's office looking like I'd won the lottery—because I'm not good at hiding expressions—then this jaunt to get a late lunch in a casual manner should throw them off.

* * *

An hour later, I still haven't heard from Char. I'm trying to use the adrenaline and dopamine from my success in the hunt to catch up on reading, but I've hit the limit for how much I can stomach about historical education practices that were so much more about compliance than learning. I decide to go back to the room and if Char doesn't show up soon, maybe I'll tell Maze first.

Char has done a whole bunch of calculations about coins of various ages and she believes the collection could be worth anything from a few thousand dollars to tens of thousands. Even a single ten thousand would be so helpful. I get financial aid from the school or I'd never be able to go here, but it doesn't cover everything, just like my folks' health insurance doesn't cover everything about my knee. If I can bring them a few thousand, that covers their deductible for a year and I could get new scans and maybe a surgery that actually works.

They try not to talk about money around me but I know there's no way they can afford college for both my brothers and my little sister. Maybe one of them won't want to go, but if they all do, they should have the chance. The best thing I can do for all of them is graduate college with solid grades and get a good-paying job. But the second-best thing I can do is win this treasure hunt! If it's on the high end of Char's estimates, like even thirty thousand, split two ways, that covers school expenses and the health plan deductible for me for the next three years.

I manage not to skip on my way back to the room, but only because the stiff pressure of the knee brace reminds me this is a bad idea.

When I open the door, I'm surprised to see Char. Why hasn't she answered my texts? She stands in the middle of the room, a pink and violet suitcase open on my bed since I'm the lower bunk. Neat stacks of clothes dominate the bed, her chair and her desk. Her expression looks pulled as tight as her severe ponytail.

"Where are you going?" I manage to ask.

"Someone called my parents. They want me to come home for a week or two and get myself together."

That makes no sense. I say, "It's not break."

"I know. But they got a call and they want me to come home." She tosses a stack of clothes into her suitcase, then takes half the stack out.

"You'll miss class and the treasure hunt. The semester is over in four weeks anyway. Why now?"

"Someone called my parents!" Char yells at me. Her slender face is a shade of red that doesn't work with the purple of her hair. She wipes a hand across her eyes and grabs half of the clothes on the desk, shoving them into the suitcase, then pulling pants out to refold them.

"My dad started driving early this morning," she says. "He'll be here in less than an hour and if I'm not ready he's going to *help* me pack."

"But the treasure hunt," I protest. I'm about to tell her I've found the next book but she cuts me off by blading her hand through the air between us.

"I'm out," she says.

"You can't quit. If you're out, I'm out."

"My parents!"

"Stay in and don't do the work," I tell her.

"That's what I have been doing. You're not hearing what I'm saying. My midterm grades are *low*. My advisor is worried about me. And someone. Called. My. Parents."

"Who would do that? That's such bullshit. I didn't think the administration paid that much attention to any of this."

"They don't," Char says.

"What are you saying?" I ask. I'm so frustrated I can't think it through.

Another tear streaks from the corner of her eye and she dashes it away, wipes her hand on her jeans and grabs clothes from the chair.

She shuts the nearly-full suitcase, then opens it. "I think someone pretending to be official called my parents to freak them out so they'd make me quit. Someone who's in this whole thing, close enough in to know that I've been struggling, to hear me complain that my parents were on me. All my info is on the rugby team emergency contact forms in the back of Coach's binder. She leaves it in the locker room often enough. Anyone on the team or near the team could've seen my parents' number. Plus it's not like I have a common last name—anybody with the basics about me could find my folks if they were willing to call a few wrong numbers."

"Brantley has access to the rugby forms and has heard you talking," I say. "And they've been hanging out with Bas a lot lately. Would either of them really do this?"

"My dad is *pissed*," Char says. "Whoever called told him I'd already been asked to drop out by my advisor and hadn't listened. Total shitpickle."

But the kind of shitpickle another student would make up. That doesn't sound like what a school official would say. I want to find who did this and punch them right in the mouth.

"Did you report it to…someone?" I ask.

A sweatshirt goes into her suitcase, followed by her toiletry bag. She shuts it and zips open the top section. "If I report it and they find out it was Bas, that takes Maze out," she says. "I've got nothing to gain doing that. My grades are shit right now. I'm going home and getting my head together—and maybe you all can find a way to win it."

I want to tell Char things are okay, but I'm too furious. I make it out of the room without slamming the door, but that's the best I can do.

* * *

I stay away as long as I can, walking too slowly away from campus and then back again. I don't want to text Maze in case she can tell something's wrong. I'm not ready to talk to her about this. I should talk to Kai but I can't. The rage is a knot in my throat with cords attached to knots in my fingers.

I want to run. Used to be that could settle me through almost anything. Furious as I might feel, the motion and the strain, the burning in my lungs and muscles would pull me into the space of my body, out of this up-swirling vortex.

Maybe weights would work, but then I'd need to be in the gym around people. Running gets me away and I need to be away. I must have something heavy in my room. If nothing else, my backpack with some books in it. I head back.

I open the door to a half-empty room. A lot of Char's stuff is here, but all her most important stuff isn't. Her favorite plushies, her backpack, important clothes from her closet—all gone. I wish I felt the emptiness of this. Maybe I do for a moment but then rage rushes back in.

Her desk is all surface: laptop gone, tablet gone, cords gone. Mine is heaped with books and papers, a notebook, a chaos of pens. Unlivable heat rises inside me.

I grab the edge of the biggest textbook on my desk and shove it into the piles of papers and books and fidgets, shove until it all falls to the floor beside the rest. Then move to the closet and tear a shirt off a hanger. This feels right. I drag a sweatshirt down next, a jacket, more shirts. I pull a drawer out and throw the socks, but they're too soft, nothing is breaking the way I am.

Back to the desk pile, kicking at it with my good leg and then crumpling into it. There's an article from education class on top of the pile, neatly stapled. I tear the top page loose and rip it in half then those halves into smaller pieces and smaller until they're too small to tear. I go to the next page and keep tearing.

I hold a handful of page shreds to my chest when I'm crying too hard to keep tearing, then return to that, back and forth for a while.

A tap on the door: Maze. She always taps instead of knocking. I've seen her wince when someone knocks hard on a door so I figure it's a sounds she hates.

Is it dinnertime? Probably Maze is here because I didn't meet her and didn't answer her texts.

I want to stay quiet until she goes away. But I need her. Maybe she'll see me like this and realize what a disaster I am and then she'll dump me and I can quit all this and go home, give up on everything.

"Yeah," I say, rough and low-pitched.

"Can I come in?" she asks through the door.

"Yeah," I repeat.

I didn't lock it when I came in. Why bother now.

Maze cracks it open and peers in, then steps through and shuts it. She observes the pile of papers and books I'm sitting in and the pile of clothes in front of the closet. I watch her register the half-empty state of Char's closet and the top of her desk.

She crosses the room and sits next to me, opens her arms.

"I'm a disaster," I tell her.

"Nope," she says.

I curl into her, tears fresh in my eyes, a few sobs struggling out from my chest.

When I've quieted, she murmurs, "Do you want to tell me?"

"Char left. Parents. Someone called them. They made her come home and drop the treasure hunt. I'm out of it."

"Okay…so I'll win and you can share the win with me."

She makes it sound so simple, her thoughts racing ahead of her feelings as usual and maybe this time ahead of mine too. I want that. But I don't think I can have it.

"You can't," I say. "And it's not the winning, it's everything. Education class, Leland's project, being here and fighting and fighting. I don't know if I can manage without rugby, without the treasure hunt."

"We still have the treasure hunt," she says. "And you've got Kai and the rest of the team."

"I feel so lost," I moan.

A long pause and she says. "I know. Nobody's teaching us what we need to know to grow up but they expect us to be good at it anyway."

I lift a handful of academic confetti and drop it to the floor. "At least I didn't break anything I can't replace. Sometimes I do."

"Yeah?"

"One feeling gets so big it overwhelms everything else," I tell her, needing to explain to myself and to her. "I read that ADHD folks can get taken over by an emotion. Something about how emotions are designed to grab attention for survival plus that thing about our brains having weak brakes."

She nods, lips compressed into a thin line. "I use music. Headphones. Painfully loud. Until I can't think or feel. Next time I'm going to tear up some shit instead. Maybe leave myself a pile for tearing. Stuff I'm angry about."

"Are you serious?"

Maze pokes at the confetti pile with a finger. "This is functional," she says.

I snort-laugh. "How?"

"I can look at it and know how you're feeling. And you didn't harm anything. I worry the music is going to mess up my hearing eventually."

"Oh."

"There's a thing Sophi's been telling me about and it kind of applies here. I think we need more outlets for emotion in ways that work for us, not the ways the neurotypical world says are acceptable."

"Maybe." I feel not exactly better, but settled. Walking and tearing things and crying worked. Maybe Maze isn't wrong that we should keep piles around for that. I peek at her eyes, narrowed with worry. Tears burn my eyes and my throat closes as I say, "I found—"

I can't complete that sentence, so I stretch across my floor to grab my bag and drag it to me. I unzip it and pull out *The Stars and the Blackness Between Them*, hand that to Maze.

Her eyebrows quirk with questions until she opens the front cover and sees the slip of paper with the next clue on it. Her mouth opens in an unvoiced, "Oh." She glances from me to the book and the clue, back to me. I don't try to stop the tears.

"Oh, Lys, this is amazing and I'm so sorry," she says.

I crawl into her arms.

CHAPTER TWENTY

Lys

This last week I've cried more than I did the whole first part of the year, though the last few days it's been half happy crying. We've gotten more accommodations videos from alumni and some are so inspiring. I have to imagine that the faculty board will be moved by these and give less weight to Professor Leland's work.

After hours of editing, interrupted by crying, I fall asleep in Kai's bed. She's still working on the videos. I figure she'll wake me up when it's time for dinner.

I wake up because she's talking, but not to me. My body is heavy in the warmth of the blankets, brain fogged with sleep.

Kai says, "Char's right about her contact info on the forms. Anybody on the team could've looked. And if Brantley is working with Bas…"

Another voice says, "You dated her, though. Do you think she'd do that?"

That's Sophi. How did she get into my room at night? I peer up at a ceiling a few feet from my face. I'm in Kai's lofted bed, not in my room. Is it night? The ceiling is mostly dark except for a square of light, the reflected glow from Kai's laptop screen.

Kai says, "You've been spending a lot more time with Bas than I have. What do you think?"

"I don't know what she'd do for money," Sophi tells her. "I like how Bas thinks about design and art. But that doesn't generalize."

Sleep catches me again and pulls me into a dream in which Bas and I are biking through a forest of huge trees. Dollar bills fall from the trees and we're trying to catch them, but we can't stop biking.

I wake up to Kai saying my name. "Lys found it. She gave it to Maze and they decided to tell us too."

Why did I get to find a book only after Char had quit and pulled me out of the hunt with her? Tears prick my eyes and I squeeze them closed. I'm so tired of crying. Kai has been super supportive and I don't want to cry in front of her again, especially not with Sophi here. They can't see me because I'm in Kai's lofted bed, but I'm not good at crying silently.

Kai says, *"The Stars and the Blackness Between Them."*

"By Junauda Petrus, a young adult novel," Sophi tells her, "I've been meaning to read it. What's the clue that goes with it?"

"Reach the end, then go back to go beyond," Kai tells her.

Sophi chuckles. "As clear as all the others. Do you think we should wake Lys if we're talking about all this?"

"Not yet. She's having such a hard week. Speaking of fiction, though, and fic," Kai says. "Did you read the one I sent you?"

"I read it," Sophi tells her. "Really fun idea. Even if that middle part got a little slow. I wanted them to kiss sooner." Her voice sounds more fluid than I've heard it, more tones. Is she teasing Kai? Should I sit up and let them know I'm awake. My body feels so heavy and half asleep under Kai's big warm blanket.

"For half a page? I was building character."

"You think you need to build the character of a woman who wrote her whole own biomythography?"

Kai asks, "Do you truly think all eight of my readers have read *Zami*?"

"I think *some* of your readers want to see more kissing on the page."

"Only *on the page*?" Kai asks, her voice rich with meaning.

"Not only," Sophi says.

It takes me a minute to register that her voice also sounds different than usual, more open and resonant, and that this means a whole lot of things—including that Kai is getting out of her seat. I'm so confused that I open my eyes and peer over the edge of the bed. Kai leans against the edge of her desk, very close to Sophi.

She bends forward. I close my eyes as they kiss.

Now I have no way of knowing when they stop kissing. But if I tell them I'm awake they'll know I saw them kiss. What if this is their first kiss and I'm making it weird?

I hear Kai sigh and the creak of the chair as Sophi shifts in it. They're still kissing and I am making this so weird. There are sounds that I should not be hearing.

I make a totally not fake (much) half-awake grumble and roll on my side away from them.

The chair creaks, the desk light clicks on and Kai asks, "Lys, you awake?"

"Barely," I mumble.

I turn toward them and open my eyes the smallest amount. Kai is back in her chair, hands on knees like she's holding herself in place. Sophi has turned toward the desk, back to me. Her arm is moving, drawing fast in her notebook.

"When you're mostly awake, we have treasure hunt things to talk about," Kai says.

"I'm awake enough," I tell her.

I climb down from the bed and grab my sweater from the pile of pillows. I find my laptop and shove it into my bag. Kai's face is shining with joy and I want her to have more of that. I'm getting out of here as soon as I can, but she waves for me to sit in the pillows.

Kai says, "I've been trying to figure out who all Bas is working with, asking around. The players in Linc's building say Bas has been over there a lot lately. Plus the other night when I went back to the gym to get my stuff, Bas was there talking to

Linc while he did weights, or tried to at least. I don't know how he doesn't break in half."

"Why would she go in person?" Sophi asks.

"Because she's paranoid that someone else is pulling the same sneaky shit she is," I say. To Kai I ask, "Did she see you?"

"No, I went up to the track to see if I left my favorite sweatshirt there. I don't think she's been to the gym enough to know to look up, and Linc was focused on the weights."

"Linc already has the combination. If he gets the lockbox..." I trail off and sink further into the pillows. We can't go through all these books and have the prize snatched away at the last moment.

"No one's been able to find that lockbox in six years," Sophi says firmly, sitting up from her drawing and turning to Kai and me. "Despite there being some super smart students here and I'm sure they went over every place they could think of—and a lockbox is not small."

"Coins could be small," Kai says. In the air she sculpts a small square and then a flat rectangle. "Maybe everyone's looking for a big box and it's really the size of my fist. That would be easy to hide. Why would Bas work with Linc, though? I'm guessing he's offered to split the treasure if he gets it—but what's in it for him?"

"He needs the inside scoop on the teams," I suggest. "Needs to know how far along we are and if anyone is coming up with ideas he hasn't yet. Since Bas is with Maze and they all know I talk to Maze, that's two teams covered."

"And I talk to you," Kai says, nodding. "Yeah, I could see Linc offering half the treasure for that info."

Sophi taps her fingers on her knee. "We need to slow them down. I've been thinking about how to get ahead of the others now that we're only one book away from the end. My best idea is to make up a lockbox location with an actual fake lockbox in it. We could feed that info to Bas and see who shows up to get it. If it's Linc, then we have proof he's the one Bas is working with—because it's possible she's the one hanging around him to get more info out of him about past years."

We stare at each other because none of us knows how to make a clue, even though we've been following them for weeks.

"I guess we should start with where we want them to go," I suggest.

Kai says, "Someplace that will be easy to spot them, because how are we going to stake it out?"

We don't have much free time. There's only a week and a half until the faculty board meeting where we'll present the accommodations videos. Plus we're in the spring rugby season where we play seven-person teams. Kai is playing and I'm trying to watch as often as I can, but there are only three weeks to finals and I'm behind in two of my classes again.

"Hide it in the gym?" Kai suggests.

I shake my head. "It's so big, though. Hard to think of a clue that's specific but still matches the other clues. Library?"

Sophi says, "Feels kind of obvious. Remember that tour Linc gave us. He said Professor Stendatter met her wife in the Admin Building. How about there?"

Kai snorts. "Yeah, hide it in the elevator and maybe it's the reason it keeps breaking."

I join her laughter. That would be so great, but I doubt we could get it hidden in the parts of the elevator we can access.

I say, "The professor met her wife in offices that are now Disability Services, Harper seems entertained by all of us doing this treasure hunt. I bet if we asked she'd keep an eye out for people showing up. And there's that old storage room past the offices—the one that's also a nap room that almost no one uses because you have to walk by everyone in Disability Services. That would be a great place to hide it."

"Wow genius!" Kai says. "I'll ask her."

"We need a decoy lockbox," Sophi points out. "With something in it that's a collection but not valuable so maybe Linc or whoever stops looking for a while, gives us time. My brother's into stamps. I'll see if I can get a bunch of low-value ones from him."

"There's another problem with the lockbox," Kai says. "Linc has the combination and we don't. We don't know how many digits it is. We don't know the right numbers. He's going to try to put in a combination and it's not going to work."

"Break it," I suggest.

"Oh yeah, like somebody already found it and broke in and decided they weren't into stamps? But then do we even need the stamps?"

"It'll take time to find the value of them, let's put some in," Sophi says.

"I've got a broken lock," Kai says. To our questioning faces she explains, "Someone wrecked it good last fall trying to steal my bike. I kept it because it looks kind of badass and symbolic. Like I should make some art about this broken lock. Except I forgot that I don't make art. I'll look for a small box it could go on. So then all we need are the hints we're going to drop."

"We don't know the last book. That's going to be hard," I say.

"What's in the nap room?" Sophi asks.

I close my eyes and picture it. I've used it a few times once I realized that going late in the day meant only Harper was there and I could have a little room all to myself. I thought about taking Maze there, but with Harper just outside we wouldn't be able to do all the things we'd want to. There's furniture in it—an old couch and end table—but that might not have been there the last six years.

"HVAC system?" I suggest. "It's got those blowers the old buildings have near the floor. Be really easy to magnet a little lockbox onto the bottom of one."

Sophi grabs her notebook and a pen off the desk, flips to a clean page and writes words, connecting them with lines and arrows and swirls. She's tilting the page toward me and Kai, but from my spot in the pillows I can only see the half that says: *nap room, HVAC, floor—grounding?, self-care as radical.*

She says, "We have a through line from *Zami* to *Stars* because of the two Audres. I watched some of the professor's old lectures and she talks about how Jewelle Gomez of *The Gilda Stories* interviewed Audre Lorde, so that's connected. We've got disability in the early part of *Zami* and illness, possibly chronic illness, in *Stars*. Definitely a lot of care in all three books."

"Do we even need an entire clue?" Kai asks. "That's a lot to go on. Lys, what if you tell all this to Maze and ask her to pass it on to Bas, saying we think we found the lockbox clue and it's from the three novels, those connections, we think it's in Disability Services in the spare room because of self-care and so on."

I'm nodding. "The message would get garbled anyway if I'm telling Maze about what you two think and then Maze passes it on to Bas. It doesn't have to be a perfect message."

I push to my feet, bringing my bag up with me, because Sophi is staring at Kai with so much curiosity and intensity. I need to be gone when Kai sees this stare so things can happen. At the door, I turn to wave good-bye, but Kai has already turned toward Sophi, lips curving into a huge grin.

CHAPTER TWENTY-ONE

Maze

I've been making notes about all the possible clues in *The Stars and the Blackness Between Them*—or, rather, starting documents on my computer, deleting them and starting over because my thoughts don't fit in the space of the screen. I want to put items that represent the clues around the room, but my roommate would move the ones on her side. That's not so bad on its own, but it will remind me of Mom doing it in my bedroom at home after I've asked her not to and that anger would get very distracting.

My chest keeps churning about Char being forced out of the treasure hunt and taking Lys out with her. This event was designed pretty informally so there aren't any rules about forming new teams two thirds of the way through. If your teammate drops out, you're out too. I guess that wasn't a big deal in previous years when people formed their own teams. Of the remaining teams, Char and Lys were the most vulnerable.

Who knew that? Everyone in the hunt this year and Linc. Professor Haille knew, but I can't believe she'd do that. And

Professor Leland probably also knew, but it seems really below him. Still he might take a perverse delight and maybe wanted to get back to at Lys for how she challenged him at dinner? Is he even following the hunt enough to know the teams?

Bas is still working for him. She could've told him. Would he ask?

The more painful question is: could Bas have done this? It's time to find out. Three days ago, Lys told me about the decoy plan that Sophi came up with. Two days ago she let me know that the decoy lockbox was in place in the Disability Services nap room.

I've spent a lot of the last two days asking myself if I want to do this. Now grudging and anxious, I send the notes about *Stars* to Bas and ask her to come over.

She texts that she's on her way. I'm still staring at that text when she knocks on the door. Am I really going to give her the decoy info from Lys? I'm afraid she'll figure it out and be pissed at me.

We were on the verge of being friends again the night of the party, until she got dumped and I got pissed about her telling me to get her jacket button from under the car. I didn't know she made her jackets. Have I even apologized about snapping at her? Should I? Is there other stuff she should apologize for first—and is there really a priority to apologies in a friendship? I need a manual about this. I wonder if Sophi has one and if I have the courage to ask her.

I open the door and say, "You got here fast." Was she lurking near my dorm so she could follow me if I figured out the clue?

She shrugs and sits in my roommate's desk chair. "I was nearby."

I sit on my bed, back against the head of it, arms crossed, facing her. "Doing what?"

"Hanging out. Why do you care?"

This is not how I wanted this conversation to go. But I don't know how to get on track, so I answer the question with the info that's been haunting me. "You're not working on this treasure hunt alone."

"I have you," she says.

"That's not what I mean. You hired someone to scan the Wi-Fi networks and that's how you got the third book."

Bas blinks at me, a soft smile on her face. "Is that what you think? I did no such thing."

I suck at reading faces so I look at her body: leaning back, affected casual, shoulders high and tight, one hand curled toward a fist but not quite there yet.

I say, "You're not lying, but you're not telling the truth either."

"I don't need to use the Wi-Fi network, I have a human network," Bas says. "And Char has a habit of muttering to herself when she's texting something important. I'm not confirming that someone overheard her and told me, but if I were going to come by some information, that's how I'd get it."

This feels less clever and more sneaky, but part of me is still impressed.

"About Char, did you force her out of the treasure hunt? Did you call her parents?"

The frown that starts on her forehead twists her mouth. She sits forward, one hand fully in a fist now. "Someone *did* that? That's garbage."

I haven't seen her show this much reaction to anything before. Come to think of it, I've never seen her angry. She's always joking and needling, but now her face is crumpled with heavy emotion.

"The caller pretended to be college staff," I tell her, "but we're pretty sure it's a student."

"What the hell," she snarls. "I know the treasure might be a lot of money, but that's so low. You don't fuck with anyone's parents. What if she had shit parents? She doesn't, does she?"

"No. Lys would've said."

Bas sighs and leans back in the chair. She pushes the heel of her hand against her forehead and the other one unclenches and grips the chair's arm.

"You okay?" I ask.

"Yeah," she says softly, then again louder, "yeah. You thought it was me?"

"One option. Kind of made sense."

"While you're judging me, think about this: if Lys was willing to make out with Linc at a party, mere weeks ago—"

"Months," I say. "And she wouldn't get her own teammate to quit."

Bas continues as if uninterrupted, "Can you be sure of her affections? Wouldn't you rather be loyal to me, since we can win this together and split the winnings fewer ways?"

"Who told you about Lys at the party?"

"Word gets around," Bas says airily. "Same as I may or may not have gotten info about what Char was texting."

On the surface, that's plausible. But I don't think Linc would want to brag about his awkward failure. I remember Lys telling me, after we went back to get her keys, that Linc had someone else in the room with him. Could it have been Bas?

"Was it you with Linc at the party after Lys and I left?" I ask.

"No," Bas scoffs. "It was Brantley, but just to talk."

"They told you that and you believe them?"

"I confirmed it," Bas says and shuts her mouth quickly.

The logical person for her to confirm it with would be Linc. Was that in a single conversation about that one night, or have they been talking more often? I scramble for more questions I can ask.

"I thought Linc had a guy, an on and off thing," I say.

"Those two are platonic life partners," Bas tells me. "Like they totally love each other and always have each other's backs, but they don't hook up usually."

This is a lot of information about Linc from someone who wasn't friends with him last fall. She has been spending time with him recently.

I need a distraction. "Yeah. Wait, are you hooking up with Brantley?"

"Who wants to know?" she asks. "Your hot ex?"

"Maybe."

Bas spins the chair lightly, kicking her feet against its base. "I did not actually have sex with Brantley. There was some making out and then Paisley showed up."

"Oh shit."

"No, he joined in for a bit, but I felt like a third wheel so I left. It's all good."

"That is *not* what I expected," I say.

"I know," she says and drags the "o" sound out like she's pitying me. "We played it up as a drama to give you lot something to dish about. They gave me their find of *The Gilda Stories* outright because I promised to give them a future answer."

That all sounds so straightforward that for a moment it's hard to believe Bas could be working with Linc. Now I really need to know.

"Did you give them a future clue?" I ask.

"Yeah. I told them about *Stars* when you told me. They're still working on it. I'm hoping they'll tell me if they get it first. Wait, did you find the next book?"

I must have some look on my face—but it's not the one Bas thinks it is. "No, not that."

"But you know something. I'm your teammate, dammit, spill."

I shake my head. "It's just talk. It's not really mine to say."

"Maze, I can help. Come on."

"Lys was hanging out with Kai and fell asleep in her bed and then Sophi came over and they were talking about the books—especially the themes from *Zami* and *Gilda* and *Stars*. Those three are really strongly connected thematically and historically. So maybe that points to the lockbox location."

"Oh shit, yeah. Is there more?"

"Lys didn't want to tell me all of it, but she said some things about self-care and community care and I got thinking about the places on campus that could be about that." I turn to the surface of my bed and pull out the historical map of campus buildings that I'd been looking at. I hold it out to Bas.

She takes it and turns it to face her. "The Admin Building. Wow, this really hasn't been remodeled in that long?"

"That's why the elevator keeps breaking. It's ancient. And that means it's a perfect place to hide a lockbox for years."

"Maybe not," Bas says. "The older buildings are the ones more likely to get remodeled."

"Older student buildings," I point out. "The ones that are only for staff get done last and there's a lot of other student buildings that still need a remodel. This won't be touched for a bunch more years."

"But it's not about care, it's admin," Bas says.

"Disability Services is on the lower level."

"Ohhh shit! Yeah. You think it's there?"

"It's a place students can get to. It's on campus but not a place where a lot of people go. And it used to have this huge storage closet that's now a nap room." I lean forward and point to the nap room. "I'll bet you could hide anything in a walk-in storage closet. But now it's cleared out and nobody found it, so if it's there, it has to be on something that wouldn't get moved."

"What doesn't move?" Bas asks and starts answering herself. "Bookshelves usually, the door. Does the room have those stupid floor heaters?"

"Yep."

"Wow, you already thought of that. Did you go look?"

"It's not open. I want to go tomorrow but I have class in the morning and then I'm supposed to have lunch with Lys. I don't want to tip her off in case I'm wrong. Don't want her to get disappointed."

"I'd go look but I'm working all morning," she says.

I know that. This is the other reason I waited two days to talk to her about this information. Kai and Sophi got the lockbox ready and into place two days ago, but then I waited until Bas would be busy and have to send someone else.

"I can go in the afternoon," I say. "I hope that Kai and Sophi don't put this all together before one of us can get there."

"No shit," she says. "Text me if you can go before lunch."

"Same," I say.

She rolls her eyes. "No way I get out of work early. We're short-staffed as it is. One of the other students got the Covid and Professor Leland needs us to get this first batch of data sorted before the faculty board meets."

"He's presenting at that meeting?" I ask, worried about what might happen if he's presenting right after Lys and Kai show their videos. Could he refute the stories?

Bas nods. "Don't you know all this? I thought Kai had spies everywhere."

"She and Lys don't tell me everything."

"The board is voting on new guidelines about giving accommodations that make sure that students have appropriate documentation," Bas says. "Leland's research uncovered some places where students are pell-mell getting all kinds of accommodations. It's wildly uneven. Some professors are super flexible and others not at all. He wants to standardize it so it's easier to measure what's working."

"Sure he does," I say. "What's appropriate documentation?"

Bas shrugs. "That you got the testing or your doctor signed off on it."

"So because I've been diagnosed with ADHD I could get accommodations for that, like a quiet room for tests, but if I have sensory issues and the sounds in the classroom hurt my brain, I'd need to get tested again for that?"

"Your doctor would give you a note," she says.

"Yeah, my privileged middle-class white self can get that," I say. "For students who are marginalized for so many reasons and don't already have a doctor, Bas, that's a huge barrier."

She flicks her hands up and out, stands up. "You've been indoctrinated. How are we going to know what works and what doesn't if everyone does whatever they want? How are we going to make sure college is fair?"

"Leland's making it less fair," I say.

"Maze." She pauses with her hand on the doorknob. "I'm telling you this to make sure that Lys and Kai know. Stop being so willing to think I'm the bad guy. I'm just a person who doesn't have all the answers like everyone except, apparently, you."

She sweeps out in a swirl of long, gray, historically-accurate coat before I can answer.

CHAPTER TWENTY-TWO

Maze

It's true that I have class this morning, but it's an optional session today. I skip it and head to Disability Services right before it opens and take a spot in the hall waiting area. Harper and the other woman who work there come down the hall, chatting. Harper pauses by me while the other woman unlocks the door and goes in.

"Do we have an appointment?" she asks.

"Uh no, I'm going to sit here for a while. Treasure hunt stuff."

She nods, shifts her coffee mug from one hand to the other to get out her keys. "Kai was in here two days ago. She went into the nap room. Should I let you in there too?"

"Maybe in a bit," I say. "I'm waiting to see who else goes in there."

She laughs. "Spy style, huh? Okay. Come on in and get tea if you want, I'm here until ten thirty but after that Terry will still be holding down the fort."

"Thanks."

I should probably read for class, but I'm jittery from misleading Bas and nervous that she's going to show up and bust me here. I read news on my phone for a bit and then text Sophi.

I ask: *any chance you have a manual about human relationships?*

I expect she'll send some laughing emojis and we'll brush it off. But she replies within minutes, saying: *I have three. Do you want analytical, colloquial or graphic novel format?*

Um yes, I tell her. *Send me all three names and I'll check them out.*

She texts: *Are you on the stakeout? Do you want me to come by?*
Yes!
Be there in 15.

Sophi shows up in flowing pants, a long sweater and a pink and purple headband that's matched by swirls around her eyes.

"You did that in fifteen minutes?" I ask waving at her eyes.

She chuckles. "No. I woke up really early and wanted to try this eye shape." She touches the outside corner of her eye. It doesn't look that different from the last time I saw her, but I am not a makeup expert. Both looks are amazing to me. She says, "Including the time watching the tutorial and the times I messed it up, it took about an hour and a half. What took fifteen minutes was getting these."

She opens her backpack and pulls out a bakery bag. Inside are frosted cinnamon buns and I take one, stomach gurgling with anticipatory happiness, and put it on a napkin from the stack she's set between us. Sophi sets out her thermos, a vibrant indigo, and reaches back into her backpack.

"I found this late last night," she says and puts a dark-brown book between us. The cover says: *Ormond; or, The Secret Witness.*

"That's it? The last one? Why is it last this year?" I ask, as I pick it up and look inside the front. "No additional clue."

Sophi shakes her head.

"Why are you telling me?"

"We've played fair with each other this whole time and I know you're planning to give your half to Lys if you win. I think you both deserve a good shot." She pauses as a smile dances across her lips. "Plus I know Kai and I are going to win."

"You might," I admit. "And even if we get the combination, there's the matter of the lockbox."

"Exactly," she says. "We have two weeks to the end of the semester. That's not a lot of time to find both, especially given how vague the clues are."

"I've been wondering if Professor Stendatter, who set up the contest, had ADHD or Autism or some kind of neurodivergence," I say. "The clues remind me of the kinds of connections my brain makes."

"Oh," she says. "Yes. That's been in the back of mind too but not with words, just this feeling that I wanted to think about the clues and how they might point to the lockbox differently than how I have been. Did you talk to Lys about how your brain works? You two seem close again."

"We are and thanks for the info. It's super helpful to know that's my brain doing a thing instead of thinking we're doing the relationship wrong."

"I don't think you two could do it wrong."

"You and Kai?" I ask.

"Lys told you."

I nod. "Not prying, though."

She grins and I blink a few times because I'm used to her wry smiles, not this big grin. "We figured out a lot," she says. "Yes, we're dating and I can see you're going to ask what we figured out. Still working out some of it, but clearly that my masking is highly effective but also drives her crazy, especially before she realized it was a mask. And, if I'm being honest, I've been a little scared of how ardent she is as a disability activist. I respect the hell out of that, but I've been afraid that she'll insist I do what she does the way she does it."

"I've been a little afraid of that too," I say. "Both from Lys and Kai, like I have to go get accommodations and speak out and do all the things."

"We do need accommodations," she says. "But in our own ways and times. I know a lot about my needs and I make my own accommodations. I allow myself to do what I need to take care of myself and I don't feel guilty about it. I like the planning that goes into making sure I have what I need—and I can do it outside of the official structures. Kai can't."

"How do you do that for yourself?"

She tears off a strip of cinnamon bun and chews it thoughtfully. "I give myself a lot of time for transitions between activities. I talk myself through them or message my big sib or online friends if something changes unexpectedly. I can deal with change if I take my time and have support. If I have to power through it, that drains my energy so fast."

"I'm good with change," I say. "That's a reason I think I'm not Autistic. Sometimes I love it when plans get disrupted, but then other times I hate it."

"Might depend on how much energy you have."

"Yeah and how set I was on the plans. I was reading more online. I don't have a lot of repetition except for fidgets. Or at least that's what I thought. But yesterday I was walking to class from Lys's room instead of mine and it felt really wrong until I switched over to the path I usually take to that class. I do use the same routes to my classes every time and I tend to eat the same thing for lunch every day. But different dinners."

"Autism and ADHD are brain differences, they're going to show up differently for different people."

She opens her bag and gets out her big notebook. I'm starting to recognize her system of notebooks, though I don't yet know the subject matter of each—and I've begun to suspect they're organized more by function than subject. This big one is for big thoughts.

The notebook has a tiny spiral binding and is already folded open. She sets it between us and I see three columns labeled: Autism, Shared, ADHD. That third one isn't filled out much.

The Shared column includes:
- Sensory issues/overwhelm
- Stims
- Webbed/interconnected thought patterns—private meaning networks
- Interest-based nervous system
- Value-based identity

- Emotional regulation changes
- Time blindness

Sophi puts her finger next to "private meaning networks" and says, "Our brains tend to find patterns and connections, but sometimes we're the only people who know what the specific connection is. I wonder if that's what's happening with the clues Professor Stendatter left us. They're meaningful to her for a bunch of reasons and she thought they'd be equally meaningful and clear to us, but they aren't. So in order to figure out the last clues, we really have to get inside her personal meanings."

I feel the map of my thoughts shifting with this new information. She's right. I need to keep more information about the professor herself in the forefront of my mind. I need to reorganize how I'm approaching this last book clue and the lockbox clue. As the back of my mind works on that, I read the list under the "Autism" heading:

- Local coherence—a focus on details first
- Detail-focus can lead to sensory overwhelm
- Repetition and routine for self-regulation
- Fixity of focus

There are more items on the list, but I want to think about this. I say, "I focus on details. But they're not like math and science details."

"They don't have to be. Some of my details are makeup and theater sets, staging, production, costumes."

"There should be something about emotions in the ADHD column," I contend. "It's like my emotions can suddenly feel really huge and take up all of my attention. And there's this thing people say about rejection sensitivity that's useful because I definitely notice negativity, but it feels even more like I thrive on positivity."

Sophi adds to the ADHD column: big emotions grab attention, thrive on positivity.

"More?" she asks.

"Let me talk to Lys. This is super helpful. I almost feel like my brain has two speeds and the fast one is very ADHD and the slow one is kind of Autistic, but the slow one isn't getting any support because everyone in my life likes it when I'm thinking fast. Do you think I should get tested for Autism?"

"Yeah you should. You have an opportunity to learn a lot about yourself."

"Are you going to?"

She draws a curly doodle by the Autism column header. "I've thought about it. Both a diagnosis and accommodations to support Kai's efforts for disability rights on campus and so I'm not doing quite as much on my own. But if I'm being honest, I'm afraid of the testing. I'm afraid they haven't seen a lot of Black Autistic women and they'll decide I'm some other way and be completely unhelpful. Or worse, decide I'm dangerous."

"Shit, yeah."

"And I think your brain and mine are a lot alike so if you get all the testing…" She trails off and grins. She adds, "If you want it."

"I want to know," I say. "And I want to not keep cannibalizing myself in order to seem more normal."

As I'm thinking about all this, Harper comes out of the office with a notepad in her hand. "Hey, Sophi. Maze, any luck?"

"Nope," I say.

"I've got a meeting but Terry knows you're out here and that you might come in for tea and coffee." She waves and heads for the stairs.

I look at the time on my phone: 10:22.

Bas works the eight to one shift today, so I need to be out of here before one. Not that I want to keep sitting in a hall for the next two-and-a-half hours, though having Sophi here makes it a lot better.

"How long can you stay?" I ask.

"I have a 1:10 class. You?"

"Should leave a little before then too. I'll text Lys and Kai and see who can replace us, but after about one thirty, it might be Bas who shows up and then we won't learn anything."

"We will if someone follows her to see if she takes the lockbox to anyone, but we'd need someone she doesn't recognize. Let me text some theater folks."

She texts, waits, texts. I pull out an article I need to read for tomorrow's class and get to work on it. After a few minutes, Sophi puts her phone away, gets her education class textbook out of her bag and starts reading.

Close to eleven, I go into the Disability Services office to get us both tea since we've run out. There's a tiny entry space with a counter, electric teapot, Keurig, tea and coffee options, mugs and paper cups. On the other side of the thin wall is Harper's office. A short hall leads to the other office at the far end, Terry's I guess, and the door to the nap room. It's invitingly half-open.

While the kettle is warming, I walk down the hall, into the nap room. I shut the door, lock it and kneel down by the baseboard heater. My hand trails along the bottom until it feels a hard edge. With my fingers I make out the shape of the small lockbox and then the lock holding it closed. Kai and Lys say that it's broken and will come open once anyone tries to spin the numbers on the combination.

I get up fast and walk back to the coffee and tea area. Coffee for me, tea for Sophi. Back in the hall, I hand her the refilled thermos.

"It's still there," I tell her.

"That's good. No one broke in last night and took it."

"Oh I hadn't even thought of that."

"Friends from theater are coming at one if no one's showed up by then," she says.

We settle back into studying. Or trying to study while also trying to not watch the minutes crawl by. I jump every time I hear the front door of the building. Cold drafts come down the stairs but no people. Registration and other student admin offices are on the first floor—pretty popular destinations.

Finally there are steps on the stairs. I peek at my phone and see that it's 11:43. That's the right amount of time for a student who had a morning class to get across campus. This could be Linc.

But not in those wingtips.

A person rounds the corner and I know my eyes have focused, but my brain has not—maybe because I'm realizing I recognize this thick brown hair over that red beard. He walks past us with barely a glance in our direction and goes into Disability Services. I stare at Sophi.

Who is staring at me, her lips parted but any possible words frozen.

Minutes later the door opens again and Professor Leland walks past us in the other direction. Is the satchel he's carrying a little thicker than it was when he went in?

I hop up and zip into the office.

The nap room door is open. I drop to hands and knees and feel under the heater. The lockbox is gone.

I run back to the hall. "He took it."

CHAPTER TWENTY-THREE

Lys

Maze texts me that Professor Leland came to get the fake lockbox and I cannot believe it. My brain stutters on that fact for hours. I'm physically in my afternoon class, but my mind has run ahead to Kai's room where we're meeting at dinnertime. I was already stuck on the news that Bas dropped about Professor Leland's motion at the faculty board meeting for stricter documentation. This is far too much.

I'm the last one there and Maze, Sophi, and Kai all look the way I've been picturing them all afternoon. Kai sits against the wall with a pillow behind her and has another pillow in her lap. Sophi is stretched out on the floor comforter, her head in Kai's lap. I catch Sophi's eye and grin—getting an awkward grin in reply, the kind of expression Sophi wouldn't make on her own, but she wants to echo mine back. She's just not great at it.

Maze sits against Kai's desk and opens her laptop in her lap. I make a spot next to her, dragging over spare pillows until I'm comfy. I wave my phone in their direction. "These texts don't make sense. Are you sure Professor Leland took the lockbox?"

"None of it makes sense," Maze says. "But he's the only one who came out of the office during the timeframe with a bag big enough to hold the lockbox. And after he left the office, it was gone. Do you think he was only pretending to hate this treasure hunt?"

"That'd be a great cover," Kai says. "Or maybe he wants to give the win to Bas as some kind of messed-up loyalty thing. Like the students who do his shit are the smartest and best and the big winners."

"That makes too much sense," I say. "I can imagine it. Maybe Bas has been talking about it and he asks questions, gets more info, decides he can save the day if he helps her figure things out."

"Still seems like a waste of time for a professor," Sophi says.

"But we don't know how much time he's spent on it. Maybe not much at all. Maybe chatting about it some but then Bas trusts him enough to ask if he'll come get it," Kai adds.

Maze lifts her phone. "Bas texted me around the time Leland showed up, saying she's working later than she thought and asking if I was going to get the lockbox after lunch. I was so shocked by Leland I didn't think of it at the time. Maybe she texted me to try to cover up sending him after he said yes."

"What happens if he realizes it's a decoy?" I ask quietly because the breath rushed out of my lungs before I could get the words out.

"He saw us," Maze says. "He'll know who set it up."

I say, "And if he knows the teams, he'll deduce that it's all four of us. If he's been talking to Bas about the treasure hunt, I'm sure she's said that Maze and I are dating."

"He can't legally fuck with you in his class about that," Kai tells me.

"He doesn't need to. I'm already doing terribly because I hate being there. He could take away any leeway he's been giving me."

"How likely is it that he figures it out?" Maze asks.

"Moderately," Sophi says. "The problem is, we don't know how many digits the combination is. So we put Kai's broken bike lock on it and that's four digits. The box opens as soon as he moves the lock around. If he only got the info from Bas and doesn't have the combination, we're fine. If Bas is also working with Linc, then they're going to realize that the combination and the lock don't match."

Kai blows out a rough breath. "I really hope Bas's secret team is her and Brantley. I don't want to know what Leland does if he realizes we played him."

Cold realization creeps up the inside of my spine. "There's another way to screw with me and all of us," I say. "Get the school to cancel the treasure hunt."

"Could he do that?" Maze asks.

Kai says, "He has a lot of connections and leverage on campus. If he can use that pressure against Professor Haille, she might have to stop giving us clues. They're in the same department but he's been there longer. I'm sure he'd know how to pressure the chair to put pressure on her."

"We have all the books," Maze says and then her eyes go wide. "But not the combination. If she's the one who gives us that and he shuts it down, we're screwed. How long do you think it would take for him to use his leverage?"

Kai says, "He'd have to call people and they'd need time to get back to him. At least a day or two."

I look around at all of us and say, "We really need to figure this out now."

"We've been working on it," Sophi tells me. "I found the clue from *Stars* last night. The final book is *Ormond*."

Sophi must've already told this to the others because Maze nods and says, "I've read *Ormond*, because it was in all the previous years, so I went by the Music Building this afternoon. There's a song in the novel that repeats, that the main characters use to find each other again. They used to sing it to each other when they were younger and then one's singing it again and the other hears and faints because she's so overcome—it's the gayest thing. But I couldn't find anything in the Music Building that seemed like a repeating song or teen lesbian love song."

"Did you check stringed instruments?" Sophi asks. "Because of the lute."

"Yep, nothing," Maze says. She seems unfazed that Sophi knows as much as she does about this book. To the rest of us, Maze explains, "One of the characters has to pawn her lute for rent money and then it's bought by this hot butch woman."

Kai grins at Sophi. "Of course you'd already read it too."

"After I'd signed up. Before the contest started." Sophi adds, "I looked around the WGSS Department because of the character Maze is calling hot and butch; there's definitely a point about gender and sexuality being made. If it's there, I didn't see it."

"What does that leave?" I ask. "I haven't read it."

"Letters," Maze says. "Since the book is a letter. And the locket. It's Constantia's and she has a photo of Sophia in it, but then she gives it to the landlord as collateral for her rent, and he pawns it—so I guess if there was a pawn shop on campus that would be a thing. When Constantia goes to get it back, she follows the trail of the locket and it leads her to Sophia, who is also looking for her. That's when the song gets important."

"And there are no giant lockets on campus?" I ask, smirking.

"Nope," Sophi says. "Maybe something made of gold? Also we need to be on the lookout for something like a lute that isn't in the Music Department, to be on the safe side. Maybe a place where students buy instruments."

Kai reminds her, "That would be off campus."

"Let's think about photos," Maze suggests. "The locket is only important to Constantia because it has Sophia's photo in it."

"Why didn't she take out the photo before she gave it to the landlord guy?" Kai asks.

"Maybe it's harder to get a photo out of a locket in 1799?" Maze suggests.

"The point of the locket is the photo," Sophi says quietly. "But what photo would be like Sophia is to Constantia?"

Kai shrugs. "A photo of someone you love. That's been here for a while."

"How would we know it's a photo of a person who's loved by…" Maze trails off as Sophi sits straight up and they stare at each other. Maze says, "We need to be in the professor's network of personal meanings."

"Exactly," Sophi says. "And the contest is fair, so therefore it can't be any photo, it has to be one we'd be reasonably expected to see. Where would we see photos of women who love each other like Constantia and Sophia, but also who are meaningful to the professor?"

"Professor Haille's office," Kai says, pushing up to standing. "She's got all those photos on the wall across from her bookshelves. Isn't there a wedding photo?"

"Is she still there?" Maze asks.

I nod. "She stays late on Wednesdays for students who need to meet with her in the evenings. I have a meeting with her next week about taking her class next year."

It's six and Professor Haille should be in her office until seven, but as we run across campus, I'm afraid she'll have been called away for some reason. I'm trying to tell myself it'll be okay if we have to wait for tomorrow morning. We still have more than a day until Professor Leland can get his resources together to shut down the contest—probably.

It's dusk and cool out, but not cold. I don't bother to zip my jacket. We're walking fast. My knee is reporting some strain, but it's not painful yet. I remind it that we're supposed to walk a lot. But when we get to the building, I take the elevator up to the Education Department.

We hurry down the hall and knock a little too enthusiastically on the professor's door. Her hair has been redyed and is piled on top of her head in a neat magenta bun. She's in a navy men's cable-knit sweater over a women's frilly peach blouse.

"Can we see your photos?" Sophi asks breathlessly.

She ushers us inside. "Are you looking for one specifically?"

There must be twenty photos on the wall in different sized frames. Photos from actual queer history going as far back as the eighties.

Maze says, "Moments that are loving?" It comes out more question.

"There's a wedding photo," the professor says, pointing to a group of formally dressed but informally goofing-off people on a bridge over a river.

Maze reaches for it. "Can I?"

The professor nods.

She turns it over, but there's nothing on the back of it. She gently hangs it back on its hook.

"Europe," Sophi says, pointing to a photo with the Eiffel Tower in the background. "That's where Constantia and Sophia go. And it's the same brides from the wedding photo."

"That's their honeymoon," the professor says and nods as Kai steps toward it.

She turns it over, holding it where we can all see the slips of paper tucked into the back corner. Sophi plucks the top slip loose and opens it. She shows it to Kai but we can all see it: 7415973

Kai breathes, "Has to be the combination. Not four digits, either."

"What kind of lock?" I ask.

"We'll know when we find it," Maze says. "Maybe it's fancy and electronic."

Sophi hands it to me and takes another slip of paper, opens it to show the same numbers. We jump up and down and hug, while the smiling professor carefully retrieves the framed photo from Kai's grip and hangs it back on the wall. If Paisley and Brantley can figure this out, there will be a copy of the combination for them as well.

"We still need the lockbox," Sophi points out and energy levels droops a bunch in all of us.

"You're sure you're not supposed to give it to us now?" Kai asks the professor.

"I honestly don't know where it is," she says.

"Do we get another clue?" I ask.

"No," she says. "I've given you everything I have."

"We've gotten through six books worth of clues," Maze says. "We can do this. Come on."

We take our leave. Maze leads us down the hallway to the Education Department lounge where there's a big table and the stuff to make tea or coffee.

"I think better when I'm moving," Kai says. "We'll go get dinner and bring it here. But if you realize stuff before we get back, you have to text us."

"We promise," I say.

CHAPTER TWENTY-FOUR

Maze

The Education Lounge is a long, narrow room like the professors' offices, but with a round table and chairs for students to meet. There's a pot that boils water and a Keurig for coffee, a microwave, utensils, and usually some leftover treat from department events. Today it's a half case of Twizzlers. I grab a few.

I make tea for me and Lys. Kai and Sophi head out to get us all falafel as soon as they have our orders. I suspect more is going to happen than a walk to the restaurant and back—and feel a surge of warmth in my chest. I like that Sophi has Kai now too. And that we all have each other.

Lys and I settle at the table, cups in front of us, looking like we haven't slept well for days. I don't know if that's true. I've been sleeping but short, waking up early, going back to the books.

Lys grumbles, "Now we all have the combination, Linc has it—as soon as Bas knows from you, I'm sure she'll tell Brantley—but nobody has the lockbox. Professor Haille says she has nothing else to give us, so Leland can't shut the hunt down that way, but he can still probably get the college to tell us to stop."

I nod. "We have to figure it out now." I want to say that I'm not leaving the Education Lounge until I do figure it out, but that's not practical. I'm not going to spend the night here. I can think as easily in my room or Lys's. But for now I want to go with the excitement, the pressure.

"Why is *Ormond last* this year?" I ask. I can't get this question off my mind. This is the one book that's in the contest every year and yeah maybe that's because it's literally the only American novel with lesbian content before the 1900s, but what if that's not it?"

"Because it's hard to read and putting it first makes folks drop the contest," Lys suggests. "And this is the last year and they want someone to win."

"I don't think so. Putting the hardest book first makes it easier on us in the long run. I don't think they want us to read five books and *then* drop out. What if it's at the end this time so we'll really pay attention. What if it's in the contest every year because it's the meta clue?"

Lys's mouth is open as she stares at me. "That makes sense."

"Yet it can't be," I say. "Because Linc would have figured that out. If the clue to the lockbox is also in *Ormond*, he's had access to all the reading lists from all the years—and he's had two years to work on it."

"*Ormond* is important," Lys says. "But the clue can't be *in Ormond*."

"We find the combination and then we find the lockbox. The combination opens the lockbox." Ideas press against the backs of my eyes.

"And in a big sense, *Ormond* is part of the combination, is that what you're saying?" Lys asks.

"Yes, but what does it unlock? A combination, a key opens something."

"Which part of *Ormond* is the key?" Lys asks.

"It can't be the part about the relationship. What if it's sort of literal? In 1799 a key would open a door, would open a house, would open…a secret passage. Right? Ormond knows what he does because of the secret passage in Constantia's house. He rents the house to her, because without her knowledge he can spy on her. He has what's-his-name use the secret passage to kill her father. He lurks in the passage to listen to Constantia and Sophia whisper to each other about their love—and that's super creepy. So if we've been given the key to that same secret passage, what are we supposed to do with it? Do we replace Ormond with ourselves? Do we become a loving presence that listens and supports them from the secret passage?"

Lys stands and walks in a circle, gesturing. "Every book! There's a love story in every book. The key to the secret passage is listening to all of them."

I jump up and grab her hands. "The whole thing is the clue! All six books and their clues are the clue to the location of the treasure."

I pull pieces of paper out of my bag and put them on the table so we can write out all the books and their clues and the love:

Zami – bridges and passages

Curious Wine – tried and true – possibly refers to the "trial" aspect of Lane's job but also the "true" aspect of their love for each other

The Gilda Stories – 1 + 2 = 8 – means the chapters. which is about finding community (Fibonacci Club is a real club hence community)

Laura Dean Keeps Breaking Up With Me – Seek-Her Reversed – How do you get together with someone you're already together with? The clue and the story are also about love and community!

The Stars and the Blackness Between Them – "reach the end, then go back to go beyond." – This is also about time therefore passages

Ormond – more passages! Secret passages!

I say, "Look at all of it! Look at the *Stars* clue—it's not only about finding the path to *Ormond*, it's about the whole contest, they all are. The professor is telling us that to find the treasure, we have to go back to the start, which is that clue about bridges and passages—and see how *Ormond* is about secret passages. There are passages and bridges between the books. They're all connected!

"She gives us Audre Lorde at the start and then Audre again in *Stars*. She shows us intense love with *Curious Wine* and its opposite in *Laura Dean* and then in *Ormond* we're back to two women caring amazingly for each other."

Lys shakes both my hands with hers. "Do you know where it is?"

"No, but I know how to think about it."

Kai and Sophi return minutes later with falafel that we all eat while Lys and I explain. Sophi pulls the pages toward her and Kai leans close to see them.

"You know where it is?" Kai asks me.

"No but we know what the clue is," I say.

"So do we. We talked it through on the way to get dinner," Sophi says. While I'm staring, she adds, "It's all the books and clues together. Moving *Ormond* last tells us to look at the whole of it. And the fact that the clue for *Stars* didn't quite match what I found clued me in to how it could also apply to the whole reading list. She's telling us that after we've read all the books, we have to go back to the start and think it through again—and look at all the clues again, together."

"Yeah," Lys agrees. "I think that first clue is really important."

"Obv," Kai says. "Because of the two Audres. But which bridges and passages? We can't scour the HVAC tunnels under the school. Well, I guess we can, but they're dangerous, I don't think she'd hide the lockbox there. Plus they're moist and not temperature controlled."

"We should look at my mindmap of all the places in the school that would be good to hide a lockbox," Sophi says. "Maybe it'll jog something loose."

"You have a mindmap of that?" Kai asks. She's grinning.

"On paper even," Sophi says with a tiny smirk. "But I can scan it for you if you want."

Lys says, "Okay, we all promise that if anyone figures it out, we tell the others. Maze and I are going back to my room to sleep on this. You two do whatever genius stuff you're going to and if nobody has it by morning we all meet for breakfast and keep going. We have to get this before Professor Leland can put anything into action to shut down the contest."

I add, "Whatever's in this collection, if it's split three ways that isn't much less than two. It's better if we work together."

"Three?" Kai asks.

"I'm giving Lys my share. But I don't know what to do about Bas."

"Let us win," Kai says. "If you figure it out, take us to the treasure. We'll claim it, win the treasure hunt and give Lys a third—if that sounds fair to you."

Sophi asks, "But, Maze, you really don't want in?"

"I don't need the money," I tell her. "I need…to have done this. I need to prove it was important, to live in a world where lesbian literature and fortunes and all our various kinds of brains intersect. If that makes sense."

"Not for nothing but that's the most sense you've ever made," Kai says.

CHAPTER TWENTY-FIVE

Maze

I fall asleep in Lys's room, cuddled up with her, and wake to Kai pounding on the door. When Lys opens it, Kai looks like she hasn't gone to bed yet. She's in the same rainbow manticore T-shirt she had on yesterday. And there's a waffle pattern on one cheek, like she fell asleep on her computer keyboard.

"You got it?" Lys asks.

"Professor Haille's office was ransacked," she says. "We're going over to see if we can help."

Stunned by the news, we toss on clothes and follow her across campus. Sophi is there with coffees and a box of donuts and gluten-free muffins. The office that we'd been in yesterday is a mess of toppled books and overturned drawers with the photos from the wall scattered everywhere. Professor Haille sits quietly in her desk chair at the apex of the mess, hair in a loose ponytail, wearing a school sweatshirt over worn jeans and boots.

Lys picks up the photo taken by the Eiffel Tower. "Whoever did this knew we were here, maybe knew we got the combination here. How?"

"I texted Bas," I say, hating that I have to add this option. "I don't think she'd do this, but maybe she told someone who did."

"Or hired someone to do it," Kai adds.

"Whoever did it had keycard access to the building," Sophi points out. "A student, faculty or staff."

"I'm sure the police are checking the logs," Professor Haille says from her desk. She sounds tired. There's a pile of stuff on top of the desk that she's trying to sort into three open drawers arranged in front of her.

"Can we help?" Lys asks. "We can put the photos back."

"Sure," Professor Haille says. She also accepts a cup of coffee from Sophi with a grateful nod and picks a donut out of the box.

Lys hangs the Eiffel Tower photo on the wall where it had been and starts gathering the others, lining them up at the base of the wall. Kai helps while Sophi and I stand near the door because we can't all fit into the office.

Who could've broken in? The doorframe is splintered by the lock. Someone must've used a pretty heavy-duty pry bar because the frame is thick. But that doesn't rule out anyone. I'm sure there are compact bars that would fit into a student backpack. Could it have been Linc? But he already has the combination. He'd have to think the treasure was in the office. I don't know why Bas would break in, since she's got as good a shot at winning by sticking with me—unless she's figured that we could cut her out by letting Sophi and Kai win, then having them split their shares with Lys.

Maybe Paisley and Brantley could do this, if they got really scared about being the one team left that didn't have the combination. They'd have the benefit of one of them to keep watch while the other went through the office. This kind of mess took some time to make. But I have a hard time believing that about people who wear paisley neckties and dress in purple and green monochrome.

I watch the mess being slowly sorted: Haille at her desk, Lys at the wall, Sophi now at the bookshelves. There's a pattern in all of this, if I can just see it.

I ask, "The notes, last night's notes, Sophi did you make a copy? Do you have it?"

She opens her bag and pulls out an artist sketchbook, opens it to the page where she copied the clues in prettier handwriting than mine. There are more notes—Kai and Sophi have been adding to it.

A rush of fear, a flush of shame because I'm standing in the middle of the room, being seen, being obvious and I know what I need to ask. "Everyone stop—can you stop moving?"

They do, and stare. I'm red in the face, I'm sure, hot all over, cold under that.

"Last night, Sophi, *Stars*, the clue, what did you say about it?"

"That it doesn't quite match. The clue is 'reach the end, then go back to go beyond.' But when I found the clue that pointed to Ormond, I hadn't gone beyond the end of the book. So I figure that clue maybe isn't *only* to get us to the next book. Maybe when she's saying go back—go beyond, she's talking about the entire treasure hunt."

I'm nodding. "And if we go back, we're at that first clue, 'bridges and passages,' which I think is also part of the meta clue. But not only which bridges and passages—look at the other books—which love pair? Which community? We've reached the end and we need to go back, but where do we go back to? *Here.* We come back here. Professor, each year you give some of the books from your office, don't you?"

"Unless another professor has them, I do. From a box or, later in the contest, from my desk drawer."

"And teams come asking you questions, right? Have you seen all the teams this year?"

She nods.

I say, "That's not a coincidence. And this used to be Professor Stendatter's office, so we've been going back to the beginning the whole time."

"But it's not in this office," Sophi points out. "Unless she could've hidden it without you knowing?"

Professor Haille shakes her head. "Two years ago when Linc got the combination, I let him go through here in immense detail. He didn't find it."

"Which means he didn't break in," Kai points out. "He wouldn't bother. He knows it's not here."

Lys says, "I don't think she'd hide it here anyway. It's too obvious and it's a little dangerous. She'd put it somewhere on campus that's easy to access but hard to figure out."

"Hard to figure out because nobody knows where to go back to," I say. "They're going back to the wrong places. They're not seeing what the books mean. Sophi, would you set the books facing out? Lys, hang the rest of the photos."

I can't believe I'm saying all this. I hate messing up spaces. No, that's not true. I love to make a big, intricate mess in my spaces, but I stopped doing it years ago and since then I've been moving through the world like a horse with blinders on. I long to make messes; I can't believe I'm making one here in a professor's office.

I feel myself distributed throughout the room, bigger than my body, filling the space around me.

Sophi and Lys get their sides of the room set and Lys says, "Nobody move, Maze is doing her thing."

"I have a thing?"

"Yeah," she says, all soft awe.

And I love the way she's seeing me—like I can absolutely stand in the middle of a room hit by a human whirlwind and she sees genius in the chaos. "You too. All your things are amazing," I tell her.

And then to everyone, I say, "Look at the books. Look at them with your heart. What do you see?"

Lys doesn't turn toward the books. She keeps her eyes on me. "Love," she says. "So much love."

Kai gently touches the corner of *Stars*. "People having each other's backs for real. Not community, that gets said too much, I mean deep, rooted group thriving."

"Power as network," Sophi says. "Emergence. Self-organizing patterns that are greater than the whole, that reach beyond and become new."

I turn toward the wall of photographs. They're in different places than yesterday except for the two that Lys remembered:

the Eiffel Tower honeymoon and the wedding photo. That's the one we looked at first—before Kai found the key on the back of the honeymoon photo. This one is Professor Stendatter and her wife on the day of their wedding, one in a light blue suit and the other in a tuxedo dress. Professor Haille is with them along with a group of friends clustered together, beaming at the camera—all of them standing by the side of the High Bridge a few miles from here.

"Love," I say. "Group thriving. Emergence. Connections— power as network." As I talk, I'm scanning the photos because there has to be one that is all of these.

I see it. A mass of people dancing behind Professor Stendatter, her wife, their close friends all at a table—a mix of genders, ages, races, and more.

I put my fingers on the edge of the frame. "Where?" I ask Professor Haille.

"The Wabasha Street Caves."

That fits, exactly, into the connections, the patterns around me. It has passages, community, history. Exactly.

I turn to everyone. "Gangsters used the caves during prohibition, there have to be secret passages there."

"It's in the caves?" Kai asks, dismayed. "That would take forever to search."

Lys looks at the professor. "Everything in the contest is on campus, right?"

"Right."

"She wouldn't put the lockbox in the caves. It's too dangerous." Lys grins at Kai. "And moist."

"But the caves are the clue," Sophi says, half-questioning.

"More than the clue," I say. "This is the map. I know where it is. And I know why nobody else found it."

"Wait," Kai says. "Don't say it. I'm not completely convinced something isn't bugged. That would be a great reason to break in here and trash the place, so no one thinks to look for a bug. Can you take us there?"

I shake my head. The problem is—now that I know, I can see it's going to be hard to get to and it could alert other folks that we're going for it.

"Where can we talk?" I ask Kai.

"Come on," she says.

We say bye to Professor Haille and follow Kai down the stairs to an empty first-floor classroom.

Kai says, "Okay, we're in a random location. If it's not in the Wabasha Street Caves, where is it?"

"It's in the *model* of the Caves that the Geology Department made. It was on display until they moved it at the start of the pandemic so they'd have more classroom space to socially distance students."

Lys's eyes light up. "Oh wow, that's that massive thing in the storage room."

I nod. "And nobody's able to find the lockbox because the professor meant it to be publicly accessible and doesn't know it got moved to storage. She never imagined a pandemic. Do we have any way to get the key to the storage room without being obvious?"

Lys looks to Kai, who shakes her head.

"One of us would have to ask for it," Lys says, meaning her and Kai. "And the whole team's been talking about this treasure hunt like crazy."

"Can we break into it?" Kai asks.

"Oh yeah and get ourselves kicked out of school. Let's not," Sophi tells her.

Lys waves her hand to get our attention. "Since I'm officially out of the contest, maybe I can ask around without raising suspicion. I just have to avoid Brantley."

Sophi leans forward, voice pitched quietly. "What's bothering me is that someone broke into Professor Haille's office. That's pretty brazen. What are they going to do to us to get the lockbox?"

CHAPTER TWENTY-SIX

Lys

We're supposed to go to the faculty board meeting and present our video clips this afternoon, but both Kai and I think we have time to check out Maze's idea and still make it to the meeting. Since I'm officially out of the contest, I go to ask for the copy of the storage room key. Everyone on the team knows that Maze and I never have enough space to ourselves. I say that we want a combined make out and study session somewhere private and I borrow the key from our assistant coach.

Kai is waiting for me by the library.

"Maze and Sophi went ahead," she says. "Do they seem real different about each other? I asked Sophi and she said they have remarkably similar brains. I don't know how to feel about that."

I love the idea. I wonder who here has my same brain. I know that mine and Maze's are very similar in some ways but not in others and I love the differences too. But what would it be like to meet someone with my same brain? I need to ask Maze more about this.

"Seems great," I tell Kai. "How long until the meeting?"

"Forty-five," she says. "And I don't think we're first up. But I texted Harper in case and she's going. She has a copy of the testimonials and said she'd start them playing if we're late and we can say our points afterward. That should buy us another fifteen maybe thirty minutes. Really hoping this doesn't take that long."

We hurry to the building basement, through the carefully propped open door. Maze and Sophi wait at the far end of the hall. Sophi has a notebook spread in her hands and Maze is pointing along the page, saying, "This is where I get all in a mess."

"Might need help there," Sophi adds.

"Do you?"

"Yeah. Siblings, though, make it easy. I'll show you what we do and you can show Lys."

"What?" I ask, completely at sea.

"We think we have the same neurotype. I'll explain later," Maze tells me and turns toward the door as Sophi closes her notebook.

I turn the key in the lock and push it open, flick on the lights. We all go to the model of the caves—the one that I remember bumping into, nearly falling on me when Maze and I were sneaking out of here five weeks ago. We'd been so close!

Maze walks around it, looks at her phone, holds her phone out over the model. "Here's the map of the caves that shows where the photo was taken. Can you guys see where that is on this model?"

"The photo is the map, literally," Sophi says. "That's genius." She holds out her hand for Maze's phone and shuffles clockwise around the model, comparing the phone and the model. Partway around she says, "Here, this big cavern."

Parts of the model break away for better access, but when we expose the cavern, we see nothing other than clay walls.

"Could it be inside?" Kai asks.

"We can't break it," I tell her.

"I was so sure," Maze says. "She wouldn't want us to break anything. What she wants is for us to work together. I bet that's a reason we have random teams this year, so we'll bond with each other. I don't get the part about not working with other teams, though. Even with the pandemic. Doesn't make sense."

"Been thinking about that too," Sophi says. "Linc told us those rules, sent out the emails. We know he still wants to win. What if he made that up?"

"Oh shit," Kai says. She turns wide eyes to Sophi and holds out a hand. Sophi takes it.

And Maze is staring wide-eyed at nothing—or nothing visible to me. She's obviously seeing a lot.

"Maze, can you tell us?" I ask.

"The photos, Professor Stendatter and her wife newly married, but not alone as a couple, they had their whole friend group taking care of them. And that's what she wants the books to be for us. They're friends taking care of us. If Linc made that up about cross-team work, it's so much more true than he knows. The professor set this whole thing up to bring us together inside a larger context of community—the authors giving us such loving works, leaving us their passages and giving us bridges to each other. We're the bridges."

Sophi says a soft, "Oh." She points around to all of us and then at the model. "Bridges and passages."

Maze nods. "How heavy do you think this model is?"

"You've got two rugby people and Sophi, we can lift it," I tell her.

The section with the cavern is really heavy, but it comes up from the table. Maze flicks on her phone's flashlight and shines it under the model. I hear her sharp inhale.

"Anyone have a knife or something I can cut tape with?" she asks, her voice hollow with wonder.

We set down the model and Sophi pulls out a small pocketknife, flicks open the longest blade. Kai raises an eyebrow at her and she shrugs.

I count to three and we heave the model section up again. There's a scraping sound from underneath and a whisper of paper.

Maze stands up from bending under the model and says, "Okay."

We set the model down.

Maze holds an envelope in her hand, letter-sized. She tears it open and lifts the flap, slides a single sheet of paper out and unfolds it.

"What is it?" Kai asks. She's bouncing on her feet lightly.

"It's a—" Maze stops at the sound of a key turning and the door opening. She has the key copy we used to get in, so this has to be someone official.

"Hold it," a sharp man's voice says. A campus security guard comes through the doorway, followed by Harper. In the dim light, her hair and glasses look brassy, sharp and cutting. What the shit?

"I told you they'd broken in here and were stealing campus property," Harper says to the guard.

Maze has the envelope in her hands, obvious.

"You lot are going to have to come with me," he says.

Kai swears softly and Sophi's jaw is clenched iron hard. I hold up my hands and step between them and the guard. He's only got a stun gun, but it's scary enough.

"I did it on a dare," I tell him. "My friends are here to talk me out of it. We didn't take anything."

"We'll see about that," Harper says.

Her face is no longer the friendly visage that brings treats to our meetings. Her eyes are narrowed, lips taut. Did she show up for meetings to listen in on our progress? She was so willing to step into our *Gilda* reenactment. She's been tracking us this whole time.

And she has access to the kind of records that include Char's parents' phone number. Plus we told her our entire plan with the decoy and she could've been the one who got Professor Leland to show up and grab the fake lockbox.

Now she's after the real one.

"You can take me in with Lys," Maze says. "I helped her. Kai and Sophi didn't do anything, though. They're here trying to keep us out of trouble."

"You're all coming in," the guard says.

"Where?" Kai asks. She's got her phone in her hands, texting. "I'm not going until you tell me where you're taking us."

"Relax," he says. "Just the Admin Building. You'll be questioned and searched and if there's nothing stolen, you can go."

Maze nudges my foot with hers. "Admin, huh. I remember picking you up there for a date once."

Why is she bringing that up? Ah, the question I should ask is: what does that connect to? Every thought she has is connected to so many others. What is she telling me? That night, the bathroom…my knee!

"Fine, we're going," I say and stomp around the side of the model, letting my foot come down wrong, twisting my leg.

The yelp I make on the way down is very real, though there isn't as much pain as I feared. I curl around it anyway.

"Stop faking," Harper says.

"She has a brace," the guard points out.

"Give her a minute," Kai says and to me, "You okay?"

"Stress, you know. Fuck." I rip open the Velcro of the brace, adjust it and pull the straps tight again. There's a dull ache, but not bad. "Help me up?"

Kai gives me a hand and I get to my feet. I hope that gave Maze the time she needed—I'm assuming to hide that envelope. It's no longer in her hands.

Harper shakes her head. "Come on. And if you think about running, we know who you are and it'll only go worse for you. If you're running, you're guilty."

She leads the way out of the building and we follow because we have to. Maze goes first, then Sophi, Kai, me in the back.

As we're coming out of the Language Arts Building, Bas runs up, coat swirling. She's bare-headed and wearing two different boots, like she heard we were on the move and all thoughts of fashion vanished.

She shouts, "You assholes! You didn't wait for me." Then she rocks back on her heels and takes in the security guard behind the lot of us. "Oh shit."

"You fucking turned us in!" Maze yells at her in a very un-Maze way.

"What the hell? I did not. Turn you in to who? The campus cops? I would *never*." To the guard she says, "If the smallest bad thing happens to any of these people, I will ruin you."

He looks like he has no idea what to do now, but he's going to push through. "Let's get moving. Sooner we do this, sooner it's over."

"Do what?" Bas asks.

"I broke into the storage room in the language arts basement to look for the lockbox," Maze says. "The others came to talk me out of it. My moms are going to be pissed. Especially my Mom Kelly. Good thing she's at work."

Bas's eyes widen. She looks from Maze to the guard to Harper. "So what you're saying is 'tried and true'?"

"Get curious," Maze says with half a grin.

The guard prods her and we start walking again, Bas falling in with us, walking next to Maze.

"It wasn't under the bridge like we thought," Maze says. "You were right about Ormond, about Martinette."

"Hey, you know I love the French and their fondness for... portraiture?"

Maze shakes her head.

"Fine, be like that," Bas says. "But call me if you need help. You know I hate being a pawn in all this," she adds.

Maze's eyes light up and she presses her lips together, crushing a smile into a twisted smirk. Bas tosses up her hands and walks away from us.

"You get all that out of your system?" Kai asks.

"I needed her to pay attention," Maze says. "You too, okay? Full *Ormond*."

"Jesus, don't let that ever become the name of a sex position," Kai says.

We're ushered into a small waiting room. The security guard goes into a back office to talk to someone important while Harper leans against a desk, glaring at us.

"You know what I want," she says. "Hand it over and this ends. Screw around and I'm going to make this hard for all of you."

"The faculty board meeting is in ten minutes," Kai says. "Who's showing our video?"

Harper shrugs. "Give me what you found and you are."

"You can't do that," I protest. "That's so mean. We've been working on that for weeks and the students need this."

"It's in your power to be there," Harper says.

"There have to be other meetings," Sophi tells Kai. "Or you could send the link to the faculty board, get individual meetings with them. We'll find a way."

"They're voting *today*," Kai says, words heavy with anguish.

"Why are you doing this?" Maze asks Harper. "Were you in the first contest?"

"I set it up," Harper says. "Helped with the whole thing, the first few years of clues. Got nothing for it, thank you very much."

"So you know what the treasure is?" Maze asks.

"No, only that it's old and valuable—which means every year it's getting more valuable. And every year teams blunder around and can't find it. You've all had enough time. This is the last year and that treasure should be mine."

"You're friends with Linc," Maze says, pointing at her. "Two years ago, did you try to help him win and get him to split it with you?"

"Of course," she says. "But we didn't find anything."

"Because it had already been moved," Maze says.

I think she shouldn't be giving all this info and helping out with Harper's villain speech, but she probably can't stop herself. She's still so excited that we found it, even if we're in the deepest shit right now. Even if I'm hearing Kai's heart break about our videos and feeling mine break along with hers.

Harper helped us get the videos that we should be showing now. She saw our edited final versions and said they were amazing. How can she do this?

Maze says, "Linc's year was spring 2020. The last part of the treasure hunt would've come after everyone switched to virtual classes. But Harper, you still had access to campus. You all might've figured it out except that's the same time when the Geology Department moved the caves model into storage. Plus you couldn't get into Professor Haille's office to see the wedding photos."

"Exactly," Harper says. "We should've won and the pandemic took that win from us."

I can't keep quiet. "Except you should *not* have won because you weren't a student."

"Unfair timing," Harper says, waving that away. "If this had started a few years earlier, I'd have been a student and could've won. I know you're stalling. Are you going to hand over what you found or are you volunteering to be the first one searched?"

"Sure," Maze says. "Search me. But let Kai and Lys go to the meeting."

"We start the search and when I get what I need, you can all go," Harper says.

"This is a shitpickle," Maze tells her, having picked up the word from Char.

She goes into the room with a woman security guard, who's been called in from her patrolling so we'll have a sort of same-gender person to search us—assuming we're all the same gender. I feel like I should do something, but what?

The room we're in is a generic admin waiting room: a row of chairs by the wall, a desk with a person who answers phones and is pointedly ignoring all of us, a water cooler, a bookshelf. Harper stands by the water cooler talking quietly with the guy guard. The woman at the desk is moving papers around while stealing looks at all of us.

I could ask to call someone, but who?

Hushed conversation comes from the inner office in low, serious tones. Maze's voice sounds upset, angry, frustrated. I bet she's trying to tell the guard all about the treasure hunt and how we rightfully won—and that's not going over well. We did essentially break into private property of the school.

After a while, the woman security guard comes out and hands an envelope to Harper—the same envelope from under the caves. Harper opens it and peers inside. "Where's the lockbox?" she asks.

"We honestly don't know," Sophi tells her.

"Storage room," Harper says, more to herself than us. "Has to be there." To the male security guard, she says, "Hold them as long as you can. I'll be back."

His lips are a tight grim line and I don't think he wants to keep us much longer, but if Harper gets to the room and finds the lockbox, it won't matter. She jets out the door.

Maze comes out of the back room looking dizzy and pale. The two guards move to the door and start a hushed conversation about what to do with us.

I've been staring at the phone for so long that when it rings, I jump. The woman at the desk picks it up and within seconds her eyes go from half-lidded and sleepy to wide. She stands up, listening intently, and turns toward the guard.

"Jack," she says, an edge in her voice. "There's a lawyer on the phone. You'd better…" She holds the phone out to the guard.

He takes it with a gruff, "Yeah." And that's all he says for the next minute.

A long, slow minute in which his jaw moves like he's chewing gum, which he isn't. He says, "Yeah" a few more times, followed by a grudging, "Okay."

Then he sets the handset on the desk and says, "Maze, your mother is on the phone. She needs to talk to you."

Maze grabs the phone and says, "Mom, hey, thanks—" And that's as far as she gets before there is a lot of loud talking from her mom on the other end. I can't make out the words, but the tone is hot. Maze winces a few times and makes a lot of sounds of agreement.

When she hangs up the phone, she turns to the guard. "So, we're leaving."

"Yeah," he says.

"That's it?" Kai asks. "You pulled all that and now we can go? You made us miss the most important meeting of this whole year."

Sophi puts a hand on her arm. "There's still time."

"We missed our time slot."

"Let's go anyway," Sophi says.

"You're coming too?"

Sophi nods. I really want to run across campus and see if there's time to show our videos in the last few minutes of this meeting, but I can't stop thinking about where Harper went.

"She's gone to find the lockbox. You hid the paper, right?" I ask Maze. "Is she going to find it?"

"I sure hope not. There might be a way we can find out and make it to the end of the meeting." Maze says. "We have to hurry."

"They're not going to let us back there," Kai says.

"We're not going back," Maze replies, all mysterious.

She leads the way out of the building.

Out front, sitting on the brick wall at the base of the steps, Bas has a bakery box on her lap. She hops up and awkwardly side-hugs Maze, who's enthusiastically hugging back.

"You all okay?" Bas asks.

"Thanks for calling my moms," Maze tells her.

"Get curious," Bas replies with a wink.

"Oh!" Sophi says. "Because one of your moms is a lawyer and in *Curious Wine*, Lane is a lawyer, your code was telling Bas who to call for help. Not bad at all."

Bas grins and holds up the box. "And then she told me to get pastry."

"I did not," Maze says. "Please tell me you didn't only get pastry."

"Teammate, I am not that much of an asshole. I did what you clumsily told me to do. Let's go eat this before it gets warm or cold or whatever."

"Faculty board first!" Kai says.

We hurry across campus but when we get to the big building with all the steps and the super official meeting rooms, professors are walking down the steps in twos and threes, talking to each other, looking at their phones.

"No," Kai groans and folds forward, hands on her knees. Sophi supports her from one side and me from the other. Kai turns into my side, crying and I duck my face into the cloth of her sweatshirt.

"Look," Sophi says. "Look up, you two. Just look."

Professor Haille hurries down the steps to us. "Your video was a big hit," she says.

"How...?"

I don't have more words than that.

"Harper sent it to me and said you might be delayed and it was really important for the college that we talk about this more."

"She *what*?" Kai asks, the words thick in her throat.

"She's the bad guy," Maze explains. "She detained us and tried to get the last clue from us. The one that points to the collection, to the treasure."

"*Oh...*" Professor Haille packs a world of surprise in that syllable.

"Don't we need to do something?" I ask. "Go find the thing? Talk to people? Stop Harper?"

"Eat a pastry," Bas says and I want to step on her toe hard, but not too hard.

She holds the white pastry box toward us and opens the lid. I see pastries but also, taped to the underside of the lid, a flat, white rectangle of folded paper. It's crinkled like it got dropped and stepped on after being pulled from an envelope.

"I could kiss you," Maze says.

"I wouldn't stop you."

Maze stares at the page, tears in her eyes. She gingerly pulls it off the lid and holds it reverently.

"What did Harper leave with?" I ask.

Maze grins. "The spare key to the storage room. Your distraction gave me time to get it out of my pocket and drop it in the envelope so there'd be something for her to find. I dropped this paper to the floor and kicked it under that ratty old guitar case. I figured we could go back for it, but then when I saw you, Bas, I realized you had to go get it in case Harper searched the room after coming up blank with us."

"That's what 'full Ormond' was about?" Kai asks.

"Yeah, Maze's obscure code was telling me to call her moms and *then* get my ass down into the basement and search anything that looked slightly like Martinette's lute. The lute that the hero had to *pawn*—hence my *cunning* pun to show Maze I got her obtuse drift."

I'm shaking my head because I can't add this up yet. "How did you get in? We have the key."

"Brantley copied it," Bas says. "Months ago."

"And gave it to you now when you asked?" Kai's words are clipped and incredulous.

"No, I promised them some of my share," Bas answers. Her downcast eyes speak to the disappointing truth of this statement. She mutters, "Rather get less than none at all if Harper got there first."

Sophi turns to Maze and asks, "How did you know you could trust Bas?"

"Yeah," Bas says. "How did you?"

Maze explains, "We told Harper about the decoy so that means if she's behind all this, she's the one who got Professor Leland to get the decoy, not you, Bas. Plus I remembered how pissed you were when you heard about Char being forced out of the hunt and then again on the lawn when you saw Harper with us and realized what she was doing. The way you froze felt like real shock to me. You've seen her before with Linc, haven't you? And you were catching on that she'd been playing you too. She was playing all of us against each other."

"The enemy of my enemy is my frenemy?" Bas asks. "After the situation with Char, some things clicked for me about how Linc was working me and Brantley—and the two of us against each other when he could. And I got to thinking maybe he wasn't working alone, especially since he wouldn't have done that to Char. I don't know if he's working with Harper as a partner or if she's using him, but what happened today confirmed that she was really bad news."

Kai takes a bearclaw out of the box. "What's on the paper, Maze? You looked at it, didn't you?"

"It's a certificate of ownership," she says. "For a collection of comic books. I believe that code we got, the seven digits, is the call number where we'll find them in the library, it's missing the period between the first three and the last four."

Kai drops her pastry back into the box. "Let's go!"

Professor Haille says, "Let me know what you find. I'm going to make sure that Harper knows she cannot detain students like she did."

We rush back across campus. The pain in my knee feels almost good. Important. The kind of pain that motivates but also warns me not to break into a run. Waiting for the library elevator takes an age and a half.

When we reach the second floor, Sophi moves ahead of us, nearly dancing down the rows, calling numbers back to us. She's louder than usual, bigger energy. Is she like that alone? Kai grins at her, follows, not small but settled.

We find the row and the shelf. There's a big bound volume in navy blue with *Theories of Construction of the Wabasha Caves Superstructure* written on the spine. It looks super boring and the top edges of the binding are thick with dust.

Maze lifts it down and opens it to show comic books in plastic bags.

"It's been here the whole time?" Sophi asks, awe in her voice.

"Genius place to hide it," I say. "Even if someone decided to search the whole library, how would they know this is the treasure? And they couldn't claim it without that certificate from under the caves model."

Kai has her phone out, typing and moving through web pages. "Did you know a woman wrote these in the 1940s? And the artist is gay. What's the first number there?"

"Thirteen," Maze says.

"Holy mudballs…if it's near mint, that's worth about twenty-five thousand. How many issues are there?"

Maze flips carefully through the sealed plastic bags. "Ten, no eleven."

Kai scrolls down a web page, lips moving as she says numbers to herself. She stops and scrolls to the top and does it again.

"What?" Sophi whispers.

"If they're near mint, all of them, this is about two hundred thousand dollars' worth of comic books."

"Why would she leave that and not sell it herself?" I ask, stunned.

"Maybe she didn't need the money?" Maze suggests.

Kai says, "Also looks like the price more than doubled in the last few years, so when she decided to leave these, they were under a hundred thou. Awesome she didn't come back for them, though."

"How many ways are we splitting this?" Bas asks.

"Four," Maze says. "And Lys gets mine."

She looks around and everyone nods.

"Who won, though?" Sophi asks. "Who gets the bragging rights?"

I remember days ago—which seems so long ago now—and Maze saying that she didn't need the money, that she needed to live into a world where lesbian literature and fortunes intersect.

Kai and Bas have started bickering about whether it matters how many winners there are and if there can be more than two. I put a hand between them so that they turn to me.

"Maze won," I say. "She found two clues, the meta clue, the certificate, and protected the certificate."

Sophi nods and elbows Kai who says, "Yeah, okay."

Bas folds her arms. "Fine, when you put it that way." But she's grinning.

As is Maze, who's not even trying to hide the tears shining in her eyes.

CHAPTER TWENTY-SEVEN

Maze – four months later

I've been marinating some chicken and tofu all day. There's rice in the Instant Pot. With the veggies Kai and Lys brought, we're all set to have a big stir-fry, followed by the variety pack of Pop-Tarts I see in the other bag. Mom has been teaching me how to cook. She was really good at it before her law practice took off and she's trying to get back into it so she can show me all her tricks.

I start washing the veggies, but Lys comes in and points to the cutting board. She takes over washing while I cut. She looks more solid. Her shoulders are dense with summer weight training and her face is tan from being outside, but also she's present in her face and shoulders. She flashes me a grin that says we are so making out as soon as I have a good excuse to show her my new bedroom.

She turns over her shoulder and asks Kai and Sophi, "Has anyone been to Disability Services? What happened with Harper?"

Sophi and Kai are sitting on the two stools at the little counter between kitchen and living room in this apartment.

Sophi's wearing a blue, brown, and gold headscarf with those colors echoed around her eyes. They're also around mine, less dramatically. She's been showing me how she does her eye makeup and I've promised to show her how I organize thoughts in the space around me.

Kai says, "Harper's gone. The school couldn't do much officially about her messing with us. By going into that storage room we really were in a place we weren't supposed to go. And nobody could completely prove that she called Char's parents, but the call was made from her office. I bet there were some pretty hardcore meetings about that. Word is out about what she did and why—her reputation is pretty trashed. Last I heard she moved out of state. I kind of hope she does okay. Is that weird? She's actually good at her job."

"It's sweet," Sophi says. "What about Professor Leland?"

Lys sets a bowl of clean mushrooms next to me and says, "Still doing that study. Bas quit, though, and I heard he's having trouble getting his work-study student positions filled. I talked to Professor Haille over the summer, setting up my fall schedule, and she let drop that the faculty board is not excited about seeing the results of the study. Someone leaked some data and professors from other schools are critiquing his methods online. I'm pretty sure Professor Haille spearheaded that—she gets a look when she talks about it—but she's not saying."

"What do you think he did with the decoy lockbox we made?" Sophi asks. "I kind of wanted to use that as art somewhere."

I toss the mushrooms into the pan. "He doesn't have it. Bas didn't send him to get the decoy lockbox. She didn't talk to him about the treasure hunt at all. But I managed to sneak some info out of Uncle Karl—they're still dating, which is gross but strangely endearing. Professor Leland didn't go to Disability Services that day to get the lockbox. He got a call from Harper telling him she had information that would help his study and asking him to pick it up."

"Then who took the lockbox?" Sophi asks. "You checked and it was gone."

I say, "My guess is that Harper had the other woman who works there get it and put it in her desk. Maybe for safekeeping or something. She set it up so we'd think it was Leland. We did tell her the whole plan and how suspicious we were about Bas—and she used that against us. Maybe it's still in a drawer at Disability Services."

Sophi nods. "She'd been playing everyone against everyone else the whole time. I've been thinking that for a while the secret team was really her and Linc. He was the one who kept sending those emails about rules changes and disqualifications."

Lys hands me the washed broccoli. "Professor Haille apologized for not paying more attention early on when Linc was telling her about rules changes that sounded strange to her. But he'd been really helpful the year before so she went with it. He probably was really helpful until Harper came up with the idea that the two of them could win it."

"I wonder if she'd have split it with him," I say.

Kai snorts. "I'm guessing not when she saw how much it was. Hey, Lys, have you seen Char yet?"

Lys laughs. "Only photos. So many photos. She asked out that cute guy in the real Fibonacci Club and they had their first in-person date this week after a month of long distance."

She finds a photo on her phone and shows it around: Char with her hair in violet pigtails leaning on the shoulder of a heavyset guy with curly hair and light brown skin.

"Cuties," Sophi says. "Academically, she okay?"

"She dropped one class and did fine on the others," Lys says, pocketing her phone. "She has a plan to make up the credits over the next two years."

I stir the veggies. "This'll be ready in about five. You all want to arrange the pillows?"

We have the big pillows from Kai's old dorm room in the living room of Sophi's and my apartment. It's a two bedroom, "garden-level" (i.e. basement) apartment that's a block and a half from campus. Sophi took the bedroom closer to the street because she's less sound-sensitive than I am but more light-sensitive and that room has a west-facing window. I adore that we could just talk about all of that while setting up this place. I guess in a way this whole apartment is my accommodation—and Sophi's.

We both love watching the other think and we're good at creating a lot of space, not interrupting. At the end of the treasure hunt as we talked more and more about what we each needed—as Mom was working on the legal part of selling the comic collection and Sophi's mom brokered the actual sale—we realized that sophomore year would be way more comfortable if we had a place to rest and recharge that was set up for how we interact with the world.

We found this place in May, before Sophi went home for the summer, and put all our stuff here. My moms helped me move more things out of my bedroom to here. Joy painted two of the rooms with me and Mom took me shopping for discount furniture. The couch does not smell like other people's questionable life choices. It smells like the churchy incense that my former roommate burned and I got used to.

"Y'all want the couch or the pillows?" Kai asks as she hops up.

"Couch," Lys says.

Her knee has been a lot better all summer, in part from the long, warm days encouraging her to move it gently and often. If it gets bad again this winter, this building has a ramp to the back entrance and no stairs—we made sure to get an accessible place, not only for Lys but for future folks we might have over. I don't know what all they're going to need, but the strategic part of my brain likes thinking through the contingencies and covering as many of them as I can.

Kai and Sophi pile up pillows and sit against the wall perpendicular to the couch. I dish up stir-fry and rice with Lys carrying plates to Kai and Sophi as I fill them. We take ours to the couch. She rests a pillow against the arm and waits for me to sit so she can stretch her legs over mine—a pose that supports her knee but also our favorite for cuddling and still being able to see each other.

We've been texting all summer—as couples and in a group text. When I visited Lys in Lansing, Kai drove over from Milwaukee. The three of us road-tripped to Cleveland to see the youth theater production Sophi had worked on all summer. Kai had done the seven-hour drive from Milwaukee to Cleveland so often by August that she was an informal and hilarious tour guide for our drive. Lys and I took the bus back to Lansing so Kai could stay in Cleveland longer.

"How's Clyde?" I ask Kai. She loves the used blue Chevy station wagon she got in June enough to have named him.

"He's a beautiful beast," she says, grinning broadly. "Got all my stuff and Sophi's up here no problem. We've been talking about winter and with the right oil, I think we've got this."

"What else are you doing with the money?" Sophi asks. "Unless that's private."

"Investing," Kai says. "My mom had a ton of good ideas. She left me a little in the bank to take care of Clyde and for stuff I might need in the next few years. You?"

Sophi nods. "Same—a little for fun and a lot for paying for college-related stuff and the future."

"Me too," Lys says. "What do you think Bas did with hers?"

The whole collection sold on auction for a bit more than the individual issues—the final total two hundred and eighty-one thousand. I agreed to take the odd one thousand to round it off and so I could buy a few things to remind myself of my victory.

Kai's mouth twitches with humor as she suggests, "I bet Bas hired folks to paint Russian House orange." Her eyes look warm, not critical.

I say, "I can't dispute that, but I know she wants to go to grad school for building design so I think that's the plan."

Sophi makes a flourishing gesture with one hand. "I expect we'll see a few more custom coats too. Oooh I wonder what fabrics she bought. I should text her. Maze, do you want to show them your books?"

I grin. "I spent my winnings on a bunch more lesbian, queer, feminist books." Lys knows this, but she hasn't seen them—particularly in their new homes.

There are two big bookshelves in this living room, against the wall with the entrance door, plus a set of shelves on the facing wall. The third wall features a window with a broad sill and there is no fourth wall because the living room opens to the kitchen. We are using the end of the counter as an additional location for books and other memory links.

We're setting up a collective three-dimensional mindmap. Sophi wanted to learn how I organized in space and I want to learn more about how she creates a whole world of accommodations for what she needs in a culture not set up for that. Plus she's been thinking about how to stage some of these lesbian/feminist/bi/queer classics and I'm so into listening to her ideas.

Lys lifts her legs so I can cross the room to the open box near the bookcases. I lift the top volume: *Black Like Us: A Century of Lesbian, Gay and Bisexual African American Fiction.*

"Middle shelf," Sophi suggests.

"Can we move it up one shelf?" I ask. "Up symbolizes future to me and I think that should definitely be in future years."

She nods and I place it. She scoots to the other side of the box and picks up *The Well of Loneliness.* "Do we want to include this one? Maybe the professor picked all American lit for the treasure hunt because the British queer lit was too depressing."

"American lit was her field of study."

"Are you guys really going to continue the treasure hunt?" Lys asks, eyes bright.

I shake my head. "I don't know. We'd need so much help. But maybe if we do fewer books and maybe one of them gets produced in the Theater Department."

Sophi says, "You know I'd love that."

I sift through the box and hold a book out to her. "What would you think about starting with *Patience and Sarah* next spring? It's set in 1816."

Her eyes unfocus as she goes into herself to review our plan. "Would we follow that with Penny Mickelbury's *Two Wings to Fly Away*, set in 1856?"

"Sounds wonderful."

I unpack more books from the box. In addition to new purchases, it has some of my old favorites and my moms' favorites. I hand *Riverfinger Women* and *The Wanderground* to Sophi and she slides them onto a bookcase shelf. I hold up Ellen Hart's *Hallowed Murder.*

"Is it a kindness or sort of mean if we get students hooked on a series?" I ask.

"More than five books in it?" Sophi asks, with a raised eyebrow that suggests she's been burned in the past by series that were shorter than she wanted them to be.

"Twenty-seven," I say.

"Oh yes. That could get a person all the way through a PhD program." She holds her hand out for the novel and puts it into our three-dimensional mindmap for future treasure hunts. We've been talking about this possibility all summer, but now that I'm in a room surrounded by all these novels, it's starting to feel real, scary and wonderful.

Sophi sweeps her hand out to indicate the space of the living room. "Maze is showing me how her mindmaps work and we're taking the one I made on paper and putting it in the space—all kinds of possible books to include. Then we have to narrow it down."

"Are we really doing this?" I ask Sophi.

An expression settles on her face that I can't read. She turns to Kai who asks, "You haven't told her yet?"

There's a hush as I realize that Kai is talking about me. She's wide-eyed and I'm not sure if that's wonder or alarm. Did Professor Leland somehow find a way to forbid future treasure hunts? I wouldn't put it past him.

"What?" I ask, trying to hold my voice steady.

"I was waiting for us to all be together," Sophi says.

She crawls through pillows to her bag and pulls out her laptop, sets it on the coffee table where we all can see, opens it. There's a video set to play.

At first I don't recognize the face on the screen. I've only seen her in photos with darker hair. Now her cropped hair is more white than gray, but the smile crinkling the corners of her eyes is familiar. This is Professor Stendatter, sitting outdoors, pale beach and deep blue sky wide behind her.

Sophi hits play.

"Congratulations all of you," she says. "I'm sending this to the official winning team but I trust you'll share. Maddie— Professor Haille told me all about it. I couldn't have wished for a better end to this treasure hunt. And I hear you want to keep it going in another form? I look forward to learning about the books you choose, new ones as well as classics. I'm making a monetary gift to the school to be used for this and to enlarge the library's holdings of lesbian, queer, bi, pan, feminist, trans, nonbinary, gay, ace—did I miss any? I mean all of them—novels, graphic novels and any other formats your generation and future generations love. You did wonderfully. You can all be very proud of yourselves. I'm eager to see what you do next."

I'm staring at the screen so hard that it takes a minute to realize my eyes are also burning from tears.

"The gift to the school includes enough for a work-study position," Kai says. "My vote is that Lys apply."

"The professor gave us her email address," Sophi says, resting her hand on my arm. "I think you should be the one who keeps her in the loop about this year's treasure hunt."

I nod and turn back to the box of books, just to have something to do. Lys slides off the couch and catches me in an enormous hug and kisses my face. My hands hold onto her shoulders and they are more solid. She's relaxed into herself, broader and stronger than before. We all are.

Bella Books, Inc.

Women. Books. Even Better Together.

P.O. Box 10543

Tallahassee, FL 32302

Phone: (800) 729-4992

www.BellaBooks.com

More Titles from Bella Books

Mabel and Everything After – Hannah Safren

978-1-64247-390-2 | 274 pgs | paperback: $17.95 | eBook: $9.99
A law student and a wannabe brewery owner find that the path to a fairy tale happily-ever-after is often the long and scenic route.

To Be With You – TJ O'Shea

978-1-64247-419-0 | 348 pgs | paperback: $19.95 | eBook: $9.99
Sometimes the choice is between loving safely or loving bravely.

I Dare You to Love Me – Lori G. Matthews

978-1-64247-389-6 | 292 pgs | paperback: $18.95 | eBook: $9.99
An enemy-to-lovers romance about daring to follow your heart, even when it's the hardest thing to do.

The Lady Adventurers Club - Karen Frost

978-1-64247-414-5 | 300 pgs | paperback: $18.95 | eBook: $9.99
Four women. One undiscovered Egyptian tomb. One (maybe) angry Egyptian goddess. What could possibly go wrong?

Golden Hour - Kat Jackson

978-1-64247-397-1 | 250 pgs | paperback: $17.95 | eBook: $9.99
Life would be so much easier if Lina were afraid of something basic—like spiders—instead of something significant. Something like real, true, healthy love.

Schuss – E. J. Noyes

978-1-64247-430-5 | 276 pgs | paperback: $17.95 | eBook: $9.99
They're best friends who both want something more, but what if admitting it ruins the best friendship either of them have had?